I0731185

The Heart of
a Storme

The Storme Brothers
Book Two

Sandra Sookoo

Copyright © 2021 Sandra Sookoo
Text by Sandra Sookoo
Cover by Dar Albert

Dragonblade Publishing, Inc. is an imprint of Kathryn Le Veque Novels, Inc.
P.O. Box 7968
La Verne CA 91750
ceo@dragonbladepublishing.com

Produced in the United States of America

First Edition July 2021
Trade Paperback Edition

Reproduction of any kind except where it pertains to short quotes in relation to advertising or promotion is strictly prohibited.

All Rights Reserved.

The characters and events portrayed in this book are fictitious. Any similarity to real persons, living or dead, is purely coincidental and not intended by the author.

ARE YOU SIGNED UP FOR DRAGONBLADE'S BLOG?

You'll get the latest news and information on exclusive giveaways, exclusive excerpts, coming releases, sales, free books, cover reveals and more.

Check out our complete list of authors, too!

No spam, no junk. That's a promise!

Sign Up Here

www.dragonbladepublishing.com

Dearest Reader;

Thank you for your support of a small press. At Dragonblade Publishing, we strive to bring you the highest quality Historical Romance from the some of the best authors in the business. Without your support, there is no 'us', so we sincerely hope you adore these stories and find some new favorite authors along the way.

Happy Reading!

CEO, Dragonblade Publishing

Additional Dragonblade books by Author Sandra Sookoo

The Storme Brother Series
The Soul of a Storme (Book 1)
The Heart of a Storme (Book 2)
The Look of A Storme (Book 3)

Dedication

To my editor Amelia Hester. Thank you for believing in me and my work, and always for your support. It means so much.

CHAPTER ONE

June 27, 1817
London, England

T HE HONORABLE PHINEAS Allan Storme—or known in polite society and perhaps in another lifetime as Major Storme—perused correspondence in the morning room. He'd been back at his childhood townhouse with his mother for nigh on three weeks, and while it wasn't a bad life, it certainly lacked the excitement or purpose that he'd had during his military career.

Of course, he'd been in England for longer than that. Hell, had it really been over two years since the battle of Waterloo and the horrors seen—and incurred—therein? He stared, temporarily unseeing, at the post in his lap, the dates blurring, but it was true. Two years ago, his life had changed permanently and had landed him into a Bath chair, but for long months following his injury on that bloody battlefield, he'd laid in various beds in various hospitals throughout England. Barely alive and weak from blood loss through the trip across France, he'd lingered for half a year or more at the first hospital, where they'd removed the fateful ball. No doubt that was the reason for his paralysis. Perhaps if it had been taken out earlier instead of left to fester and play havoc… well, no sense thinking upon the "what ifs." Finally, when he had been deemed well enough to go to a rehabilitation facility in

Bath, they'd given him a wheeled chair.

And basically wished him good fortune in the new life he now lived, for there had been nothing further they could do for him.

With a shake of his head, Finn shoved away his maudlin thoughts and put himself back into the present, concentrated on the bright sunlight that streamed in through the open windows where a summer breeze carried familiar scents of London: savory aromas of roasted foods that vendors sold from handcarts on the streets, the sharper scents of horseflesh and excrement from the same, the heady smells of the blooming flowers in the small garden below. No, this life was as different from his military days as night was from day.

Then he glanced once more at the correspondence he held in his hand, actually began to comprehend some of the words printed on the thick card stock as his vision sharpened. "Good Lord." He held up the missive. "Another invitation to yet another rout or ball or musicale evening." Honestly, he didn't give a fig for what it was. "And it's addressed to Major Storme." Anger slashed, hot and sharp, through his chest. "I haven't been that man for two years."

No matter how much he'd give anything to return to those days, a continuance of his military career was well beyond his ken. Hell, some semblance of normality before his body had turned on him would be welcomed, but without a miracle, it simply wasn't possible.

The Dowager Countess of Hadleigh—his mother—glanced up from her own letter, but her face had drained of all color. She flashed a smile that had no strength behind it. "Give the *ton* time. They only know you as the major—war hero and courageous young man."

Finn snorted, and as bitterness climbed his throat, he swallowed it. "I'm no longer young either." As for being courageous, he had his doubts. If that were true, he wouldn't be sitting in a Bath chair and his best friend in the world wouldn't have perished on that damned battlefield. "No doubt the *ton* wishes to gawk and whisper." He wanted to chuck the lot of letters into the fireplace and set them ablaze, but it was too much effort. The last thing he desired now that he was finally home in London was to make the societal rounds, do the pretty, or put himself on display for the *haute ton* to gape at and wonder about. At the ripe old age of seven and thirty, he'd become an oddity, fit for curiosity shows or menageries. No longer was he a man.

Damn my eyes. Why did he care about what anyone thought? Because, regardless of his injury, he retained dreams and hopes for the future.

"Don't worry over such things, Phineas." Did his mother refer to his formal address or his fears? Not that she could even guess at what he struggled with, for he took great pains in only showing emotion in front of his valet—never his family.

Unless, of course, it was his arrogant older brother Drew. Then he could never quite manage to shutter the anger that his sibling always brought out.

As if sensing the twisted warrens of his thoughts, his cat, Wellington, announced herself with a soft meow as she jumped off the window seat and moved toward his chair. When he patted his leg, she hopped into his lap, stretched to touch her pink nose to his, and then settled into a tight ball, purring all the while.

He sighed and forced himself to take a few deep breaths to quiet his musings. Wellington—named after the famed duke of Waterloo and one of Finn's personal heroes, and had been given the moniker before he realized what sex she was—had come to him while he'd been in France following that battle. The long, tortuous journey to England had been made better by the young kitten, who refused to leave his bedside, no matter how many times he'd tried to encourage her away. For whatever reason, the blue-gray, sleek-furred animal had adopted him. Over the weeks during his travel through France and finally into England, he'd discovered that her particular breed had originated in Persia but had proliferated in France over the years.

Since then, he and Wellington the cat had been inseparable. She always knew when he was upset, and she certainly helped bring him back from the edge whenever the nightmares assaulted him, or depression intruded.

That was how far he'd come... or fallen. The only female in his life was a cat, and sometimes she didn't bother to concern herself with his presence unless it suited her to do so.

"I think you might wish to look at this," his mother continued as she passed the letter to him with a shaking hand. "This is from your brother."

"Brand?" Finn rather missed his younger sibling and couldn't wait to see him again... whenever that was. Brand wasn't exactly one to haunt London's hallowed halls ever since Father gave him that ultimatum after his brother had caused enough scandal for two lifetimes with his rakish ways.

Before they'd both gone to war and were forever changed...

"No, Andrew." Speculation clouded her eyes as she watched him. "I'm not certain what to make of him at the moment."

He grunted. "What more do you need to know, Mother? He's an arse, and we're better off without him underfoot." Drew had always been on the commanding side. Favored as their father's heir, he took to the attitude of an earl quickly, made sure the brothers fell into his plans and machinations else he'd throw a tantrum. Father had indulged him calling it leadership qualities.

And he hadn't found grace as he'd grown older. In fact, before Drew had run from London in a foul temper, he and Finn had had a fight. Hurtful words had been said that couldn't be retracted, and even if he regretted them now, it didn't matter. Drew was gone; it was highly unlikely he'd return to London any time soon.

"Behave, Phineas." But the corners of his mother's lips twitched with the beginnings of a smile. "Please, read the letter and tell me what you make of it."

Finn settled into looking over the missive while idly stroking Wellington's sleek head. Drew's strong handwriting filled the page, as arrogant and priggish as his brother's personality. There wasn't much to tell, honestly, once he'd moved past the pleasantries, but the news contained therein was shocking, to be sure. With a slight uptick of his pulse, he glanced at his mother. "Drew is engaged?"

What the deuce did that mean? It was as if the words jumbled together on the page to create a mystery he couldn't fathom.

"Apparently he is, yet the letter is already a week old." A slight trace of annoyance filtered into his mother's voice. "What's more, the ceremony was two days ago." She threw up a hand in exasperation. "I can't believe this!"

"Neither can I." His brother engaged—nay, married—and to a woman they'd not met. Hell, from the words in the letter, Drew barely knew her. What had brought him to that pass? Even more, would it help or hinder his already volatile temper? "What are your thoughts? I must confess, I'm a bit nonplussed at the moment." He passed the letter back but saw the offense in her eyes.

Damn you, Drew! Why must you be so selfish that you hurt others?

"I'm not sure, since I haven't had time to properly think on it." She shook her head while shock lined her face. In the span of minutes, she'd gone from a vibrant, older woman to a pale shell of herself. "Andrew wrote that he wished to do his duty to the title and perhaps secure an heir, that he might as well have them both done in one fell swoop." A shrug lifted her shoulders. "Yet in the next sentence he said he'd only just met this Sarah person. How can any of this be happening? And why did he think he should do this in secrecy?" Her voice had risen an octave, a definite indicator of her upset.

"It's happened, Mother. Past tense." Finn's chest grew tight with a mélange of emotions, and he continued to pet Wellington in the hopes that his ire would fade. "Perhaps we shall discover the why of it with time."

God help the poor woman who'd agreed to marry his broth-er. She was in for a tough battle, indeed, if not heartbreak, for

Drew wasn't fit to assume a husbandly role.

His mother stared at him with wide eyes full of disbelief. "But, he's *married* and without any of us in attendance or having met her!" She wrung her hands. "Plus, there's no indication that he intends to come up to London and introduce us."

Out of necessity, Finn tuned his mother's words out. Twin spears of anger and jealousy stabbed through him, both white-hot and tipped sharply as they pierced his soul. Of course his lauded older brother would do something enormously selfish like this for attention, for he always had to have everyone's eyes on him—the perfect heir, the oldest son, the man not touched or scarred by war.

Wellington raised her head as his fingers tightened on her fur. She meowed, stretched out a long leg and rested a dainty paw on his belly. The only one who understood what Finn suffered with was a damned cat who couldn't comfort him with words.

"Sorry, old girl," he murmured to the creature who watched him with light blue eyes. He glanced at his mother, who had continued to speak but he didn't hear her, his vision unseeing, as the knife of bitterness proceeded to gut him like a fish. Envy soon followed, and she twisted the knife deeper, for Finn would never have a fiancée, let alone marry. Who the hell would want him, paralyzed, and in a Bath chair for the rest of his days, to say nothing of the depression he constantly fought?

He gritted his teeth. One deuced lucky shot, one well-placed ball in his back had led to a spinal cord injury that had necessitated him being dragged off the field in embarrassment and excruciating pain, leaving him to watch helpless as his best friend was struck down not two minutes later.

The man he'd pledged to protect and bring home alive.

Memories of that day slammed into him. No matter that two years separated him from that battle, the recollections plagued him at inconvenient times. Sweat broke out on his upper lip and forehead. Cannon fire roared in his ears, along with the screams of dying men and horses. Acrid smoke filled his nostrils. The initial pain of the ball striking him ricocheted through his person.

Christ, but the memories—the nightmares—were beginning to haunt his waking hours instead of keeping confined to his sleep. Finn shook, his whole body shivering as he struggled to pull himself out of that time before depression could come for him next. Wellington's bewhiskered face swam into view and he blinked, focusing on the cat. She stood on his lap, her front paws on his chest. When his gaze connected with hers, the feline meowed and licked the tip of his nose.

"Phineas, are you quite well?"

The sound of his mother's voice and the concern therein yanked him away and temporarily scattered his thoughts. He glanced at her, disoriented, as he hugged the cat to his chest, but then finally, he nodded. "I'm all right. Merely lost in thought." Another meow and then Wellington hopped from his lap to sit on his shoulder. She nuzzled his hair, the steady purr in his ear working to further put him at ease. With a shuddering sigh, Finn pulled a handkerchief from a pocket and dabbed at his face. Damn, but he needed a distraction else he'd lose himself to the past.

And though he missed many aspects of that life, he didn't wish to become trapped there.

"Good." His mother nodded, but the worry didn't leave her eyes, and that sent warm guilt scudding through his gut. "I've already had to let one son go as he battles with himself. I'd rather not lose another."

"Of course," Finn whispered, for who would ever think the depression in the mind of a returned and wounded soldier mattered? Not that he would burden her with his struggles. He shifted in his chair, for the pain from his life-altering wound—or at least the phantom pain therein—flared as it did when he overtaxed himself. His surgeon in London had prescribed laudanum, both for the pain and to help him sleep due to the nightmares. At times it was a godsend, but in other moments he felt it becoming a crutch, so he tried to take it sparingly. But that was the only comfort the man had for him.

She returned her attention to the letter. "I assumed Andrew might have asked my opinion, at least, before he did something rash."

"Surely you jest." Finn snorted. "He never has before." When his mother folded the letter with her mouth set in a hard line, he stifled a sigh. Was she aggravated with him or Drew? "I'm sorry, Mother. Drew will have to live with the consequences of his actions."

"What if she's not right for him?"

A bitter laugh escaped before he could recall it. "No woman would be, but Sarah must have had her reasons to wed him." He leaned over and touched her hand. Wellington protested the action and jumped to the floor. "Perhaps we'll meet her soon."

Then he'd give his brother a well-deserved dressing down for abandoning their mother. Finn was all she had at the moment, and the knowledge grated. *I am not a damned companion*, but that's exactly what he felt like. With Drew in Derbyshire and Brand no doubt causing scandal God only knew where, no one gave a bloody fig to his well-being, or had even inquired about his health or plans for the future.

Perhaps they assumed he had none.

Why am I always wedged firmly in the middle and forgotten?

Another swath of resentment overcame him, and he narrowed his eyes as Wellington sauntered from the room. Hell, perhaps he should take out an advertisement for a companion for himself. A paid friend, since those were few and far between anymore. The men he'd known before the war—before his injury—had either died in battle or pretended not to know him now. But with a companion, he could travel, would always have someone to talk with or rely on when he couldn't do things for himself. Summoning a footman every time he wished to traverse floors or manipulate a carriage was an embarrassment. To say nothing to general hygiene or personal needs. At times, he was prone to accidents and would soil his clothing... well, more like the bloody towel wrapped about his privates.

Another reason I don't need to re-enter society.

Oh, God. Heat rose up the back of his neck. His hand tightened and crushed the stack of letters and invitations in his lap. Who cared that he might have had dreams or plans before he'd been injured? It no longer mattered that he'd wanted to retire to Hadleigh Hall in Derbyshire and run the estate, bring it to more modern standards of efficiency and profit. None of that was possible until Drew sorted himself, for they couldn't reside at the same property together without inciting arguments.

And honestly, Finn was much too exhausted for that. He craved peace and a place of security he could call his own. Let life forget about him in the hopes he could finally forget too…

He frowned and shrank further into his chair. Away from London, society wouldn't stare or whisper.

Or pity.

"I shall write to Drew and find out more of his plans. If he wishes to return and occupy this townhouse, it would be prudent for me to move out and give the newlyweds time alone."

The thought brought gathering dark clouds of depression scudding through Finn's mind. Newlyweds. *Bah!* Even in this Drew had won. "Perhaps," was his noncommittal response. Unable to remain stationary, he wheeled himself across the floor to stare out the window at the Mayfair streets below. He ignored how nice the summer breeze felt on his face, for he wasn't of a mind to look for the good in the situation just now. All the people down there who went about their daily lives without care or consequence while he sat here, a prisoner in a make-believe tower, growing into more of a grumpy ghoul, deformed and trapped, with each day that passed.

The irony of it all wasn't lost on him. Perhaps he'd spent entirely too much time reading fairy stories and ancient tales from around the world. It had become a habit of sorts during his recuperation period, and recently he'd taken it into his head that he might like to pen a story of his own along those lines, featuring a hero of his ilk, and not in the usual style.

For everyone should be able to read about the hero of a storybook who overcame his struggles. *Except... I've not done that for myself anyway.*

"Perhaps I should remove to the Brighton townhouse."

To think. To hide. To let the memories and depression have at him. Or, if he didn't find himself lost to the nightmares, he might be able to concentrate on writing the meat of his story, and perhaps send out inquiries to publishers. Imagine seeing himself as a published author and returning to London with the knowledge that something he'd plucked from his mind would soon be in book form, displayed in shop windows. It was a bit of good he could put into the world to counter some of the bad.

His mother made a sound of displeasure in her throat. "I'd like you to stay here with me. I've barely spent time with you since you've been home."

Was that a criticism couched in love? For he had kept to his rooms much of the time, especially after his last row with Drew. Depression had got hold of him and it had taken a few days and talking with Rodgers, his valet, to beat it back enough that he could function. The days where he didn't wish to remove from bed—couldn't really—were the worst, for then he'd lie there and wonder how the family would function if he weren't there amidst them. It was enough to chill his blood. "I don't belong in London, Mother."

I don't belong bloody anywhere.

"Nonsense." Her tinkling laughter sounded a tad forced. Perhaps they were all on edge and had been since his father had died over two years ago, a month before Finn's own injury. "The Season hasn't started so Town isn't crowded. It's a good time to ease you back into society." The tones of her voice had lightened. "We have a rout to attend tomorrow evening at Viscount Nattingly's home. You'll look so handsome."

His stomach lurched. Finn tamped on the urge to dry heave at the thought of wheeling himself into a society event and feeling the weight of all those stares. "Except for my chair. Can't disguise that with fancy clothes or a well-knotted cravat or hair tamed with pomade." Now, he drew the line at that particular cosmetic.

"Oh, hush." A rustle of fabric indicated that she'd stood. Seconds later, she came abreast of him. "You need to circulate now that you're home, and you need people—life—around you. I don't like how you sequester yourself away from everything."

"I've had my fill of people, thank you."

She laid a hand on his shoulder. "You *need* to marry."

Finn rolled his eyes. "As if that will happen. I can't even take a mistress, for *that part* of me doesn't exactly... perform." His bark of laughter was a mangled sound. No, he was worse than useless if his prick didn't work. Visual stimulation or thinking about erotic things didn't affect his member. At times he had what was called a reflex erection if fabric moved directly over his penis or if he tried to self-stimulate the shaft, but the hardness didn't last long enough. Alternately, a handful of times he'd woken in the middle of the night to a spontaneous erection, but without any integrity, it had soon faded. No chance to shoot his wad by his own hand, and definitely no hope of being able to pleasure a woman, let alone impregnate her.

"You won't marry for the physical sake, of course," his mother responded breezily as if it didn't matter to her that he'd never again find release nor pleasure a woman. "For the friendship. Life is better with someone you love and who supports your endeavors. You can overcome many obstacles with that."

"Oh, please. I could never sentence a woman to a marriage that didn't contain the promise—or hope—of being physical. To say nothing about having children. That dream has been quite dashed." Finn tossed his correspondence to the floor. Once upon a time he had wished for children, in the early years of his military career. But as time and violence and killing had dragged on, he'd changed his mind. In no way did he want to bring offspring into such a deadly and cold world. Now he didn't need to worry about it. "All of it is out of my purview, so if you'll excuse me? I'd rather like to sit in the garden for some air and to think. If you'll ring for a footman or even Rodgers?"

At least alone he could scribble in his notebook in peace. And dream impossible things for his characters, for they had more of a chance at meeting them than he did.

For the foreseeable future, he would brood and attempt to lose himself in his writing. And if the nightmares or depression didn't slay him, then he would see about doing... something with the rest of his life.

CHAPTER TWO

June 28, 1817

L ADY JANE MARDEN, only daughter to the Earl of Worchester, looked askance at her maid in the dressing table's mirror. "Why must I wear my hair up tonight? I detest all these combs and pins." The faint whine in her voice set even her teeth on edge.

Her maid, Anna, snorted as she stuck a tortoiseshell comb into Jane's red tresses anyway. "It's necessary, my lady. Your hair is too heavy otherwise. We can't have it tumbling down in the middle of a conversation."

"Of course not. It might ignite a war." Jane rolled her eyes and couldn't quite quell her penchant for sarcasm. But she submitted to the unique form of genteel torture known to the world as a toilette. Really, Anna was quite handy, and the twists and curls she'd coaxed from the updo pleased her. When the maid slipped emerald-encrusted pins into her locks, Jane sighed. Sure, the jewels complimented the bright hue of her hair marvelously, but that didn't mean she liked the color any more. She'd had two and thirty years to accept that her hair would never be anything other than red, but oh how she wished it otherwise.

The equally detestable sprinkling of freckles on her cheeks

and the bridge of her nose had always vexed her. No amount of lemon juice could erase those spots from her fair skin, which had come from her mother's side. Mama had Irish roots a few generations removed, for her grandmother had been the daughter of a high born noble. Along with the looks, Jane had inherited a slight temper that she constantly fought to contain as well as the insatiable curiosity to explore... everything. She was well read and possessed an imagination hindered only by her own abilities.

But her aversion to bugs of all kinds as well as the dark were all her own, carryovers from her childhood and always spending time alone. Except when her cousin Trevor and his family came to call. That boy had teased her mercilessly. Now, that boy was a man a few years older than she, and he was a favorite of her two brothers.

Ugh. Men. She renewed her focus on her image in the mirror and frowned. "Argh." She poked a finger into her upswept coif. Her hair was heavy, and the comb teeth dug into her apparently sensitive scalp. "Perhaps I should wear a turban. One of those velvet affairs with an ostrich plume or perhaps a large, jeweled broach on the front." It would prevent the need for combs plus hide her tresses.

Women with red hair were never in fashion. Last year, blondes were in favor; this year, brunettes were. Not to mention tall and willowy figures were always sought after regardless of personality or lock color; last year, petite, slim pocket misses had taken the Season by storm. No man ever preferred a red-haired short woman with too many curves because she couldn't keep away from the tea tray. It was another gift from her heritage—the voluptuous body, not the penchant for sweets.

Of course, those curves hadn't become the bane of her existence until her first engagement when she'd willingly given herself to her fiancé, and once that had occurred, she'd thought nothing of doing the same with her second betrothed...

Does that make me soiled goods now?

14

The sound of Anna's voice broke into her thoughts. "Turbans are for older or ugly ladies." She gave Jane a cheeky grin. "You are neither." She finished the coiffure with one last sparkling pin. "In that watered green silk, the men will fall at your feet, my lady."

"Ha!" Jane snorted but flashed a pleased smile. "I'd rather they try to steal a kiss or strike up an intelligent conversation." She rather enjoyed kissing, and when done right, the act had the ability to transport a lady to another world... where heat and desire and everything wonderful resided. Then her humor faded. "That is if I wanted to attract anyone romantically." Would her history prevent her from making another match should she want it?

"You don't wish for a courtship or to wed?" The maid brought out a pearl choker with a large peridot stone in the middle. When she slipped it about Jane's neck, the stone settled between her collarbones.

"Perhaps I'd encourage a courtship for the mere fun of it, the romance of it, but not the engagement. I haven't been so fortunate in reaching the actual wedding portion of such."

"That's fate, not your fault." Anna stood back and gave Jane a pair of elbow-length white gloves. "Your father is anxious for you to marry though."

The heat of embarrassment went through her cheeks. Was her dismal love life talked about in the servants' hall then? How disappointing. "I know he is, but I suppose I'm too picky to merely pluck a man from my circle of admirers." She stood and smoothed the wrinkles from her gown. The gold embroidery in a Grecian pattern that lined the hem made her smile, as did the matching line of it around the square-cut bodice. "However, I fear that many of those men are only after the dowry Papa has placed on my head."

Anna scoffed. "More incentive for a wider pool?"

"Perhaps." She shrugged. "If I don't feel *something* in my heart, in my soul upon meeting a gentleman, I don't want to put time into the relationship." She'd given both freely when she'd been engaged twice, yet both of those men had died before their times. And her heart had broken with those deaths. Perhaps it couldn't be mended for a third time.

I don't have the strength to give all that I am and see those hopes wither if tragedy strikes again.

"Oh, my lady, such things you think." The maid chuckled. "True love doesn't happen in this world. Life is not a fairy story like the ones you favor. No one lives happily ever after. It's a chore and fighting and bearing children."

Jane huffed out a breath of frustration, for she adored every one of those tales, couldn't have enough of them. Even now, every available flat surface in her bedroom lay covered with stacks of books. "It *should* be, for there's already enough heart-break in this world, enough destruction, enough grim news." She looked at Anna while pulling on her gloves. "It's too bad. Fairy stories give the reader hope and a sense of anticipation that the couple will fall in love, or the people in those tales will overcome all obstacles to have the life they've fought for."

"Sounds like too much work." The maid shrugged. "It's not difficult. You find a man you get on with and hope for friendship. Love comes later if you're lucky, but even if you're not, at least you won't be alone. You'll have the man and his heirs."

As if I don't have a say in anything. "I suppose Papa does wish for grandchildren." A trace of guilt moved through her chest, for she'd failed on that part, and neither of her brothers had wed as of yet.

"If you're lucky, your man will put a babe in your belly at the first go 'round." Anna shrugged. "Then you won't need to lie with him again."

How... dismal to think like that of the man she would wed. *I want the love, the romance, the belonging.* "You're wrong."

Or else she was flawed. Despite a bevy of female friends, loneliness *did* touch her life. Her father's duty to the title kept him busy and rarely at home. Both of her older brothers had lives of their own, and both had taken residence in a townhouse of their own a few streets over. They often haunted the small surgery and clinic they'd opened in the Marylebone neighborhood. She was left to knock about the London townhouse with her maid for company, unless she lent a hand at the clinic. Despite having two brothers and doing what she could to lift injured soldiers' spirits, she had no male friends, found it difficult to relate to the opposite sex. Though jokesters, her siblings were… well, crude and smelly at times.

It was the world she lived in, and men ruled that world. No amount of wishing would change that. Marriage was expected of her, and her father had been lenient through both her engagements and the deaths of her fiancés, yet her duty was coming due no matter what she wanted for her own life. If she'd had her druthers, she'd take her dowry and funnel it into her brothers' clinic. One of the things she enjoyed was sitting with the men there and helping them change the way they thought about their new lives after an injury. Some needed support or placement with society, and if given the chance, she'd like to lend a hand with that aspect too. *Or perhaps I shall raise funds for the clinic through the ton.* She did have skill enough—as well as the figure—to make lecherous old men with more coin than God donate if he thought he might have a glimpse at her in a shadowy corner.

She heaved a sigh. All of that was a speculation, though. No doubt her father would cry foul. So would she on the marriage front unless she found a man who touched her soul.

"Well, I should go downstairs before Papa bellows." Yet the excitement for the event had temporarily faded. Sometimes being caught between responsibility and her heart felt like a quagmire.

I wish Grandmother were alive. She used to give the best advice. Perhaps it was time to start remembering it.

SHE SMILED AT the crush. For an off-Season event, this rout already had a good showing. Viscount Nattingly must be popular or else the members of the *ton* who'd remained in Town were bored. It didn't matter to her, for her best friend lived here, and she couldn't wait to see Fanny again.

"Jane!" The squeal cut through the ambient noise in the hall and reached her ears.

"Fanny!" She met her friend in the middle of the corridor and clasped hands with her. "It's been an age since I was here."

"True, but then I've only just arrived back in London from being in the country visiting my grandparents." Excitement sparkled in Fanny's blue eyes. "You received my letters?"

"I did, but correspondence isn't the same as a gab in person." Despite the people milling around them, Jane hugged her friend. "Did anything of significance happen in Sussex?"

"Of course not." Fanny chuckled. "What about with you? Break another heart?"

"Don't even joke about that." She linked arms with her friend, determined to steer the conversation away from beaus and courtship. "I adore your gown." The navy-blue silk sparkled with tiny silver beads and suited the brunette well.

Fanny shook her head. "We can discuss wardrobes later." Gently, she pulled Jane aside and out of the way of others milling about the corridor. Lowering her voice to a conspiratorial whisper, she said, "There are several unattached men of note here tonight."

Oh, bother. "I'm not looking for a match. You know that."

"You might once you discover how dashing the Duke of Ballantrae is this evening. I've never seen a more gorgeous man in my life."

She tamped the urge to roll her eyes. "A duke is something I definitely don't aspire to land." If she thought hard, she could summon his image in her mind, and he was quite the Adonis, and a young newly minted duke at that. Apparently, his father had suffered a seizure then a stroke that had killed him quite suddenly.

"You could do worse," her friend was quick to point out.

"I could do better," Jane responded in a sharper tone than she'd intended.

"Than a duke? Don't be too quick to write him off. Mama says he's on the prowl for a duchess, and you would be the perfect fit. And how cute a couple the two of you would make!" Mischief twinkled in Fanny's eyes. "I might be of a mind to play matchmaker."

Something akin to panic swirled through Jane's stomach. She clutched her friend's hand. "Please don't." Having her position so elevated in society wouldn't leave much time for her dreams. She'd never wanted to attract anyone of consequence or title though her father no doubt expected it. The panic slowly grew into fear. Once her father realized the duke was here, would he endeavor to wrangle an invitation?

Of course, he would, for then, he needn't worry over her future any longer.

Drat, drat, drat.

Never had she wanted to hide from a society event more. "Please don't," she repeated in a weaker voice.

"All right." Fanny frowned as she regarded her. "There are other men who've been invited tonight. Papa wanted a nice showing of military officers. For instance, Major Storme is here." Excitement wove through her tone.

"Oh?" A frisson of interest buzzed at the base of Jane's spine. Now that *was* news. She'd followed reports of his exploits in *The Times* during the war as she'd hunted for her last fiancé's name or even for her brothers on the lists of the dead. From all accounts, he'd been heroically brave and tragically wounded during Waterloo. Now *that* was the perfect storybook hero. For years she'd daydreamed about him, what he looked like, the battles he'd entered, what she would say if she were ever to meet him. "How wonderful." Surreptitiously, she cast a glance around the corridor. Would she even know what he looked like?

"Isn't it?" Fanny's eyes sparkled. "I can't wait."

What was this then? Jane narrowed her eyes. "Do you fancy him?" All her make-believe castles built in clouds came tumbling down around her ears.

"Oh, no, but I aspire to have an ounce of his courage. Perhaps I could if I talked with him."

"Why? You are plenty brave, I think." In childhood, Fanny had fallen from a horse and broke her ankle. It didn't heal correctly, leaving her with a permanent limp that she was self-conscious about every time she went out. "I've often felt inspired by you."

"Pish posh." Fanny smacked Jane's arm in a teasing fashion. "Do stop." But her smile was glorious. If she kept that up, she'd be the one matched in short order. "However, Major Storme is in a Bath chair." She dropped her voice. "Paralyzed or so the rumors go."

"I hadn't heard that." There'd been no more articles about him after he'd been injured at Waterloo and sent home. No doubt he'd been in hospital for a while.

Fanny went on regardless of Jane's tendency to slip into thoughts. "If he can appear in public like that, surely I can manage to *not* hide like a wallflower behind potted ferns due to my limp when the attitude turns to dancing. Mama said she hoped there would be some tonight." She shrugged. "It's sad, I know."

Jane slipped an arm around her friend's shoulders as she propelled the girl forward, slowing her stride to accommodate said limp. They moved along the corridor toward the drawing room where laughter and the buzz of conversation carried to her ears. "You don't need to hide."

"I do." A tremble moved through her body and transferred to Jane. "I'm ashamed that my limp makes me different."

"Only in how you walk. The rest of you is adorable and smart." She shot a smile at her friend. "Anyone halfway interesting is different. You merely need to change your thinking."

"Ha!" Fanny squeezed her arm. "So says my beautiful friend."

"With red hair." Beauty was suggestive. "Men only follow me about due to my dowry. How they discovered the amount has always bothered me." Surely that tidbit wasn't something her parents had willingly let slip in order to dangle her like a carrot before a donkey... Plus, Papa's hints that he wished her wed didn't help. Her steps faltered for an instant before she resumed her usual gait. Why couldn't gentlemen chase her for who she was instead of the price on her head? And, if she were crass, her looks. At times, having a well-endowed bosom wasn't worth the hassle. *Their loss*, but the thought took away some of the brightness from this event. At the door to the drawing room, she paused. "There is quite the crush in there."

"Oh yes." Fanny nodded. "Mama is pleased. I think she hopes I'll find a suitor, but I can feel my courage deserting me as we speak." She gave a self-depreciating laugh. "Mama wants to see you tonight before you leave, by the way."

"I'll make certain of it." Jane nodded, for Fanny's mother had been her surrogate mama in years past whenever she needed a female shoulder to cry on or ask questions of. There were certain things in life a girl needed to know that couldn't be discovered in a household of men. "Steady on, girl. I believe you can do anything you set your mind to." Beyond the conversation in the drawing room, no doubt there would be cards in the morning room, literature discussions in the parlor, and gossip in the retiring room. Events like this were always the same. "What should we choose to do first?"

"Perhaps gossip? That way I won't completely collapse, for no men are allowed in that room." Fanny attempted to steer Jane away from the drawing room door. "Then I promise to mingle."

"We're going to work on your courage..." Her words trailed away, for the crowds parted and she saw *him*. Major Storme sat in his Bath chair at the far end of the room, and even from the distance, he looked dark and delicious and entirely too swoon worthy. It could have easily been a different solider in a different chair, but somehow she just *knew*. "Oh, my."

Fanny followed her gaze and then snorted. "He's quite splendid even if he is in a Bath chair."

A trace of annoyance lanced through Jane. "That doesn't mean he's unattractive."

"Mmhmm." Her friend regarded her with speculation. "I heard he's a big war hero."

"Oh, he is." She nodded. "I can't wait to hear him tell the tales in his own words."

"That's why Papa invited him and a handful of other military men," Fanny went on. "I suppose they all love to talk about battles and things."

"I wonder..." But she didn't spare a glance to her, for she couldn't take her eyes from the man in the Bath chair.

"And no doubt away from women, for they'll tell us it's not fit for our ears." Fanny huffed with frustration.

"Perhaps some do, and some don't. Certain topics might cause more harm than good for someone who doesn't wish to relive a traumatic element." She stood aside when a couple of tittering young ladies in pastel colors entered the drawing rooms. The crowd shifted again, hiding the major from her view. The urge to sigh grew strong, but she quelled it. It took all of three heartbeats for her to make a decision. "I'm going over to him."

Fanny's eyes widened. "Without an introduction?"

"Of course not." Jane smoothed her gloved hands down the front of her gown. She squared her shoulders. "You can do that for me."

"But—"

"Come on." She tugged at Fanny's hand and cut the protest short. "Perhaps the two of you will find love at first sight." Though the tiny imp inside her brain really hoped that wasn't true.

By the time they'd made their way to the man, knots had formed in her stomach. Fanny's cheeks were ablaze with a blush, and when the major glanced at them, Jane lost the ability to breathe.

Dear Lord, it should be a crime for a man to be so handsome. Sapphire eyes intense enough to pierce her soul, midnight black hair that stuck up in tufts here and there as if he cared not to tame it, broad shoulders his well-tailored evening jacket only highlighted, a jaw so sharp she had the decided urge to touch, strong-looking legs regardless of him using the chair.

"Uh…" When Fanny didn't offer any other words, Jane gently elbowed her in the ribs. "Major Storme, this is my best friend, Lady Jane Marden, and I'm…" Her swallow was audible. "I'm going to go somewhere… else." She fled so fast her skirts flapped about her ankles.

Oh, Fanny. Yes, they would need to work on screwing her friend's courage to the sticking point. When the man narrowed his sapphire eyes, she sighed. "I must tell you how much I've admired you over the years."

"How is that possible? You and I have never met." He didn't try to hide the annoyance that threaded through his voice.

"I read about your exploits in the papers." There was simply no need for him to know why she'd perused those pages to begin with.

"Exploits?" he hissed and dropped one hand to a wheel of his chair. "I'd argue that it was survival. The French were merciless."

"True." Her nerves felt strung too tight. Butterflies both tickled her belly and help tighten the knots that already existed. Every intelligent thought flew out of her mind. "The weather is quite perfect for this time of year, wouldn't you say?" Internally, she berated herself. What sort of falderol was she speaking? It was as if she'd no breeding or intelligence behind her. And why the devil did this one man have the power to take away her ability to think?

His feathery eyebrows drew together with a frown. "That largely depends on what one wishes to do in said weather."

A wave of heat swamped her. Jane resisted the urge to fan herself with a hand. As of yet, no one else had approached. Perhaps she dealt with a touch of hero-worship now that she stood before this man. And, oh goodness, he smelled so good! Hints of citrus and sage and something spicy tickled her nostrils. It was all she could do not to lean closer. "There's quite a crush here tonight. I hope that's a good thing for Fanny's chances."

Botheration, I'm babbling. Like an idiot. Which I'm not.

He stared at her as if she were little more interesting than a mouse upon the floor. "It matters not. I only came to make an appearance to appease my mother. Now that I have, I shall take my leave." Emotions roiled in his eyes, but she couldn't discern just one.

And it fascinated her. What was this man thinking, and why? "I'm sorry to hear that."

"Why?" That intense gaze met hers once more, and she drew in a swift breath.

Something danced through her lower belly. "Why?" Jane was the world's dullest parrot. Deep down in her soul she felt a connection that pulled in his direction, and despite her being tongue-tied now, she wanted—needed—to explore why that was. "I believe my path was supposed to cross with yours." She held up a hand, palm outward, when his sensual lips parted to protest. "It sounds impossibly insane, quite mad in fact, I know, but I also realize that one should never discount a gut instinct, for that first impression is oftentimes the truest emotion." She smiled. "If you have the time, I'd like to remain in your company for a little while."

"What if I don't wish to converse?"

"Then I'll sit with you in the silence."

Emotion flared in his eyes. She caught a quick glimpse of longing before it was hidden beneath boredom once more.

This would either be the greatest folly of her life or the most wonderful decision she'd ever made.

CHAPTER THREE

F INN WASN'T IN the proper mood to do the pretty—now or any other time. His mother had deserted him to chat with a friend. That left him fair game for gawkers and gossips.

And apparently for women who didn't know better.

God, how he detested conversations about the weather and the number of guests in attendance at this event. Was it too much to hope for a woman who might discuss things that mattered? He flicked his gaze to the lady who'd most recently announced that she'd had an instinct about him, or rather *them*. Which he still found the biggest load of gammon he'd ever heard. But her suggestion to sit with him merely to be with him had given him pause… and a myriad of questions.

"I apologize, Miss—"

"Lady," she interrupted with amusement dancing in her pretty emerald eyes. "Lady Jane. We were just introduced, remember."

How could he forget? Her companion had fled as soon as she'd gotten a good look at him while this one had wrongly assumed they'd been meant to cross paths as she'd indulged in inane chatter. "I apologize, Lady Jane, and I'm quite flattered you've followed my career—which is in itself quite disturbing—but I'm not good company tonight." What sort of woman would do that?

Instead of taking her leave as anyone with half a shred of common sense or propriety would, the petite intruder perched on the bolstered arm of a crushed velvet sofa near to his position. The mauve color was an interesting contrast to her moss green gown. "I'll wager you aren't good company *any* night. However, you could be if you let your charm come out."

What sort of game was this? Finn glanced about the room. No one paid him the slightest mind, yet a few men in the room cast interested looks at his temporary conversation partner. He curled his fingers into a fist upon his knee. No doubt one of those men would win her over this night, for she was a woman who needed a man. That he felt deep inside, and damn it all, it made his curiosity bloom. "How do you know I have any charm whatsoever?"

"You have that look."

Surely she was in jest. He snorted. "Are you truly seeing me?" With some theatrical finesse, he gestured to encompass his form. "This—me—is *not* charming."

She flicked her gaze up and down his person. "Of course not."

"Beg pardon?" What the devil ailed the woman?

"Of course, *you* wouldn't think yourself charming." She clasped her gloved fingers in her lap. "You will if you change your mindset." The woman smiled, and he stared at her lips. How could he not? He might be paralyzed, but he wasn't dead.

Both were lush and plump and would form a perfect pout. Currently, they were curved in a relaxed sort of way while she peered at him, clearly waiting for him to respond. Before his damned injury, merely thinking about what such lips could do beyond kissing would have him hard in an instant, but not anymore. Bitterness sat heavy on his shoulders. No, now he could only imagine illicit acts such as those without the accompanying lust rushing through his member. Visual and aural stimulation no longer affected his shaft. It was both a relief and a curse.

But bloody frustrating.

With a sound that was a cross between a growl and a sigh,

Finn snapped his attention back to hers. "I rather think you know nothing about it." He didn't care if his tone was rude or clipped. "You are fully able-bodied." So saying, he couldn't help sweeping his gaze up and down her person and how she easily perched there, watching him.

"That is true enough, I suppose." Lady Jane possessed the perfect body that men would go to war to possess. Hell, they'd kill a man merely for a chance to kiss her. Voluptuous curves to tempt a monk, short enough to tuck beneath a man's chin if he held her close, thick luxurious hair a man could tangle his fingers in, and the tresses a glorious red—fiery and vibrant. Hair a man—he—might grasp and gently tug upon until her head tipped backward and—

Well, there it would end. The thoughts as well as any such deed. He was consigned to this chair and that was all. Realizing she still looked at him, now with speculation in those eyes that glittered like jewels, he blew out a breath. "I'm sorry, what?"

"I imagine you feel your world is rather small in the present."

"Are you mad?" He gawked at her. The woman made no sense. It was as if she'd popped out of the forest like an errant tree sprite or a fairy.

Another thought, purely random, infiltrated his brain and he cocked his head. *I need to write that down for use later.* Slowly, as if any fast action on his part might frighten her away, he lifted a hand and delved into an interior jacket pocket for a small notebook and the nub of a pencil. Yes, she might make the perfect inspiration for a lead in his book…

If she wasn't insane, perhaps he was, for he now had the niggling of a character dancing through his brain, and all because of a chance meeting with this not-so-usual lady.

"I am not, but I do see potential in you. Right now, you have the air of a fish stuck in a tiny bowl after being given the run of a vast ocean. Despite everything, you're rather too comfortable in said fishbowl, but deep down you know there is a big, bright world out there, and you remember it."

His eyebrows lifted. "Is that so? What else do you see?" If nothing else, she gave him ideas, which he would then feed to his muse. As unobtrusively as possible, he opened the notebook to a clean page and scribbled a few thoughts.

She shrugged, which pulled her gown tight across those full breasts. "You're afraid, both of the world and your abilities to live in that world." When her inquisitive gaze fell to his notebook, questions populated in her eyes though she asked none of them. "You don't wish to know what you might still do because you can't do everything from before."

"I... I..." The gall of this woman! Finn gripped his pencil tighter. That this petite menace thought to tell him how to live his own life... *And then a rather large and hungry wolf ate the wood sprite in one gulp.* Savagely, he shoved the notebook and pencil back into his jacket pocket. There was no point in remaining in her company. "Goodnight, Lady Jane." He wheeled himself across the room without needing to weave between party guests, for they gave him wide birth. As if he could somehow transmit paralysis by touch. *Bloody hell.* When he arrived at one of the windows, he stared unseeing outside while annoyance seethed through his blood.

Why the deuce does she upset me? It's not like he hadn't fielded insensitive suggestions by well-meaning individuals before. If it was due to her being female, many others had wormed their way beneath his skin... before his injury.

"That was rude, Major Storme."

Of course she followed him. Why not? The evening had already been trying enough.

"So, you intend to become a hermit then? Shun everyone, society, your family, all of it, and live by yourself like a troll beneath a bridge, growling at passersby?" Both amusement and aggravation dueled for dominance in her tone. "Perhaps swiping at them when you're bored."

"If I do, it's none of your affair." He watched her reflection in the window glass, made possible by the darkness outside.

Grudgingly, Finn admitted to himself that she made quite a fetching picture, all pale skin and fiery Titian hair that glittered with jewel-encrusted pins. "And I don't growl." Why had she chosen that particular analogy? Did she suspect his fondness for fairy stories? Perhaps she was a witch hiding in plain sight with the *ton*.

Get hold of yourself, man. None of this equates to magic and make believe found in fiction, and neither is she a good model for a book.

"You're doing it right now." Obviously not deterred by that, she came abreast, looking at him in the window glass. "You'll grow old in that chair because you feel your life is over, helpless as the world moves on without you."

"My life *is* over," he ground out from around clenched teeth.

"That's where you're wrong. The life you knew *before* is over. This one is new with unlimited possibilities."

"How dare you!" His intense whisper didn't put her off. Finn sputtered as he attempted to form his next words. How had he been so unfortunate as to have himself beset by the likes of her? "What difference does it make? My new life is a prison." He hadn't meant to tell her that; the words had merely tumbled out.

"Not from what I can see." Her tone rang with merriment, and every jolly inflection made him frown and his chest tighten with irritation. Again, she assumed to make judgments, no doubt erroneous.

"Then, pray, enlighten me. Finn rolled his eyes as he turned his head to glance at her. "For *I* see a life cut short of activity and purpose, but long on dullness and depression." Why he'd told her the barest truth of what he was living, feeling, he couldn't imagine. Perhaps he was indeed in desperate need of conversation with someone other than his mother or his valet.

Or his cat.

"Hmm. That's unfortunate." She shrugged. The light scent of orange blossoms filled the air—sunny, like her damnable personality. "You're handsome and vital. A member of good standing in the *ton*. Well connected. A war hero—"

"Stop." The order was just shy of a snarl. "I am *not* a hero." Didn't he possess the ring that proved it? The ring he'd been too much a coward to return to its rightful owner? Surreptitiously, he moved a forefinger over his waistcoat pocket where the slight outline of the trinket rested. The ring that his best friend had entrusted him with giving to his intended? It sat like a hot coal in the small pocket. A shaft of guilt speared through his chest, stealing his breath. He could have saved his best friend, but he'd failed. Hell, he'd failed at the one task the man had given him. What good was he? The heavy weight of depression sank in on him. "The rest doesn't matter," he finished in a whisper and wished like mad he was alone.

As if he'd left the battlefield mere seconds ago, hot, all-consuming pain shot through his back. The muscles in his legs were heavy and didn't obey his brain's command to move with alacrity. Cannon fire thundered in his ears. The earth beneath his prone body trembled. Closer and closer the charge of the enemy came...

"Major Storme?" The sound of a woman's concerned voice yanked him from the nightmare. Her fleeting touch on his shoulder sent heat through his chest. "Major Storme? Are you with me?"

Finn wiped at the sweat on his upper lip and gave a shaky nod. "Yes. A memory suddenly terrorized me." It was the only way to explain it. "What were you saying?" He needed to concentrate on something other than the past

"Uh, I said, I think you're wrong."

"Is that so?" God, did she know how to say anything else? He didn't have time to argue with the woman, for it would take all his concentration not to let the gripping sadness consume him while in polite society. His curiosity bloomed. He turned his chair to face her. There was nothing in her expression to indicate she'd found fault with his temporary foray into insanity. Damn, but she was a daring miss to play with his brand of fire. Nothing good could come from it, and the thought both impressed and annoyed him. "Why is that?" Was it in answer to her question or his thought?

"Yes." The addlepated lady nodded as if she had no idea how her tossed off words had affected him. "You don't need working legs to feel self-worth. There is a whole life ahead of you, Major Storme. Don't let bitterness or jealousy rot your soul or jade your attitude." Concern shadowed her eyes. "Neither will help."

Though he wanted to deliver her a sound dressing down, Finn shook his head while anger mounted in his chest and the voices in his head told him he was useless as a man now. "You know nothing of it." There was nothing else to say. "We're done here." He attempted to wheel away and put much-needed distance between them, but Lady Jane blocked his path. The silk of her gown brushed his knee and slid over his left leg.

Oh, but he wished he could feel the rasp of that fabric or ascertain the warmth therein against his lower extremities. How long had it been since he'd touched anything having to do with a woman who wasn't his mother? He knew how long, of course. Once the initial wound had healed and he realized his paralysis was permanent. Forcing the thoughts away, he glared up at her while heartily resenting her optimistic outlook, her easy smile that brought out a dimple in her right cheek, her damned inexplicable interest in him.

"What do you want, Lady Jane?" he finally asked, though he would no doubt begrudge her answer. She knew him not at all and he wished to keep it that way. Before he glimpsed pity in her eyes or disgust in her face.

As everyone showed eventually.

The crowd in the room shifted, and he started in surprise. For the moments that he'd spoken—sparred—with her, he'd forgotten the presence of other people. Before she could answer, a young gentleman came over to her.

"Good evening, Lady Jane," he said, his words tripping over themselves in his haste to secure her full attention. The man completely ignored Finn. "Your friend Fanny told me I should come talk with you."

"How wonderful. I'll have to remember to thank her," she replied, and the melodious tones of her voice reflected the same graciousness that was in her expression. She shot a glance at Finn and shrugged in apology. "However, I was in the middle of a conversation with—"

"I missed you at the last event you and I both attended," the man rushed on, interrupting her.

"Oh. I'm afraid I don't recall your name." She blinked and a frowned creased the smooth perfection of her forehead. "I hope you're enjoying yourself."

Finn ignored their conversation. He took the opportunity to study her in profile. The flare of her hips and the swell of her breasts offset her narrow waist. The creamy tops of those globes caught his attention purely for the aesthetics, for they certainly didn't provoke a reaction from his shaft thanks to the damned injury. In that time since his rehabilitation and his return to England, he'd never let himself think about a woman erotically, for there was no point. However, now, staring at her, breathing in her sunny scent, he couldn't help himself from wondering.

What did her skin feel like? If he were to kiss her, would her pillowy lips cradle his? When her hair was let down, would it brush her bum? Were the curls hiding her sex the same color or a bit darker? For that matter, if the two of them knew each other better, would she consent to use those luscious lips on various portions of his anatomy in order to stimulate an erection?

For the love of God, man, rein yourself in! Even if that were possible and she were willing, you can't maintain enough hardness to actually pleasure her.

Heat sneaked up the back of his neck, due to desire or shame he couldn't say. Both held him in their grip, and at least with them present, he had a good chance of keeping depression at bay. It was when he was alone that the blackness would strike. Why the thoughts of doing anything carnal now? Suddenly needing something to do with his hands, he fussed with the folds of his cravat and fiddled with the buttons of his jacket. Perhaps he should record her description in his notebook. He had a feeling that until he rid her from his system by writing, she would continue to haunt him.

Then another thought occurred that cheered him immensely. On the page, he could do whatever he wanted with a character who strongly resembled her. Why had it not occurred to him before?

"Oh, *there* you are, Phineas."

He jerked his head in the direction of his mother's voice as she bore down on him with a young lady in tow. Thoughts of Lady Jane—real or imagined—scattered. "I want you to meet the Honorable Lillian St. Augustus. I talked about you so much to her that she had to meet you." A hopeful note resonated within his mother's breezy tones.

Oh, kill me now. Finn glanced at the slim blonde with the wide blue eyes that reflected both fear and disgust. Of course they did. The one person he'd met tonight who hadn't showed such a reaction was the talkative Lady Jane. Why was that? But under his mother's scrutiny, he elected to do the pretty instead of dwell. Extending a hand, he reached to take one of Miss St. Augustus'. She tugged it away before he could draw her fingers to his lips. *Ungrateful debutante.* It crumbled the foundation of his faith in humanity. "Good evening, Miss St. Augustus. I trust you're enjoying yourself." Honestly, he didn't care. If a person couldn't see past his chair, he didn't wish to further their acquaintance. His chest tightened. What he wouldn't give to have Wellington in his lap right now.

"I am." While he narrowed his eyes at her high-pitched voice, she glanced at his mother, who gave her a nod. "Uh, would you like to talk over punch?" Her expression suggested she'd rather do twelve other things instead of spending one more second in his company.

"Ah." Now he understood. She was desperate to wed before the Season began or her father needed an infusion of coin, which meant she had to attract a wealthy man, regardless of whether said man could walk. *I'm so sick of artifice.* Finn swallowed down the sour cynicism in his throat. "No, thank you. I find I'm fatigued at the moment and will make my goodbyes shortly."

It wasn't a lie. If it hadn't been for Lady Jane's delay, he would already have done it.

Relief flitted across Miss Augustus' expression. Really, she should learn how to school her expression better. Before she could answer, his mother sailed in.

"You've only just arrived, Finn." She frowned. "Won't you stay a bit longer? It's good for you."

"So is not being here. Sorry to disappoint you." He looked at the young woman. "Enjoy your evening, Miss Augustus." Then he wheeled away from the knot of people as well as Lady Jane and her growing circle of eager admirers. The blonde didn't hold his attention like a certain redhead.

"Coward."

Perhaps it was his own conscience who berated him.

"I can't believe you're leaving."

No, it was *her*. The softly uttered words in her voice gave him pause. He stopped the effort of moving his chair forward. The baby fine hairs on the back of his neck prickled. "I have never acted the coward in all my life." Except the day when he hesitated on the battlefield on his way to push his best friend out of harm's way.

Lady Jane came into his sight line. Faint annoyance framed her mouth. "No? Well you're certainly acting like it now." She propped her gloved hands on her rounded hips and stared him down. "You didn't tell me goodbye. That was rude."

"You were otherwise engaged." He shrugged. "Besides, I'm not a very likable fellow." She knew him not at all and he wished to keep it that way. The less she discovered of him, the less of a mess he'd have to overcome to maintain a friendship. Not that he wanted one.

"You certainly aren't in this moment."

"Then let me take my leave."

She lowered her voice as she stepped to the side. "Anxious to return to that troll bridge?"

"Well, I'm fairly certain this Bath chair won't turn into a pumpkin at midnight, so I suppose, yes I am." The corners of his mouth twitched with the urge to grin. If she wished to needle him, he wouldn't go down without a fight.

One of her finely feathered eyebrows rose. "So bent on keeping people away before they can make their own decisions about you?"

"It's easier that way."

"Going through challenges gives a man strength and the ability to press onward." She shook her head. Disappointment clouded her eyes for a second, gone at her next blink. "I wasn't done talking to you, so this isn't our last meeting, Major Storme."

Finn's lower jaw dropped slightly open as his mind spun. "Why is that?" Despite himself, he truly wanted to know what this maddening woman was thinking.

A soft smile curved her lips, and his gaze once again dropped to her mouth. "I'm going to show you that you still have worth, even if you don't believe it." With a saucy wink, Lady Jane turned on her heel and then disappeared into another knot of laughing, chatting people.

Finn stared at the empty space she'd previously occupied. What the devil was wrong with the woman that she wished to further their acquaintance?

"Who were you talking with? She's quite striking," his mother said as she joined him.

"And quite assertive," he murmured, but his interest had been piqued for the moment. "As for who she is, I suppose we'll discover that together. It was too difficult for me to ask many questions tonight."

A band of worry tightened his chest. Did he even wish to encourage her?

CHAPTER FOUR

July 1, 1817

A PAIR OF sapphire blue eyes surfaced into her consciousness. Jane huffed in exasperation as she neared the end of her walk through Mayfair. Why was she thinking of Major Storme yet again? It had been three days since she'd last seen him, and though she'd attended two other society functions, he hadn't attended those. Yes, he was handsome and striking, and yes, she'd been a bit tongue-tied when she'd first met him, and yes, he smelled outrageously delicious, but he had a few struggles facing him while he came to terms with his altered reality. In fact, he'd been injured two years before. Wouldn't that have been plenty of time for him to discover his new path?

That alone should make her worry. A man who wasn't at peace with himself wouldn't find the same with anyone else. Yet she felt nothing but calm and curiosity regarding the major.

She'd meant what she'd said. Something in her called out to something in him. Why, she had no idea. The same thing had happened with her fiancés as well, so she'd be a fool to ignore the odd connection. Not that she wanted to marry again. It would take much more than grudging charm and intense blue eyes to change her mind on that point. But… he'd taken her troll bridge comment in stride. Did he read such tales, or did he consider them pedestrian to other literature?

There'd been something in those eyes, however, which had tugged at her heartstrings. That need to be understood, to fit in made her want to help him find the answers he sought. Chances were high he'd misinterpret her motivation as charity or even pity, but her natural confidence wouldn't let that possibility deter her. With a gloved hand on the door latch of Brummel and Basil Booksellers, she tilted up her chin.

The only way to find out was to further her acquaintance with the surly major. Once she'd completed this errand, she'd call at his townhouse, the possibility of societal rumors be damned.

She pushed open the door to the shop. Located in an alleyway off Brook Street, the cozy tucked away area conjured up images of magic and mystery. Whenever her mind was in a tither, she came here to lose herself in the smell of books and ink for a couple of hours. Usually, after browsing the stacks, the answers to her problems made themselves known.

Would that the shop provided insight today regarding the major.

As she stepped inside, a slight tinkling of a tin bell over the shop door made her smile. That cheerful jingle was a magnificent sound. "Good afternoon, Mr. Basil," she called as she headed for the shelves containing books from around the world.

"What are you after today, my lady? Another thrilling novel?" Fondness echoed in his voice, for he and she had been friends for years.

"I'm in the mood for fairy stories." All the teasing of the major had fired her imagination and her appetite. "Something beyond the usual." How easily she could picture him clad in dented and scratched armor, riding upon a white horse into battle.

"Well, I don't know if anything has changed with my inventory since your last visit, but you're welcome to look."

"Thank you."

"You'll have the run of the shop. At the moment, there's only one other customer browsing."

"Just the way I like it." She preferred the book shop empty, for she craved the quiet. Such an atmosphere made it easier to commune with the books while she ascertained which one would accompany her home. With a wave, Jane made her way between the narrow aisles then was obliged to stop short at her destination. The object of her recent musings sat in his Bath chair, glaring up at the shelves. Her heart skipped a beat... and then another before resuming its normal rhythm. "Major Storme, what a surprise." Her traitorous pulse kept up its rapid beat, and when he turned his head to rest that intense sapphire gaze on her, tingles raced down her spine.

Oh, my.

A muttered, "Bloody hell," escaped him before his facial features returned to the usual blank mask of indifference. "Lady Jane. Not really a surprise though, is it?" He expelled a breath and glanced once more at a higher shelf. "To what do I owe this intrusion? Here to berate me more on how I should live my life? Or have you had me followed so you can memorize my daily schedule?"

"Of course I haven't. I'm merely out doing errands." Jane stood at the end of the aisle, temporarily flummoxed. Words skittered about her brain, but her tongue refused to let any of them loose. Outside of a society event and in the public eye where her confidence basked in the attention, she was suddenly at a loss of how to interact with him on a personal level. Drat her inability to befriend a male of the species.

"Ah, so you were gripped with the need to purchase a new book then? I somehow have the feeling you are well-read and don't suffer the absence of reading material." He didn't look at her again. Instead, he leaned slightly forward in his chair with narrowed eyes on the shelf, as if willing a book from the location.

"As a matter of fact, you're right. My bedchamber is filled with books, much to my maid's chagrin and my brothers' exasperation. They are all of a mind that keeping a nose buried in a book will somehow do me harm."

He snorted. "Imbeciles, all."

While she agreed with the sentiment, she didn't say so aloud. Instead, she took a step toward him. "Also, this is my favorite book shop. Mr. Basil keeps a good selection of books on hand to satisfy any reading whim."

The major grunted. "It is mine too." But he didn't spare her a glance.

Well, at least they had that in common. Excitement circled through her insides to know that he was a booklover, which made him intelligent. Her respect for him edged upward. "How interesting." As she trailed gloved fingertips along book spines and spun mental tales around the foreign-sounding titles, she covertly studied him.

Midnight hair in the same disorder she'd seen it the other night. It stuck up in places as if he'd just shoved his hands through it. Was it soft? Her fingers itched to comb the tresses into some semblance of order. His jaw was set at the stubborn angle she knew all too well, but that didn't stop the thought that if she peppered that underside with kisses, would he respond in kind? A shiver danced down her spine while she continued her inspection. His aristocratic nose was straight, which meant he'd never broken it while in the military, and his pristine cravat was slightly undone, giving off a devil-may-care attitude even though he was out in public. Seeing that bit of skin behind the loosened knot hitched her breathing. His clothing, like the other night, was impeccably tailored and impossibly expensive. They fit his lean body as if they were a second skin.

Why, he's a veritable Beau Brummel except he's three times as handsome!

"Are you quite finished staring at me?"

Startled out of her thoughts, Jane gawked at him as if she were a schoolgirl instead of a woman grown of two and thirty. "What?"

"You're staring at me. Did you wish for me to move my chair

so you can better see me or devour me with your eyes?" One of his dark eyebrows rose in challenge. "Unless you merely suffer from bad manners."

Heat slipped into her cheeks. Was her interest that obvious? "Uh…" Every word she'd wanted to say flew out of her head. It was so unfair that being in his proximity severely reduced her intelligence. Instead, she changed the subject. "It's a happy coincidence you and I both like this book shop. Don't you think?"

"I do not." He scowled and then returned his attention to the shelf.

As her natural confidence came soaring back, Jane smiled. It was much easier to converse with him while he was on the defensive. "What are you looking for? Perhaps I can assist you."

"I can manage."

"Can you? It's not a weakness to ask for help." She glanced at the books nearby. He'd been studying… fairy stories, the same ones she'd been after. Her heartbeat quickened. "Which one do you want?"

"Again, I don't need your help." A growl infused the words.

"Ah, you've decided on being the troll today. How disappointing. Then, since you've eschewed my assistance twice, I'll assume you're perfectly capable." Leaving him to his own devices, Jane perused the books on the shelf nearest her. Titles danced before her eyes but every portion of her being concentrated on him: the slightly accelerated sound of his breathing, the way he tapped a forefinger on the armrest of his chair, the tiny creak of the chair's rattan backrest as he shifted his weight, the clean wintertime scent of him that filled the air around her. His presence was big and bold, and it consumed the space.

Eventually, the major cleared his throat. When she met his gaze, he said, "I'd like to see a book there on the top shelf."

"All right." Jane came toward him slowly as if she would approach an out-of-sorts dog. "Which one?"

"The book entitled *The Arabian Nights Entertainment*."

"What a marvelous choice." Did he enjoy fairy tales? Tamping on her inherent curiosity and excitement, she prowled a step closer. When she couldn't reach the shelf indicated, and with no footstool in sight, she hiked up her skirts, climbed upon a lower shelf, stretched out an arm, and grabbed the red linen-covered book that featured faded gold lettering on the spine. Once on the floor, she handed it to him with a smile. "I've not read that one yet."

"This will be my third time around." The major dropped the volume into his lap. A muscle ticked in his cheek. "My last copy was lost when I was forced to exit the battlefield unexpectedly." He shrugged, turning his face to the shelf once more. "Made for a good way to pass the time and avert worry."

"I can only imagine." As questions bounced through her mind like soap bubbles, she scanned the shelves near his location. Ah, there was an interesting one. She tugged a slim copy of American folk tales from the shelf. Perhaps not exactly fairy stories but it should prove interesting all the same. The neighboring book flew off the shelf and tumbled into his lap. "I'm so sorry."

He stared first at the book then at her, his eyes wide with wonder and confusion. "Do that again," he asked in a whisper graveled with emotion she couldn't name.

"Do what?" Why was it so difficult to follow a conversation with him today?

"Drop this in my lap. Er, actually on my right thigh specifically." His hand shook as he held out the book.

"Why?" Jane grabbed the volume with a frown. She held hers close to her chest.

"Please, humor me for one second."

"All right."

"And drop it from the same height of where it fell before."

She couldn't fathom why he'd ask such an outrageous thing, but she followed instructions. As the book fell, the corner of the spine hit his thigh.

"Bloody hell!" Excitement shot through his whispered exclamation. The book tumbled to the floor.

"What?" God, could she sound duller than she did this afternoon? "What has happened?"

Red mottled color filled his cheeks and crept above his collar at his neck. "I felt that."

"I'm sorry to appear stupid, but felt what?" She simply couldn't understand.

The major blew out a breath. He picked up the book from the floor. "I felt the book fall on me."

Finally, she understood. "But you're paralyzed."

"You're quite astute today, my lady." There was a fair amount of sarcasm in his voice as his gaze connected with hers. Then his expression lightened. "Yes, I am, so *feeling* anything shouldn't be possible."

"Oh." She flicked her gaze from his thigh to his face and back again. "If I may?" When he quirked an eyebrow, she rushed to explain. "For research purposes."

"Very well."

Jane's hand trembled as she placed it on his thigh, so close to his equipage one little slip would have her fingers brushing that spot. "Do you feel that?"

"Not all, but in a small place."

She nodded. "What about this?" Daring much, she pinched his leg through the fabric. "How about now?"

"Yes!" He grabbed her hand. "I felt that pinch on my skin. *I felt it.*"

Warmth emanated from the point of contact, but her heart constricted. "That's wonderful!" She took the unwanted book from him and propped it on a shelf. "What does it mean?"

"I have no idea, but I'll make an appointment with my surgeon." When he realized he still held her hand, he released her as if she'd burned him. "I beg your pardon for the unusual favor."

"I'm merely glad to be part of something positive." The enormity of what that might mean for his life staggered her, but with spinal cord injury, one never knew. At least, she assumed that was what caused him to become paralyzed. Needing to put space between them lest she burst into inconsequential babble again, she moved farther along the aisle.

He worked at maneuvering his chair around in the narrow confines while she pressed her lips together to keep from smiling. It was adorable how he tried to hide his elation beneath his customary scowl. After a few curses escaped him, she broke her reserve.

"Would you like assistance?"

"As much as I'd love to say no, reality dictates otherwise." He sighed. Resignation settled over his features to obscure the previous excitement. "Especially while I'll have to face the door and the pavement..."

"It will be my pleasure." Helping people underscored her own dreams and confirmed that she followed the correct path.

The major rolled his eyes. "Must you act as though everything in life is delightful?"

"Must you act as if everything is drudgery?" Jane smiled as she tucked her book beneath an arm and slipped to stand behind his chair. "We balance each other out, wouldn't you say?"

"Or encourage a storm to form," he said in a grumble.

"I guess we'll see which one of us has the stronger will." Anticipation buzzed at the base of her spine while she changed his chair's trajectory, pushed him from the aisle and up to the front of the shop.

A few newly arrived patrons glanced up for no other reason than to stare at him. None of them said hello.

"Ungrateful dodgers," she whispered for the major's ears alone.

Mr. Basil peered at them both from over the rims of his half-moon spectacles. "Did you find what you need?"

"Yes." Major Storme gave over his book. "I'll pay for Lady Jane's as well." When she sputtered in protest, he inclined his chin a notch. Dear Lord, a slight dent occupied that feature. "In exchange for your mobility assistance."

"I... I..." She took a deep breath and then let it out as Mr.

Basil frowned. "Thank you." She handed the older man her book. The unexpected kindness as well as that chin dimple worked to set her at sixes and sevens. When was the last time that had happened?

Once the transaction had concluded, she accompanied the major to the door, which she held for him. She joined him on the pavement and once more took control of his chair, pushing him through Mayfair toward her other favorite place.

"Where the devil are you taking me?" The major put his hands on the chair wheels, effectively halting their forward momentum regardless of the pedestrian traffic flowing around them.

"To the chocolate house."

The mottled red color had returned to his cheeks and neck. "Why?"

"To repay your kindness with some of my own." She smiled as he glowered. "We can talk more privately there if you want."

"And if I don't?"

Jane resumed pushing him. "Then you can scowl at me and the rest of the patrons while I enjoy a snack." A self-conscious laugh escaped her. "Perhaps I like such outings too much else I wouldn't look so chubby."

"What utter poppycock."

Did he refer to her looks or her words or her presumption to take him to the chocolate house? And why did she suddenly hope he found her attractive despite her curves?

By the time they were seated at a small round table inside the chocolate house, his face was bright red with embarrassment, for she'd had to help him with his chair at the doorway. Jane pretended not to notice, for calling attention to it would only make matters worse. She'd gone through it with her brother when he returned from war missing an arm. The fact that she was nearly enamored with the major didn't help, but if his faith in himself ever restored itself, he would be fine.

Silence rolled between them except for when they both

placed an order.

"I'm glad you're encouraged by that bit of feeling returning to your leg," she began in a bid for conversation."

"It probably won't last." He kept his gloved hands palm flat on the table across from her.

If she reached out, she could easily touch them. But she didn't dare. "Will you keep me appraised of any new development?"

He grunted. "I don't believe my health is any of your business, my lady."

Jane sighed. She held out a hand. "Please, my name is Jane. There is no need for the title. I don't wish for us to remain formal with each other."

"Very well." He took her hand and briefly squeezed her fingers. "Phineas, but I prefer Finn."

"Ooh, so do I, but Phineas is interesting too."

The corners of his lips twitched with the beginnings of a smile. "I'm merely glad that I didn't land my younger brother's name of Francis Hildebrand."

She snorted but composed herself when a man in a Parisian-style apron approached them. He set a tea service on the table along with the typical pastries and a small silver tray for oval-shaped chocolates. Each one was decorated with sugared flower petals.

Alone again, she poured out a cup of tea. "Shall we talk about you? I find you fascinating despite your dedication to an off-putting attitude." When she handed him the dainty china cup, their fingers brushed.

Dratted gloves.

"I'd rather not. For the time being, you know everything about me that you need to."

"Very well." He was also stubborn as a mule. After filling a small plate with all her favorite sweets, she took a sip of tea. "I have two older brothers. One is a surgeon while the other is interested in everything from surgery to psychology to biology."

"Do I really need subjected to your history?" Though he eyed one of the chocolates, he sipped his tea instead.

"Perhaps not, but I refuse to sit here in cold silence merely because you're in another rotten mood. God only knows why this time." She shot him a smile. "I'm a bit awkward talking to men."

"Is that right?" One of his midnight eyebrows rose. "I hadn't noticed." Sarcasm fairly dripped from his words, but he grinned. That was a good sign.

"It's true. One would think that after I'd been engaged twice, I wouldn't have such a problem, but I do." She shrugged and plucked a honey cake from her plate. In two bites, it was gone. "My first fiancé died tragically while riding his horse in Hyde Park. I was two and twenty at the time. Young with my head in the clouds. I thought I would have years with him, and we'd live happily ever after."

Why did she disclose such secrets to this man she hardly knew? From his stiff body language, he didn't care one whit about her.

"Ah, now I understand why you're partial to fairy stories and why you reference them often." There was no mockery in the words, but his eyes held a light of interest. "I imagine you were heartbroken."

"I was." She took a gulp of tea as unexpected tears formed in her throat. "In fact, I thought my life had ended." A trace of heat pushed into her cheeks. "Like I said, I was young and thought my world—and chances—had ended."

He nodded. "Understandable. What of your second fiancé?"

"I met him once I came out of mourning. He was a soldier and had been invited to a ball I attended. We struck up a conversation. I felt I'd known him forever after those hours."

"Let me guess, you were engaged soon following." Finn took a piece of the pretty chocolate, popped it into his mouth, and chewed.

She stared, her attention drawn to his lips and the tiny smear of chocolate at the corner of his mouth. What she wouldn't give to lick the sweet away. "Yes. I'm not one to hesitate when I want something." A sigh of relief left her when he dabbed at smudge and it came away on his linen napkin. "I had two glorious weeks with him before he was sent to the Continent to fight Napoleon."

"He died there, didn't he?"

"Yes." She nodded. "During the Battle of Toulouse." The bit of pastry she'd chewed tasted of sawdust. Her belly knotted as a wave of grief rose up to crash over her so hard, she gasped. "One doesn't quite forget the dead, but as soon as the grief has been carefully tucked away, it surfaces again."

"This is a truth none of us can escape." Finn's eyes took on a faraway look. "So many men left on so many battlefields. Never will their bodies return home again." He touched his waistcoat pocket with his right hand while an expression of such sadness lined his face that tears filled her eyes at the sight. "None of us wanted to fight, but we weren't given a choice."

"Too many men thought the wars were a lark. William assumed he'd be back in a year." Of course he wasn't, and sporadic letters weren't the same as having the man home in person.

"In the three years since he'd died, you haven't tried for a third engagement?"

"No."

"Do you want to marry again?"

Jane cocked her head and regarded him. Already fragile from unexpected feelings, she needed to tread carefully lest she become a watering pot in front of him. "I will only marry if it's a love match. I'll not waste my time on anything else."

"Perhaps that's asking too much these days. There is precious little love to go around." Bitterness etched lines on his face. His eyes took on the hard glint of glass. "Compassion has fled."

"You say that because it's the only thing you see. If you wished to find joy in the world, that's what you'd discover." She took a shuddering sigh. "Regardless, a love match is what I want, and that's my final say on the matter."

Finn nodded. "You're a woman of intelligence. I have no doubt you'll soon land the man of your dreams." He met her gaze, but she couldn't read the emotions in his. "Do you want children?"

Despite her best efforts, tears once more sprang to her eyes. She'd been with child once after she'd laid with her second fiancé. Unfortunately, she'd lost the babe a few months into the pregnancy. No one, not even her father, had known. The one person aware of the secret had been her maid, Anna, for she'd had to empty the chamber pot. Jane wiped at an escaped tear on her cheek. It was a loss she would never forget, and she'd grieved alone. No doubt her story was one of many that had played out within the *ton* and all over England, for war was an exacting master and didn't confine itself to class.

"Jane? Have I said something to offend?" He snaked a hand through the clutter on the table to briefly touch her fingers. "If so, I apologize." Gone was the gruff bitterness from his voice. In its place was concern.

"It's not you. I hadn't intended to become a watering pot today, for I rarely allow myself to dwell on sad or angry emotions."

"Perhaps you should," he said in a soft voice. "You can't pick and choose what emotions you want to show to the world, for it will cause other problems later in life."

"So says the man who dwells only in the negative."

"Point taken." For the first time since she'd met him, a genuine smile curved his lips. The delicate skin at the corners of his eyes crinkled. "Perhaps we're both a bit broken."

She snitted, and though the human connection of his hand on hers kept her anchored in the present, she was the first to pull away, for his touch added confusion to her already overwrought nerves. "I'm not certain children are in my future, for I haven't given the possibility thought." Not since she'd lost her babe. It was another reason why she was leery of marrying. Opening herself up to that heartbreak again was too much.

"What of your personal aspirations then? Do you intend to force men like me into a positive way of thinking until we die?"

"Oh, hush." She shook her head in exasperation. "No, but I do wish to help people like you, perhaps more deeply understand their circumstances, and find new ways to assist them to live with their altered realities. Perhaps I'll extend that support to widows and others who've suddenly found themselves adrift by various forms of loss."

It would have been quite helpful to have that sort of program available after she'd suffered her miscarriage. A young woman in the *ton* couldn't exactly talk about such things without ruining her reputation, but if she—or other women—could do so anonymously…

"I see." Finn gawked at her as if he couldn't quite believe she were real. Hope lit the depths of his eyes. "Why would you do that?"

"I feel it's my purpose, that's it's stamped upon my heart. Yes, it's quite unexplainable and sounds a touch mad, but it's been with me ever since my brother returned from the war, injured. Perhaps before then, for my heart breaks each time I see a soldier shunned by society and unable to find work or a compassionate ear." She shrugged, and since her appetite had fled, she pushed her plate away. "I believe I *can* help, and I *can* give hope. That's important."

His jaw dropped. "You're not wrong." For the space of a heartbeat, he remained silent. Then, a slow grin curved his mouth, and it was her turn to stare. "God, you're amazing."

Both of her eyebrows rose. Warmth from his compliment infused her cheeks and chest. Finally, he'd paid attention to her instead of treated her like an annoying bug. "Not really. I'm merely me, and I know what needs to be done."

"So you'll manage your way through? Come through everyone's life like a great, swirling storm that clears the air?" The words weren't hurled at her with anger or bitterness. Instead, his tone suggested he thought over what she'd said. He shook his head, but the wonder remained in his expression. "Jane, truly, you have no idea. The world needs more women like you."

"If I can help one person heal, to come to terms with what they're fighting against, I'll consider that a good first step." She sat there, smiling at him while his hand remained on the table amidst the tea things. "Besides, it'll feel like home. I assist my brothers in their clinic."

"Oh?"

"Yes." Her gaze dropped to his mouth. What would it feel like to share a kiss with this man? Even she wasn't so bold to try and steal one in such a public setting, but if they were alone, she might. "It's small and cozy. I like to lift spirits of the patients, but the actual nursing part makes me ill. It's a failing I've yet to overcome."

"Then you *do* intend to positive them to death." Some of the light faded from his eyes. "You'll have to get your hands dirty to make a considerable difference." The stubborn set of his jaw had returned. "A man's mental state can only be stimulated so much. The rest of his life is messy and raw and real."

Why couldn't he understand what drove her? She bit the inside of her lip as tears once again prickled the backs of her eyelids. Her father didn't want her to lend a hand in the clinic either. "I'll bear that in mind. Thank you." It had been a horrible idea to bring him here to the chocolate house. They'd made some headway, but now it had stalled.

Gone was his easy grin. In its place was a fierce frown that pulled his eyebrows downward. "Permanent injuries aren't the romance and heroism found in story books. Men don't heal fast or magically, if that's what you think." His eyes narrowed. "We sometimes struggle with depression, with darkness, that whispers things in our ears and tells us we're worthless. A sunny disposition won't fix that, and neither can we will it away by changing our mindset."

"I can but try." Being in his company was as intense as he was.

Finn huffed. "It's not a matter of cheerfulness or happy thoughts. Sometimes, you need to sit quietly with a man in support without trying to put him back together."

"We shall see what happens in time." She glanced around the small café. "If you're finished, I'd rather like to return home." There was much to think about, and she needed to repair her flagging confidence. "I'm suddenly fatigued."

He peered into her face, looking for only God knew what, but she feared she lacked whatever it was. "You can't run when things grow too real, my lady. Only cowards do that," he said in a barely audible voice.

Is that what he thinks I am? The thought made her want to weep. "There is no harm in trying my way."

"Agreed, but if that way fails, promise me—yourself—you won't abandon the men you wish to help." He lowered his voice. "It's not their fault England treats them as outcasts."

Jane nodded, for Finn had given her much to think about.

Fifteen minutes later, she walked beside him through Mayfair. Neither of them spoke, but a certain companionable silence had fallen between them.

"Where do you live?" she finally asked after another long stretch of silence.

"Just here. Number twelve, but shall I escort you home?" He came to a stop at a wrought iron gate. "I don't mind the trip."

She glanced at him as her pulse jumped. Under his layers of grumpy bitterness, he was quite the gentleman. "Thank you, but there's no need. I'm only ten houses down from you and on the next street over." They'd spent perhaps an hour together, yet she could have sworn it had been years instead of mere minutes. Why? Perhaps he was an old soul-type of man, the sort of man who'd seen things beyond the usual ken of others, and that, in turn, attracted her soul like a moth to flame. There was a comfort in that, but she was at sixes and sevens in his presence. "Do you go to the Adkins dinner tonight?"

"I do not." He laid a hand on the gate. "I've grown tired of being in society, so until my mother demands I do the pretty again, I'll stay in."

"Well, goodbye then." Why was her chest so tight at the thought of leaving him? They were barely friends.

"Jane?"

"Yes?"

His grin held a wicked edge that sent her heartbeat soaring and butterflies dancing in her belly. "This isn't our last meeting."

She returned his grin, for he'd repeated her words to him that she'd uttered when they'd met. "I'm counting on that." With a cheerful wave, she continued on her way.

What it all meant she couldn't say, but she couldn't wait to find out.

CHAPTER FIVE

July 3, 1817

"MUST WE DO this every day?" A groan escaped him when Rodgers extended Finn's leg and then folded it against his chest. He hated the exercise sessions. Lying so ignobly on the floor was embarrassing. Not to mention Wellington thought it all a great game, for she'd taken to pouncing on his chest from her position beneath any close piece of furniture.

No matter the challenges, it *was* conducive to thinking. Already, the next scene in his novel had come to him as he let the valet do what he must, and his fingers itched to write it down. Of course, that might also have much to do with the fact that he couldn't evict a certain petite marvel from his mind.

"You know we do, yet you grouse about it every morning." There was no mockery in the valet's voice nor pity; only understanding. "We must keep your muscles pliant and healthy."

"What the devil for? It's not as if I'll ever walk again." Except, since the day at the book shop, he'd continued to have feeling in various portions of his right leg every so often. When he'd awoke this morning, it had been to a curious tingling through the limb.

The man never paused in his task. He switched to the other leg, first massaging the hardened knots of muscles, and then moving the leg and stretching said muscles. "You don't know that." When Wellington took a swat at him, he gently batted her away.

Finn sucked in a breath when a tweak of pain made itself known. Never had he experienced that before. "I suppose I should tell you of a change in my right leg."

Rodgers met his gaze with a raised eyebrow. "What's wrong?"

Even Wellington stopped teasing the valet and stared at him with a soft *meow*.

"I'm not certain yet." Briefly, he explained about the falling book. "It's occurred a few times since then, but never in the same place, and right now, I can feel the knots in the muscle you massaged, feel the pressure of your fingers." He watched the valet's face carefully for any sign of his thoughts. "What do you think it means?"

"Perhaps your original surgeon was wrong." The valet shrugged. "Is it possible to regain the use of your legs?"

"I'm too frightened to think of what might happen." Could he truly be restored to his former self before that Waterloo incident had changed his life? "Besides, it's only the one."

"Let's try an experiment." Rodgers took hold of Finn's right foot. "Can you wriggle your toes?"

No matter that he had the thought, told his brain he wanted to move his toes, nothing happened to said phalanges. Streaks of cold disappointment moved through his chest. "It's useless. No doubt these random patches are merely aberrations."

Wellington climbed onto his bare chest. Her purring soothed the worst of his emotions, and she hunched down, her front paws stretched out to his chin, her blue eyes never leaving his face.

"It's more than you had in the last two years, and I've chosen not to give up hope."

Finn blew out a frustrated breath. He stroked a hand down the cat's sleek back. "Then you're a fool, Rodgers." So had he been for one shining moment in that book shop.

"Perhaps I am, but so are you if you believe not having the

use of your legs means the end of your life."

The sound that left his throat was a mix of a strangled sigh and a scoff. "Not you too." When his cat meowed and moved her face closer to his, he scratched her behind an ear.

"I'm afraid I don't know what you mean, sir." Rodgers continued to exercise Finn's muscles while he regarded him with speculation in his eyes.

"You're exactly like Lady Jane and her perpetual sunny attitude that solves nothing." It had been two days since their meeting at the book shop and subsequent tea at the chocolate house. Two days since she'd given him a brief history of her life and the subject matter that had made her cry. Two days since he'd decided that perhaps having her around as a friend or a companion wouldn't be such an annoyance after all. Never in his life had he known a woman more open and trusting than her. When tears had made an appearance, he could finally understand her in that grief.

Rodgers' eyebrows lifted into his hairline. "I wasn't aware you have a lady in your life at the moment." Shock reflected in his hazel eyes and he paused the exercises. "How did you meet? For that matter, where? I've been with you for the duration."

Heat crept up the back of Finn's neck. He fixed his gaze to the ceiling, uncommonly aware both the valet and the cat stared at him. "You have, except when I went to the book seller." He lifted his arms above his head, stretching, and then rested them on the floor.

"Ah, that was my day off." Rodgers nodded. "Try to push your leg into my hand."

"She and I met by accident, I suppose." Try as he might, Finn couldn't make his leg or foot obey his brain's command to fight against the valet's hold. Had he imagined those random pockets of feeling? He shook his head. Obviously, the nerves were permanently damaged. Perhaps they were dodgier than he'd thought, which had resulted in the bits of sensitivity. "I met her at the Nattingly rout nearly a week ago." When all his aggravation—and his interest—had begun.

"Oh? Did you get on with her?"

"Not at first, but she's a rather tenacious individual." And she had the most adorable splash of freckles across her cheeks and the bridge of her nose. "I met her again a couple of days ago at the book shop. She was as managing then as she was at the rout." He frowned at the towel wrapped around his private parts like a damned baby's nappie. It circumvented embarrassment while out in public.

Just another reason he could never be with a woman.

Wellington, ever observant to his change of mood, stood and licked the tip of his nose. She stared at him, whiskers quivering, until he lifted her up and set her on the floor beside him.

"Managing how? Try as I might, I don't recall you speaking to a female that evening." Rodgers narrowed his eyes.

"She dressed me down for what she calls my grumpy attitude. Then she attempted to tell me that my outlook was flawed, and that everything would improve if I changed my thinking." Not to mention she *was* a rather pleasing eyeful.

"I'm sorry I missed that." Rodgers took both Finn's feet in his hands and moved them to mimic marching. "Do you intend to call on her, or see her socially again?"

Did he? "Call on her? Decidedly not, for that would assume an interest I don't have. I can't do anything about society. If she's at an event I am, so be it."

When Wellington decided to snag a claw in the towel and tugged, the scrape of the fabric over his shaft caused a bit of hardening.

"Stop," he hissed at the cat as he replaced the towel. Too damned bad he couldn't have such a reaction when looking at Jane.

"Ah." The valet continued the exercise in silence. Finally, he said, "Do you attend the Primrose rout with the dowager tonight?"

"I hadn't planned on it." Finn frowned. "Why?"

Rodgers shrugged. "Lady Jane might be there. If you went and struck up a conversation with her, perhaps you could better judge whether you'd like to call on her in the future."

"Please don't say you're playing matchmaker." Why the devil did everyone in his life wish to see him wed? Having a wife underfoot wouldn't take away his demons.

"Of course not, sir." The ghost of a grin tugged at Rodgers' mouth. "However—"

"Oh, God," Finn muttered and rolled his eyes.

"Is she the model for the heroine in your novel?"

He blew out a breath, for each evening Finn read aloud from his writings for Rodgers' feedback and input. "Perhaps."

"Then don't you owe it to the story to further your research? If that's the only reason you can find to attend the rout, it would be well worth the headache."

"This is true." He stretched out his arms again. Wellington immediately pounced, and he spent the next several seconds pretending his hand was a spider for her to play with. "That being said, you might press my light blue waistcoat…"

Later that evening

REMARKABLY, FINN'S NERVES didn't plague him as he wheeled himself into the large, elegantly appointed drawing room done in gilt and sage green. The Mayfair home belonged to an earl who apparently didn't care that his lavish tastes had nearly run to ostentatious. The low ebb and flow of conversation filled the room. A footman in dark clothes circulated and offered the guests flutes of champagne. From somewhere down the hall and removed from the drawing room, the faint clink of coin and masculine laughter drifted. Obviously, gaming was in full force this night.

And perched on a low sofa with a scalloped wooden back was

Lady Jane, chatting happily with a blonde man who resembled a damned Adonis in the candlelight. God, she was gorgeous tonight, clad in a gown of navy satin trimmed with seed pearls and tiny clear glass beads around the hem and bodice. Diamonds sparkled in her upswept Titian hair and around one of her gloved wrists, but around her neck, a thin golden chain sparkled. A small cloisonne heart rested between her collarbones, which only called attention to the swell of her perfect breasts.

A low groan left his throat. What he wouldn't give to have her undivided attention.

"Oh, look, Phineas. The Duke of Ballantrae is in attendance this evening," his mother whispered at his side. "And isn't that the lady you spoke to the other night? They make a handsome pair." Her chatter fell like dropped brass in his ears. "Gossip holds that he's looking for a duchess."

"Indeed." Something akin to jealousy darted through his chest with lightning sharp accuracy. "Perhaps it's time the duke learns about disappointment," he whispered, not caring if his mother heard the aside or not.

She patted his shoulder. "I see my friend Lady Caulder. Excuse me for a moment. After I talk to her, we'll make the rounds. If all goes well, we'll find a lady who catches your eye."

"I'm certain I can take care of myself." Though he loved his mother, the matchmaking attempts had begun to grate. "Have a lovely time." Then he squared his shoulders and wheeled himself toward that settee. "Good evening, Lady Jane. Your Grace."

"Finn! Er, I mean Major Storme." Genuine joy lit her emerald eyes when she looked at him. "I'm so glad you're here."

The duke inclined his chin. He and Finn stared each other down. "Good evening, Major. I trust you're enjoying yourself."

"Not more than usual." He didn't care if he sounded surly. What he wanted was for the man to vacate the settee and leave Jane alone. "If you don't mind, I'd like to chat with the lady for a few moments." He left no room in his request for the duke to linger.

"Of course." Smoothly, the blonde man rose to his feet. He took one of Jane's hands and brought it to his lips. "If I don't come back to you tonight, I shall see you at my ball later this month. Be sure to save me a dance then." Their gazes connected and a faint blush filled Jane's pale cheeks.

"I will." She waved him off and then turned her full attention on Finn. "I'm happy you decided to come tonight."

Now that the duke had vacated, Finn relaxed slightly. He brought his Bath chair close enough to her that their knees touched. Of course he felt nothing at the contact, but a tiny inhalation issued from her. He gave her what he hoped was his most charming grin. "I am too now that I find myself in your company."

"See? I knew you had it in you to act like a polite gentleman instead of a troll beneath a foot bridge." Amusement sparkled in her eyes as she raised a hand and poked a finger into her coif.

"At times, the bridge becomes boring." When her orange blossom scent hit his nose, he stifled the urge to groan. "That gown suits you." What an asinine thing to say. She probably already knew it.

"Thank you for noticing." She laid a hand on her stomach. "I like to think it resembles the midnight sky on a starry night."

"That it does." When was the last time he'd ever taken notice of the nighttime sky? Not since he'd left Belgium, certainly. Finn glanced toward the French-paned doors at the opposite side of the room that had been thrown open to catch the night breeze. "Too bad it's overcast tonight, else we could move outdoors and star gaze." What an idiotic thing to say. He swung his attention back at her and hoped she didn't think him a nodcock.

"I wouldn't mind that, for the crush is growing in here." When he didn't move, she lifted a red eyebrow, clearly waiting, but his courage gave out. She pressed her lips together, and he stared at her mouth, those luscious lips made for kissing. "Have you continued to have feeling in your leg?"

Glad of the interruption to his thoughts, he nodded. "Some,

SANDRA SOOKOO

yes. In random spots, but nothing significant."

"Still, you should see your surgeon. Perhaps something has changed with the nerves in your spine." She leaned forward and briefly touched a hand to his knee. "Regardless, it's encouraging."

"Perhaps, but I refuse to have my hopes buoyed in the event they come crashing down." He'd come to crave her optimistic attitude and her sunny smiles. "Ah, how well do you know the duke?"

"We're acquaintances." She dropped her gaze. "My father wishes for me to encourage his attentions."

"I see." It took all his willpower not to turn about and check to see if the man lurked in the room, biding his time. "Do you intend to encourage him?"

"At the moment, no. As I told you, I refuse to marry unless love is involved." She glanced up and waved to what he assumed was an acquaintance.

Finn glanced over his shoulder. When a pair of young men approached, he growled and glared, making it clear that he wouldn't let them join the lady while he had her attention. They diverted on their path, and he smiled without mirth. When Jane snickered, he looked at her. "What?"

"It's cute how you're jealous."

"I am not." He ignored the heat creeping up the back of his neck. "I merely don't wish to have our conversation interrupted." She could take from that what she would. "How have you been?"

"Well." The smile that flirted with her mouth teased him beyond measure, and his chest tightened with a need he hadn't felt in years. "I finished the book you bought for me."

"Oh? How did you find it?"

She shrugged, and the candlelight winked on her heart-shaped pendant. "I didn't enjoy it as well as the classic fairy stories." A throaty laugh escaped her. "I'm not certain if the wild ways of American living are one of my interests."

"Understandable." Would that he was a whole man and could claim the cushion beside her, encourage a chance brush of his sleeve against her arm instead of being removed from her due to the Bath chair.

"I enjoyed our conversation at the chocolate house."

"As did I." In some shock, he realized he spoke the truth.

"Good." She nodded and once more poked a gloved finger into her hair.

He frowned. "I beg your pardon, but are you suffering from lice?"

"Finn!" Her outraged squeak tugged a grin from him at his effrontery. "How dare you." Yet amusement continued to glimmer in the green pools of her eyes. "I do not. However, I despise hair combs and pins. They hurt my scalp and generally make my head hurt."

An image of her with her fiery hair flowing free about her shoulders and back took up residence in his mind. The fact that, in his imaginings, her gown was loose and sagging on her arms, barely clinging to those voluptuous globes of her breasts had no relevance.

"Then I hope you find relief soon."

"Since I can't exactly let down my hair in a public setting, perhaps you should tell me about your family. I wish to understand the man beneath the surly disposition."

"I can't help who I am."

"Pish posh. I believe you can, but you're too lazy." When he bristled, she winked. "Settle, Finn. I'm teasing."

Why would she do such a thing? "Fine. Where shall I start?"

"Where were you when your father died?"

The directness of her inquiry stole his breath. "Somewhere in Belgium." He waved a hand. "I'm told Father died shortly before the Battle of Waterloo." Even if he hadn't been fighting to survive, if he had been notified that his father was near death, he wouldn't have made it home in time for a last goodbye. Besides, there had been his best friend to consider, and the promise he'd made.

"I imagine you were devastated." Her eyes were luminous

and clouded with concern and grief. "I was when my mother died, but then, I was a young girl at the time."

"Truth to tell, I wasn't given the chance to properly grieve, for we were preparing for the battle, and then it was upon us." Shock from the admission sent pain ricocheting through his chest. "After that, I was wounded, struggling to survive in a whole different arena than war had made." With his hands tightly clenched on the arms of his chair, he shifted his position. Tingling sensation pushed through his right buttock and leg but faded before he could marvel at it. "I thought about many things during the long period of convalescence but mostly my thoughts concentrated on the fact that I would never walk again."

"I'm sorry." She leaned forward and again touched his knee. "You have gone through more than most men do in an entire lifetime."

And where were the thanks for it? Certainly not here or in any of the homes he'd been invited to. No, the only thing people wanted from him were stories from the battlefront, the gorier the better. One little word of gratitude for the sacrifices he'd made on England's behalf would have gone a long way in the last two years.

The thoughts sent a wave of bitterness crashing into him.

"You're scowling," she was quick to point out.

"I'm entitled to it." He waved a hand to encompass the artifice in the room. "Ungrateful lot, all. Half of these nobs didn't deign to fight, yet their lifestyle is possible because of men like me who held Napoleon back." The words were clipped and thrown like daggers.

What was wrong with him that talking to her pulled the secrets from his soul as if by magic?

Jane retrieved two glasses of champagne from the footman as he came around again. One she handed to Finn. "I'm eternally grateful for what you, my brother, and countless others did out there. Never think I'm not." When she took a sip of her drink, he once more stared at her lush lips.

Damn. What he wouldn't give to taste that wine from those two pillowy pieces of flesh. But he couldn't; he didn't have that right, and what the devil did he think would happen after that? With more haste than finesse, Finn took a large gulp of his own drink. The bubbles tickled his throat and made his eyes water.

"Gah!" He swallowed again. "How does anyone enjoy this?"

"I think it's wonderful." She smiled and her eyes twinkled. "Where is your brother, or rather the Earl of Hadleigh, now?"

"In Derbyshire, on the family's country estate. And from all accounts, he's wedded a woman he scarcely knows." Another swath of jealousy reared and slashed its way through Finn's chest. He downed the remainder of his drink in the hope that it would drown those emotions for things he would never have. "Father always favored Drew because he was the heir and would one day become the earl. My parents expected much from him, held him to a different standard, I suppose."

"That's how it is with my oldest brother and my father. They bicker and fight all the time over his expected future."

Finn cocked an eyebrow. "Your brother the surgeon?"

"Oh, yes. While he knows that will ultimately be his fate, in the meantime, he follows where his heart leads, for as he said, why should he train for the Earl of Worchester while my father is hale and hearty?"

Unbidden, a grin tugged at the corners of Finn's mouths. "My youngest brother Brand is the baby, so he was always coddled and spoiled, no matter what, until his behavior became too scandalous."

"What happened?" She took another sip of her champagne, and when she pulled the glass away, a tiny drop of the wine clung to her lower lip. Finn held his breath until she licked it away, but that only stoked the need to kiss her. If he were alone in his own bedchamber, he might stroke his length merely to remind himself that he was still a living, breathing male who could hold desire for a woman.

"He had an affair with the wrong married woman whose

husband took exception to the whole thing." A chuckle escaped him. "So Father ordered Brand into the Navy or the church. Brand went for the Navy and never looked back."

"Has he been informed about your brother's marriage?"

"I have no idea. Mother is the one who sends letters." He leaned over and placed his empty flute on the floor next to his right wheel.

She scanned the room before giving him her full attention again. "Does your mother get on with Drew's wife?"

"None of us have met the woman." He shrugged. "Mother was quite hurt at the news."

"No doubt she was." Jane stared, questions clouding her eyes, the heart on its golden chain glimmering each time she moved. "Were you also hurt?"

The conversation had veered into territory that was too personal, and he refused to rip off barely formed scabs from deep wounds, especially in front of her.

"Finn." Jane set her glass on a small round table at her elbow. She came forward on the sofa and laid a hand on his knee, her touch lingering. Damn fate for making him paralyzed, for he couldn't feel the comfort or her heat. "How did your brother's marriage make you feel? Have it all out now."

"Why, so I have might a chance of acting sunny and carefree like you?" The words snapped in the air between them while her eyes rounded and hurt etched into her expression. He sighed. "I apologize. The subject matter is newly raw for me."

"I understand." She didn't remove her hand even though such an action would link their names in gossip if anyone were to witness their exchange. "It must have brought home your own mortality like a slap in the face."

"It did." How could she know what he struggled with, and him not saying a word? "I felt terrible, was extremely jealous. How could Drew with his arrogance and rage, convince a woman to marry him?" A growl had entered his voice. To cover his confusion and anger, he reversed his Bath chair and put distance between them so that her hand fell away. "Marriage is something I'll never have. Where I would have appreciated such a thing, Drew never will."

"You don't know that for certain. Perhaps he's changed in the time he's been away."

"Ha! Drew won't change." Finn shook his head. Darkness crept in to sit heavy on his shoulders. Depression whispered into his ear that he'd never be good enough, would never know any of what his brother had because no woman would want half a man. He took a shuddering breath while debating whether he should leave the rout early.

"There is nothing stopping you from wedding, if that's what you truly desire," she said in a soft voice that had him thinking of waking up next to her and seeing that glorious hair spilled over his pillows.

Bloody, bloody hell. What was this woman doing to him?

To cover his confusion, he snorted. "I'm paralyzed. Damaged. A waste of a man."

She shook her head. "You can still love, laugh, contribute and be present. There is much life ahead of you."

"Enough with your saccharine sweet outlook," he all but hissed. Her eyes widened but he continued. "There are other... *things* I can't do. Important things that a woman—a wife—will expect."

"Oh, Finn." Jane rose to her feet and shook out her skirts. The smile she flashed him held a sad edge, a pitying edge no doubt. "Physical intimacy is only one part of a bigger whole."

While he wanted to lash out at her in anger, she who stood there in her very perfectness, a temptation to every man in that room, he tamped the urge. "It's not fair!" he hissed, fearful of making a scene more than he already had.

A handful of people turned to stare from his outburst.

"Come with me." Without waiting for consent, Jane took command. She slipped behind him and pushed his chair through the crowds and across the room. Easily, she guided it out onto the terrace. No one else took advantage of the night air, for a light mist of rain cooled his overheated face. At the stone railing, she turned his chair and then came to stand in front of him. "No, it's not fair, but it *is* your life."

"As if I hadn't noticed." God, he was acting the prick, but any man would when faced with the same facts.

Jane blew out a breath. "What I meant is why spend the next thirty years mourning what you're not when you could live that time celebrating what you are?" She peered into his upturned face, but it was too dark for him to see what was reflected in her eyes.

Before he could respond, a dark-haired woman appeared at the doorway. "Jane, the Duke of Ballantrae is looking for you and the dancing will start soon. They're getting ready to roll back the rugs."

White-hot jealousy combined with cold bitterness to stab through his chest in duel attacks so intense Finn caught his breath and pressed a hand to his heart. It was only natural that a woman like Jane would want a man who could dance with her, stand up with her, be everything she needed him to be.

Everything I am not.

She glanced at the interloper. "Thank you, Fanny. I'll be right there." Once they were alone, Jane touched his shoulder. The diamonds in her bracelet sparkled in the dim light. "To the right lady, none of that will matter. Please think about what I've said."

The words had the power to disarm his emotions and leave him gaping at her. How did she do it? How could she know what to say that would both feel like a call to arms and a soothing balm at the same time? But it left him wanting so much more from her. "I will." He nodded. "Jane?" He caught her hand when she would have left the terrace.

"Yes?" Confusion echoed in that one-word.

"Just this." Before he could think the idea through, Finn tugged her down. When her face was close to his, he took full advantage and brushed his lips against hers. This wasn't the venue to kiss her as properly as he would have liked, but it was a start. At least she would know the gist of his feelings. As he released her hand, he said, "Thank you."

"For the kiss or the conversation?" She pressed a gloved had to her lips.

"That's for you to discern." For the first time in a long while, a bit of joy rose inside him to beat back the darkness.

"I'll call on you soon."

"I…" Annoyance circled through his chest, for she was doing things that a man should—making calls, plans for a next meeting…

"Remember, Finn, a man who risks nothing, has nothing—is nothing—and will never grasp his own potential, different though it may look now." The words were so low he had to strain to hear them as she moved toward the door.

Did that mean she wished for him to rise to the mark? Before his courage could desert him, he asked in a rush, "Will you come driving with me tomorrow afternoon?"

Delight twinkled in her eyes from the light of the room at her back. "I would like that."

"Good." He couldn't contain his grin. "Look for me around three o'clock."

"Enjoy your evening." She fled the terrace, vanishing into the room beyond that suddenly teemed with activity as folks prepared for dancing.

Did that mean they were having a courtship now? His chest tightened with worry. Did he want that? She was chatty, nosy, and managing, but she felt like sunshine and… hope. Suddenly, he wished to return home to work on his writing, for she'd inspired him.

In more ways than one.

There were worse ways to spend his time.

CHAPTER SIX

July 4, 1817

"NO, NOT THAT one. The sky-blue with the white daises embroidered on the hem," Jane directed her maid. Butterflies continued to dance in her belly. Had Finn truly kissed her last night? Well, it wasn't a real kiss, but that brief touch of lips had been a step in the right direction. When Anna held up the day dress, she nodded. "Yes, that will do. And the darling straw bonnet with the white ribbon and blue silk flowers." The brim on the headgear was stubby, which meant it wouldn't obstruct her vision... or anything else she might wish to do while on a drive.

"What does it matter the dress today? Do you have an outing planned?"

"I'm going driving with a... friend," What exactly was she to Finn beyond that? After she slipped the dress over her head and while Anna did up the short row of buttons, Jane pressed a finger to her lips. That fleeting sensation when his mouth had brushed against hers remained even now. "Besides, aren't you the one who keeps badgering me to get out of the house more instead of read?"

Anna twisted Jane's tresses into a loose chignon and secured it with a handful of plain hairpins. "It's good to take in the air." She pointed to a pair of sky-blue satin slippers embroidered with white scrollwork. "Best finish your toilette." Then the maid peered into Jane's face. "You're different today."

She ignored the heat that jumped into her cheeks. "Such gammon. I'm the same person I was yesterday and the day before that." To avoid meeting her maid's gaze, she busied herself with her slippers. Then she donned her grandmother's heart necklace.

"No, it's definitely something," Anna continued as she grabbed a white shawl from the cheval mirror where it hung. "You're more... illuminated I suppose."

"I don't know how." Jane encouraged a few curls from the knot to hang loose at her temples. "I haven't done anything scandalous." Except spend time with the major. She took the shawl and her reticule then moved to the door. "Feel free to take the afternoon off. I don't expect to return home until well after teatime. And there's not a society event to prepare for tonight." Hastily, she stepped into the corridor in order to avoid another barrage of questioning. "It'll be nice to have an at-home this evening."

She fled to the breakfast room and once arrived, tossed the shawl and reticule into an empty chair. Unfortunately, both her brothers were in attendance, but her heart leapt, for she rarely saw them outside of their work. "What a nice surprise this morning. I thought you would have already gone to the clinic. Why are you here?"

"It's Friday. We open an hour later. You know this, and I was in the mood for a decent breakfast. Mrs. Halsey is fine enough as a housekeeper, but she's rather rubbish as a cook." Royce, her oldest brother, frowned at her before shoveling a large forkful of hamsteak into his mouth.

True, she *did* know that but had forgotten what day it was, for every extra thought she had lay centered on Finn. Could meeting one man make her lose track of the calendar? She glanced at him with his dark suit and collar not as high as fashion demanded. The black cravat gave him a bit of understated elegance, and the pomade that tamed his auburn hair that wanted to curl had turned his mischievous self into a staid and proper surgeon.

"Pomade again?" She wrinkled her nose as she passed him on the way to the sideboard. "Why? I like you better when your hair is wild."

He snorted. "Why do you care?"

"You might have better luck with the ladies if you didn't use that nasty, foul-smelling goo in your hair." Thank goodness Finn hadn't resorted to such vanity. She rather liked seeing his hair sticking up in whatever way it would. It gave him more personality. With a slight smile, she filled her plate with all her favorites and brought it to the table, where she took a seat across from both her brothers. A mere eleven months separated them, but they resembled twins so strongly they'd often fooled many a governess and family member in their youth.

"That assumes I'm in the market for a permanent lady," Royce shot back in between bites of his breakfast. He followed the mouthfuls with a gulp of coffee. "At present, my time is well and truly spoken for, so the women I do select aren't looking for a commitment."

"I don't know how you have time to play the rogue while being a surgeon." She nodded when the butler hovered at her elbow with a teapot.

Royce sighed. "Leave it alone, little sister. You'll never understand the inner workings of a man's mind."

"Mmmm." She popped a bit of toast with marmalade into her mouth and chewed, but her focus was on Finn and what they would talk about this time.

"Jane." Her brother snapped his fingers until he had her attention.

"I despise when you do that." He often employed the same on patients who had difficulty concentrating. "It's quite demeaning."

He pulled a face. "You're woolgathering."

"I'm not." She hid her smile behind sipping tea. Royce didn't like not being the center of attention. Perhaps that was why he'd chosen to become a surgeon.

"You were, and you certainly weren't paying attention to me." He stared all the harder. "Ah, I see now. You have a new project."

"I don't." Jane didn't give him a glance, but instead spread marmalade on her toast. Ever since she'd begun working at the clinic, they'd teased her about the people she chose to minister to. "Why must you bedevil me?" Despite him, she couldn't tamp down the urge to grin. If she'd been alone, she might have hummed a few bars of a favorite song.

"Because it's entertaining," her brother went on with a grin. He speared a piece of hamsteak with his fork. "And, you *do* have a new project. You're only this happy when you've found someone you can fix."

"I don't fix people." But she refused to meet his gaze. It was enough that her other brother Trey kept staring without saying anything.

"Fine, but you work your magic on them, so they will fix themselves."

Jane took a sip of her tea. She bounced her glance between her red-haired brothers, who both looked back at her with expectation. "It's not about fixing. I simply wish for your patients to look at life in a different perspective." Perhaps Royce was right. She *did* feel happy, but then, Finn had that effect on her even if he was grumpy more than he wasn't. He had an air about him that made her want to share secrets with him and delve into everything that he was.

Her brother snorted. "Who is it this time?"

Lud, but he was relentless. She rolled her eyes. "He's not a project, just so you know." In fact, she'd never been as intrigued with a man as she was with Finn.

"*He?*" Royce's eyes nearly bugged from his head. He exchanged a glance with Trey, who shrugged. "Who, he?"

"You sound like an arse." Jane narrowed her eyes at her

brother while calmly continuing to eat her breakfast.

"That's because he is one." Trey chose that moment to join the conversation. "So," he waggled his bushy red eyebrows. "Who is the lucky man? For let's face it, you wouldn't continue to spend time with said man—"

"Project," Royce interrupted.

Trey shot their brother an annoyed look. "Man, unless you had an interest that transcended the purpose of the clinic." Returning from the war hadn't damaged his joking attitude. To his credit, Trey had accepted the loss of his left arm with grace and humor. It was refreshing and she wished Finn could find that too.

Oh, dear. Heat sank into her cheeks. "He's a friend, and I didn't meet him at the clinic." A friend who'd kissed her. Hastily to be sure, but she could still feel the flutters that had come from that kiss in her belly.

"Ah, a *friend*, you say." Royce made a theatrical gesture. "Pardon me, but does a friend who is male put such color in a lady's cheeks if that's all he is?"

"Quite right," Trey added with his own theatrics, fluttering his eyelids, and waving his linen serviette about as if he were a female actress on stage. "She's got that look, wouldn't you say?"

"What look?" With a frown, she glared at both of them. Why, oh why had she been born into a family with only brothers? "What look?"

"That look which says said friend is something more," Royce went on with a grin. "So, what is he to you, exactly?"

"Nothing more than a friend. Just what I said." It was hardly a lie. After all, one tiny almost-nothing-kiss didn't count. It had been a product of the moment, undoubtedly.

"Why do I think you're lying?" Royce's grin would be thought of as charming to anyone else except her. She knew that grin all too well. It had been a part of her childhood when Royce had bedeviled her, chased her around with bugs in his hands. "What do you think, Trey?"

"Oh, she's definitely lying." Her second brother leaned across the table, and with his fork, he speared a piece of her toast, quickly taking it back to his side. "I mean, her freckles only stand out like that when she's under high emotion, and there's no other emotion like looooove." The way he said it made it sound silly and demeaning.

"Well, she does have an inordinate interest in fairy stories and illicit novels. No doubt they've rotted her brain," Royce said with a nod. He threw a glance her way. "So, are we right?"

Both of them nodcocks. "No!" Jane shook her head despite the heat in her cheeks. They didn't need to know that each time she read such stories now, Finn was always the hero in her mind. Why didn't she put powder over her freckles before coming down to breakfast? Of course, she had no idea these two jokers would try to reenact the bloody Spanish Inquisition. "We're friends. The end."

"Since you're committed to that answer, I have no choice except to accept it for the moment, but I'll be watching." Royce held up a hand while Trey finished his stolen toast. "Does this manly friend have a name?"

Should she tell them? If she didn't, they'd badger her until she gave up the information. Besides, she was proud of Finn, and was desperate to talk about him to someone. "He's Major Storme." When another wave of heat infused her face, she huffed. "Satisfied?" *I am much too old to keep blushing like a girl fresh out of school.* There was no reason for it. She'd been engaged twice before and wasn't inexperienced. "As I said before, we're friends."

"Major Storme, huh?" Royce turned his head and looked at Trey, who widened his eyes and frowned. Then they both stared at her as if they couldn't believe what she'd said.

The hair on her nape prickled. "What?" They knew something that she didn't. Something big.

"Nothing. It's not entirely relevant at the moment." He stabbed at another piece of hamsteak. "Where did you meet the major? I was under the impression he didn't go out into society that often."

How did *he* know Finn? "We met at a rout last week. At Fanny's home." She couldn't help but smile once more while pushing the food about her plate with her fork. Her appetite was no longer prevalent. How could it be when anticipation regarding her imminent drive with Finn thrummed through her veins with every heartbeat? Happiness continued to bubble up in her chest. "He's fascinating. Despite being in a Bath chair, he's managed to acclimate himself to that fact better than most." To be sure, there was bitterness in his attitude, but no man could banish it altogether. "I'm hoping my support will help him accept his new reality and his abilities."

Trey snorted. "So, he's a project." He sat back in his chair and shook his head. "Unsurprising."

"No, he's not!" Jane took refuge in draining her teacup. When the butler stepped forward, she nodded for a refill. "I truly enjoy talking with him, but the major thinks he's too broken to be of use in today's society. I'm trying to convince him to change his mindset." When they'd met at the bookseller and he liked the same books she did, her interest in him increased.

But when he'd brushed his lips against hers? *Something* had changed between them, and she'd be a fool if she didn't explore it.

Wouldn't she?

Royce cleared his throat. The small sound yanked her from her musings. "Some men who returned from the war fall into that trap. They feel hopeless and worthless. Depression is often their Achilles' heel, if you will." His expression sobered. "At times, their thought processes are too damaged to come about. Any sort of life at that point is littered with pitfalls."

"Yes." Trey nodded. "The mind, once compromised, is difficult to return to normal." Of course, he would say that, for her brother studied everything, including psychology, among his many medical interests. If there was something wrong with a brain, Trey would dig until he discovered why.

"Perhaps normal is overrated." Indeed, Finn wasn't like any

other man she'd ever met. Jane narrowed her eyes. "However, he and I haven't spoken about his time in the military." She sighed. "He's quite adept at changing the subject when I introduce it." That didn't mean he was flawed.

"Interesting." Royce stroked his fingers along his chin as he stared.

"Indeed," Trey said while he shoveled his fork through a pile of golden scrambled eggs. "Does he behave erratically or have mad starts of temper?"

"Not that I'm aware of." She took a gulp of tea. Really, it was outside of enough that her brothers couldn't let this go. They hadn't cared that much about her last beau, who had also been in the military... not that Finn was a potential romantic partner.

Was he? Intriguing thought, that.

"Is he violent?" Trey wanted to know next.

"Absolutely not. He's charming when he wills it, and he's quite gentle." She shrugged. "I think he has a cat, for I've seen stray hairs on his jacket a couple of times."

The men exchanged another glance.

Royce cleared his throat. "Is he different from your other projects?"

"Don't be more of an arse than you can help," she bit off and set her teacup onto the table with more force than necessary. Amber liquid sloshed over the rim. "He is not a project! In fact, we're going driving this afternoon." Oh dear, she hadn't meant to mention that.

Her brothers gawked, and in Trey's case, his lower jaw dropped.

"Perhaps you've bats in your belfry, sister dear, for your protests and your actions do not align," Trey began in the voice he used to counsel patients. "Are you interested in Major Storme as a *man* over that of a project?"

Oh, how blessed annoying the pair of them were! However, it was a fair question. "Perhaps." She certainly wished to pursue the avenue that kiss had started. "It's quite an intriguing theory, isn't it?"

Again, her brothers exchanged glances, this time of unease.

Royce laid down his fork and met her gaze. Concern roiled in his. "If he conducts himself as less than a gentleman or tries to get handsy, please let me know and I will call on him."

"You mean threaten him?" Jane shook her head. Really, this had gone too far. "The major is nothing but proper." More's the pity, that. "He's not scandalous in the slightest." It was quite sad, really, for he would no doubt be a wonderful kisser. Butterflies erupted in her belly as a testament to that thought.

"Very well, but please be mindful. A man like the major isn't who I'd choose for you."

A stab of annoyance cut through her chest. "Because he's not whole?" Never would she think Royce such a pompous, prejudice arse.

"No, because falling in love with a wounded, military veteran is a rocky, uphill path to trod. Every step will be a battle, for he's at war with his demons that could take a toll on everything between you."

Trey nodded. "It's harsh, but it's the truth. Royce and I see it every day in our work."

"I'm trying to protect you." Royce went on. "I'd rather you know only happiness instead of frustration, for you've already had more sorrow than a woman should." His words were without guile, and the concern in his eyes tugged at her heart.

"Thank you for that," Jane said in a soft voice. "I promise to keep that in mind."

Nothing more was said, for her father entered the room at that moment. His big, barrel-chested form seemed to fill the space, and no one would guess he was nearing the age of sixty. "Good morning, children." He glanced at her brothers. "To what do I owe the pleasure of having the two of you at breakfast? I scarcely see you anymore."

Royce shrugged. "We're quite busy at the clinic. It's turned out to be a terrific business venture."

"That's good to hear. Mind you don't become too acclimated to the work; you're destined to hold the earl's title and that's where your concentration should lie."

Jane looked at Royce. All the pride and confidence had leeched from him for a moment, and he wilted before he straightened his spine and frowned. "Royce is a wonderful surgeon, Papa. He's talented, and I'm proud of what he does."

"That doesn't excuse tradition or duty. Sullying one's hands at work in exchange for coin might do well for the merchant class, but it's crass and beneath those in the *ton*." Her father's steely gaze alighted on her. "Speaking of which, Jane dear, it's time you settled down and marry. I'm not getting any younger and I'd like grandchildren."

Not this again. She huffed out a breath that ruffled an escaped curl on her forehead. "You have two sons who are older than me. Harangue them to marry."

Her father dropped into a chair while he accepted a cup of tea from the butler. Then he swung his attention to her. The intensity there made her want to hide beneath the table as she'd done when she was a little girl. "Men are different. Women, however, need the wedded state, for it's unseemly to remain single at your advanced age."

"I won't marry without love, Papa. Thus far, I haven't found it."

"Enough of that." He held up a hand. "I've been patient with you due to your abysmal luck in bringing a man to the altar. But it's time to move on with your life." He nodded his thanks at the butler when that man placed a loaded plate in front of him. "I've accepted an invitation to a ball later this month, hosted by the Duke of Ballantrae. I'd like to see you talk and dance with him. You're beautiful enough to capture his interest." He nodded. "He's a good man and will make you a fine husband."

All the happiness and anticipation she'd had previously faded away in the face of her responsibility. "Do I have a choice?"

"You do not. I've made my decision, and if the duke is of a

mind, I'll give him my permission to pay his addresses to you." He took up his fork while her brothers remained deathly quiet on the other side of the table. "It's unseemly for you to gallivant all over London by yourself or continue to attend *ton* events with nothing to show for it."

"But—"

"No more excuses. I want you engaged by the end of the month. Ballantrae will do nicely. If your mother were alive, she would agree."

A swath of grief fell over her. Jane pushed her plate away. "Mama would have wanted me to marry for love and friendship."

"True. You take after her more than the other two." Her father chewed thoughtfully, and once he swallowed, he continued. "Perhaps marriage will quell your penchant for the fanciful. Out of all the men I know, Ballantrae will suit. You'll find purpose in being his duchess."

She glanced at her brothers, but they both had their attention fixed to their plates. No help from that quarter. *Cowards.* "What if I'm interested in a different man?" Not that Finn was remotely thinking of marriage. He'd not yet indicated any sort of curiosity in her as a woman outside of that poor excuse of a kiss.

"Who?" The question was more of a demand than a polite inquiry.

Did she dare? On the heels of a hard swallow, Jane said, "Major Storme. He's the second son of the Earl of Hadleigh."

Her father snorted. "Absolutely not. That man is paralyzed if the rumors are true. He has no hope of fathering children, let alone doing anything else needful or of import." He narrowed his eyes as he looked at her. "You'll marry the duke, and that's final. I won't hear more of your nonsense or delays."

Finally, Royce nodded. "It's the more sensible choice, Jane."

As if Finn wasn't worth anything and should be tossed away into the gutter with rubbish.

In a fit of anger, she stood up from the table with such force her chair sailed over the floor. "The lot of you don't understand how unfair this world is for women. You assume that because your sexual organs are phallic-shaped and on the outside of your body, they make you more powerful or the only ones who are capable of thinking, but you're wrong." Her throat tightened with unshed tears, and the last thing she wanted to do was break down in front of them.

The glob of golden scrambled eggs held on Royce's fork halfway to his mouth fell to his plate with a soft *plop!*

Not even that could make her smile. "If you excuse me? I suddenly find myself sick to my stomach. Perhaps it's the company." Without waiting for an answer, she fled the room seconds before the first few tears fell to her cheeks.

An uphill path indeed, and she'd just lost the first step. She touched the fingers of one hand to the heart pendant her grandmother had given her. When it came time for a decision, would she have the courage to follow her heart over duty and responsibility?

Only time would tell. Too bad that was quickly running out.

JANE FORGOT ALL the hurt and confusion the second Finn pulled up at the curb in front of her townhouse. The flashy phaeton featured red-painted wheels while two gorgeous bay mares pulled the equipage. Her heart skipped a beat as she exited the house, tying her bonnet's ribbon beneath her chin as she went. Finn was so handsome and dashing sitting there with the reins in his gloved hands.

"Good afternoon, Major," she said with a grin as she approached.

"It remains to be seen how good it is," came his reply couched around a growl. "Playing with scandal if you don't bring a maid, aren't you?"

"I'm old enough to know how to deport myself." She ignored

his ill-humor. After stroking one of the horse's noses, Jane hitched up her skirts and then climbed into the carriage. When she sat on the luxurious squabbed bench next to him, tingles danced down her spine. His citrus and sage scent enveloped her, and she sighed. "I, for one, am choosing to believe this afternoon will be quite joyous."

"You would." With a click of his tongue and a slight slap of the reins, Finn set the carriage into motion.

"Did you have difficulty coming out from under your bridge this morning?" She refused to let his mood foul the day. Instead, she turned her head and drew her gaze up and down his person. Gray breeches were tucked into shiny Hessian boots, a gray satin waistcoat embroidered with green ivy vines and tiny blue flowers called her attention to his flat abdomen, and his royal blue superfine jacket perfectly complimented his broad shoulders and muscled arms. At the last second, she stifled a sigh of pure appreciation.

Too bad a good portion of the *ton* was gone from London this time of year, for she wanted everyone to see him while they drove. He was the perfect picture of masculine elegance.

Finn grunted. "That never fails to amuse." A grudging grin pulled at the corners of his mouth. "However, no. Suffice it to say that my disposition has come from my inability to find the correct way forward in my book."

"Your book?" She straightened her posture. "Never say you're writing one."

He narrowed his eyes. "Does this surprise you?"

"Quite frankly, yes, but it's fantastic!" She turned toward him in her enthusiasm. "What seems to be the problem?"

"I cannot make my characters do what they don't want." Those sensuous lips turned down in a frown. "They wish to do things not relevant to the story."

"Such as?"

"Romantic endeavors." He shook his head, and her gaze fell to the careless knot of his cravat. "It has no bearing on the plot, but how can I remain true to the piece if I don't at least hear what they want to say?" Such passion infused his voice that she gawked at him.

"Every good story, no matter the type, should have some element of romance. At the heart of every person, they want love and acceptance." She delighted at hearing him speak of things that had nothing to do with the war or his injury or outlook. "May I read it?"

"No!" Then he cleared his throat. "That is to say, not at the moment. I'd like to finish it first before I ask for impressions."

"Very well." She glanced at him, but his attention was on the street. "Will you tell me what it's about?"

"I will not." But when he turned his head and met her gaze, he grinned. Butterflies erupted in her belly, for it was quite potent. "I want you to remain surprised." Why did a slight flush cover his neck above his cravat?

Jane smiled. She adored this side of him. Deciding to change the subject, she said, "I'm impressed you drove yourself today. Your horses and carriage are quite smashing."

A frown once more chased away his grin. "I'm not an invalid, Jane. It's a matter of me trusting the horses and my ability." Censure rang in his voice.

Oh, Finn. "I didn't mean offense." Daring much, she briefly touched his arm. The muscles beneath her fingertips flexed. "I simply meant that it's good to see you out—"

"Of my chair and looking normal?" Annoyance growled through his tone.

"No." With a sigh of frustration, she turned toward him again. This time her knee brushed his. Sensation zipped up her limb from the point of contact. "Why does your mind instantly go to the negative?"

"Habit."

"Well, stop. I don't appreciate it." Her words were sharper than she'd intended. "Honestly, you and I should be beyond that by now."

Several moments of tension-charged silence brewed between them as he drove toward Hyde Park. Finally, he blew out a breath.

"I apologize. Most times I assume people only have an interest in me due to pity or gathering fuel for gossip."

She glanced at him, caught the resignation in his expression, and softened. "There are more good people in the world than bad."

"Like you?"

"And my brothers." Jane laid her hand on his arm and this time left it there. He didn't dissuade her, and she smiled. "They're quite the pair and do great work at the clinic. I admire them for that."

"What of you? Have you inherited the same nature?"

"You know I have. The days I help at the clinic are quite fulfilling, and I like to hope that I do some good." She shrugged. "I've felt... compelled, I suppose, to lend a hand ever since the carriage accident that took my first fiancé."

"Were you with him when it happened?"

"Yes." It seemed such a long time ago. "I was quite young. Barely turned twenty. He was reckless, wanting to impress me you could say. Had a phaeton like this, but one of those higher versions. And he liked to drive fast, taking turns like a madman." Jane looked away and bit her bottom lip. "Hyde Park was a crush of people that afternoon, but Richard was overly confident. He raced through Rotten Row, but when he was obliged to swerve to avoid pedestrians, he careened into the path of an oncoming carriage."

"Oh, no."

She nodded. "His vehicle flipped. We were thrown. He broke his neck. I was stuck in the wreckage. One of the horses yanked the equipage over me, resulting in an eight-inch scar on my left side." A sigh escaped her. "It required a mass of stitches and weeks of bedrest to heal." Quick tears sprang to her eyes at the remembrance of that tragic day. "I wasn't able to tell Richard goodbye or even have a last word before his funeral."

"I'm sorry for your loss." Finn put the reins in his right hand and squeezed her fingers with his left. "I'm glad you weren't taken in the same accident, for the world would have grieved the loss of your sunshine."

"Thank you." She wiped at the tears on her cheeks. "I'm quite unlucky at romance. Every time I find myself in love with a man, something occurs to take him from me."

"There is always a risk in anything… even giving our heart to someone." He released her hand in order to concentrate on the street. "Only you can decide if that risk is worth the price."

"Love is always worth it," she whispered.

He snorted. "I wouldn't know."

"You've never had a lady in your life you've felt that way for?" She stared at him in mild shock.

"I have not. For more than ten years, the military has occupied my full attention."

"I'm surprised. You're quite handsome, and when you're charming, it's devastating to a woman's peace of mind." *Drat*, she hadn't meant to say that. "Not even a mistress?"

"Jane!" A strangled sort of sound escaped him. Mottled red color rose into his cheeks. "This is hardly proper conversation."

Merciful heavens, he's adorable. She leaned into him. There was something lovely in seeing him discomfited. "In the event you haven't noticed, Major Storme, I am not a proper lady."

"Oh, I've noticed. Make no mistake." He turned his head and met her gaze. Amusement and something darker lurked in his sapphire eyes, but she couldn't quite read it. "In my younger days while in Town, I had a mistress here and there, but once I entered the military, I didn't." He shrugged. "I won't say I was celibate during those years, because that's not reasonable, but I never treated a woman badly. At times on the march, the only comfort a soldier could find was taking refuge in perfumed arms and honeyed heat."

Heat blazed in her cheeks while hot jealousy lanced through

her chest. How she envied those women who'd known him in such a way. "I like a man who has had life experiences and doesn't apologize for them."

Would he be shocked to know she'd done the same?

CHAPTER SEVEN

E VERYTHING SHE'D EVER said had managed to surprise him. Why did he think this would be any different? Finn shot her a glance as shock and interest took up residence within his chest. Thank goodness for his well-trained bay mares who knew the trip to Hyde Park as well as they knew the mews behind the townhouse.

"Yes, well, some of the experiences I've had haunt me to this day." He glanced at her while her attention centered on the street ahead. The sky-blue dress she'd chosen complimented her ivory complexion and brought out a richness to her emerald eyes. Her russet hair gleamed in the sunshine beneath a pretty little bonnet, and that same hair streamed through his dreams, for he thought of her when the nightmares didn't beset him. She was easily the finest damned sight he'd laid eyes on in a long time.

"Do you often think about the war?" A matching reticule swung from her wrist when she lifted her left hand and waved to an apparent acquaintance strolling the pavement.

Surreptitiously, he peered past her to look at the person she'd acknowledged. A sigh of relief shuddered through him to see that it wasn't a male. "More than I'd like while awake, but when I'm sleeping, I'm powerless against the nightmares that comes with alarming regularity."

"Trey has them too."

He frowned as jealousy stabbed through him. "Who is Trey?"

"Oh, he's my second brother. It's short for Trenton." She met his gaze with a cheerful smile. "When he returned from the war—a few years ahead of you—he did so missing his left arm. Cannon fire caught him and blew it clean off." Compassion clouded her eyes. "He dreams of that time, and when he lived under our father's roof, I used to hear him cry out at night. It was horrible knowing I couldn't help him."

"Yes, rarely is there opportunity for a cessation of the nightmares." He swallowed down the wad of tears lodged in his suddenly tight throat. "They're quite real, I can assure you." Even now, talking about what he struggled with, the muscles in his arms went taut and he swore he heard the reports of cannon fire ring in his ears.

Oh, God, please don't let me have a nightmare in front of her.

"What do you do when they come?" Jane's eyes were wide, and she'd once more laid a hand on his arm.

Finn rather liked the warmth and the support she imparted. "Suffer through," he admitted in a low voice. "Hope I survive them without becoming lost." His breathing became a touch ragged. "It's as if I'm doomed to live the war twice... or hundreds of times." He shook his head. "On the nights when they're unbearable or I can't sleep due to the dark thoughts that plague me, that tell me I'm not good enough, or whole enough to remain alive, I take a dose of laudanum."

"Does it help?"

"When I take the drug, I don't dream at all, but it's a double edged sword, for if I rely on it too much, I'll become addicted. That will bring a new host of problems." And then what would she think of him?

"I've heard that, and sometimes, the men who arrive at the clinic are addicts who can't break the hold of the opium." She tightened her fingers on his arm. "War is a terrible, tenacious monster that sinks its repercussions onto everyone years later like the most horrible sharp teeth."

"That's a fair representation." Perhaps he wasn't the only one with a gift for words. That brought a certain satisfaction he hadn't known before. Imagine having a partner in life who could assist him with drafting books or even offering support when he needed it.

Which brought another, more interesting thought. What, exactly, did he want from this woman beyond the tentative friendship they enjoyed presently?

"See, though? That solidifies my point. If you make a conscientious effort to look on the bright side, perhaps it would help with the nightmares."

Despite her good intentions and the genuine smile that curved her kissable lips, he shook his head in disgust. "Can't you understand that depression can't be swept away merely from thinking of happier times? I can't magically snap my fingers and smile, for the darkness I battle with won't shy away from that." A decided growl had set up in his voice, but he didn't care. She must be made to see where he came from. His fingers tightened on the reins. One of the horses tossed her head, and he slowly relaxed. "I know you're an intelligent woman. That's why it upsets me you're being so flippant about this."

Jane sucked in a breath. "Once again, I didn't mean to offend." When she turned her head to look at him, a wash of tears made those gorgeous eyes luminous. "This is the only way I know to help." She pressed her lips together. "No one, except you, has ever taken exception to it."

Why would they when she presented such a tempting and wholly mouth-watering picture? One look at the curve of her hips or bosom and men wouldn't care what she said. "I'm trying to tell you the truth before you meet someone who won't be as nice about it as I am."

"Truth?" She huffed and crossed her arms beneath her ample breasts, pushing those globes tight against the rounded bodice of her dress. "I've had quite enough of *that* today. Thank you."

What the devil did that mean? He certainly didn't know, and

she'd gone silent.

After another lingering peek at her decolletage, he focused on the street. They would soon enter Hyde Park, and since it was such a fine day, anyone worth knowing in London would be out to promenade. But by God, what sort of man was he to sit beside this woman and not pull the phaeton into a private alley and then ravish the hell out of her?

I'm not a whole man, that's why.

Silence had sprung between them as the carriage passed through one of the more popular entrance gates of the park.

Jane played with the strings on her reticule. "What *is* the best way to help people like you? I'm always interested in learning."

At least she was willing. "You can listen to us, really listen, and though you haven't gone through the same circumstances, sitting with us in the quiet is a form of support that's sorely needed." He shrugged. "Some of us will want to talk; some won't, but it's not your duty to judge how we're healing." When she nodded but said nothing, he gathered the reins into his right hand and took one of hers in the other. "Above all, never stop shining your sunshine. When men like me aren't locked in nightmares or playing at being grumpy bridge trolls, we appreciate it."

"That is good to know."

It was as if the sun had gone behind the clouds, for she didn't smile at him again. Finn racked his brain for a way to bring back her natural happiness. "Did you want to hear about the battles I've been in?" If he stayed at society functions too late, the conversation usually came around to battles.

"Not if you don't wish to speak of them." She didn't look at him. "Trey never wants to talk of such, especially to me. I can't say that I blame him. It must have been terrifying to stand there facing down the enemy, not knowing if you'll live or die."

"Quite." She didn't need to know of the deep, profound fear that knocked a man's knees together or caused him to shit his pants the night before the last charge would begin. A lady of breeding shouldn't be privy to the sheer number of men who had died on those battlefields, the way their blood ran like rivers over the land, or how boys as young as sixteen bolted from cowardice only to be shot in the back by a superior officer for desertion.

To say nothing of the French brutality and torture that happened if one were unfortunate enough to fall prisoner.

"No man should ever have to experience the ravages of war, whether they agree with the politics behind it or not," Finn said quietly. "The only thing war serves is the rich and the legislators and the unscrupulous merchants who transport goods on demand for a price." Bitterness clogged his throat, choking him on the sour taste. "There is money to be made when war wages, and none of that coin falls to the men fighting or the people left behind to pick up the pieces."

"Oh, Finn, I'm so sorry for what you've been through." Jane turned toward him and threaded her arm through his, regardless of the crush of carriages around them. The scent of orange blossoms wafted through the air. "Forgive me if my naiveté has caused you grief."

"There is nothing to forgive. The effects of the war will continue to be felt for years to come, I'll wager." Ignoring her for a time, he guided the horses through the maze of carriages and pedestrians until they'd cleared the mess that was Rotten Row. "Did you wish to linger on the promenade, or should we follow the other paths through the park to more quiet, private locales?"

"A spot removed from the throng is most welcome." The smoky quality of her voice sent gooseflesh over his skin. How he wished he could feel that desire in his prick and stones. Just once and then he'd be satisfied with his lot.

As soon as the thought knocked about his mind, he realized it wasn't true. Not at all, and not when this tempting, caring, compassionate bit of womanhood sat beside him all peaches and light with her warmth seeping into his side.

"Very well. Let's find a shady place to park. Then I shall answer any question you put forth to me." Upon his honor he would, even if it were distasteful to him. She deserved that.

"I'll hold you to it." Then she smiled at him and his world came about right once more.

"I don't doubt it." He clicked his tongue and pulled on the reins, guiding the mares on a path away from the hub of polite society. "In the meanwhile, tell me the significance of that heart pendant you wear. I've seen it twice now." The colorful cloisonne bits sparkled and winked in the sunlight each time she moved or drew a breath. "It's quite pretty."

"Thank you." She touched a gloved fingertip to the heart. "It belonged to my grandmother. Oh, she'd had adventures in her day, and I'll wager she hadn't even told me all her stories before she died." A smile lingered in her melodical tones, and it brought one to his face. "She was a pillar of strength and the one I turned to when times were rough."

"I remember my grandmothers. One died when I was a boy, but oh, she was a veritable whirling dervish. Managed us all."

"That was my gran too." Jane giggled. "When I was a young girl, after my mother died, my grandmother used to tell me stories of long-ago knights and maidens who were rescued by those brave men." She shrugged. "They were tales to help me forget the pain of loss, I'm sure, but I ate them up and begged for more."

"The root of your love for fairy stories," he said softly with a nod.

"Of course."

"I had a similar experience, though it was my grandfather who fed my addiction, with those same tales of knights and King Arthur you probably heard."

"To live in such a gallant age." A sigh escaped her, and she pulled her arm from his. Immediately, Finn missed her touch. "Grandmother was the foundation stone of our family. On her death bed, she gave me this pendant, told me to always follow my heart regardless of what was expected of me, regardless of duty. I asked her why, for I couldn't fathom a time in my life that I'd need to heed that advice."

"What did she say?" He was enthralled in her tale as if she read from the most popular book of fiction.

"She laughed and said I should save it as a reminder for when the time comes." Again, Jane passed a fingertip over the heart. "I'm still waiting for that crossroad."

"Perhaps it's a good thing you haven't encountered it yet."

"Yes, but I know that it's coming." A touch of despair had entered her voice.

"How do you know?"

"My father wishes for me to eventually accept the Duke of Ballantrae as a husband. Right now, he wants me to do the pretty and flirt with the man at the next social event we attend together." She stared at her hands which we're twisted in her lap. "I'm in a quandary over what I should do."

Choose me over him.

A shaft of jealousy lanced through his chest so sharp he caught his breath. His fingers tightened on the reins. The horses tossed their heads and slowed their forward momentum. Of course, that's what fate would do to him. When he'd found a woman who might accept him for who he was, she was all but promised to another. By increments, he forced himself to relax. The horses regained their previous momentum, but his breath was labored. Each inhalation hurt.

"What is there to think about? If a duke is interested in you, then don't hesitate to take advantage of that." Good Lord, why did it hurt so much when Jane was nothing more to him than a friend? "You shall have a nice life as a duchess."

"At this moment, I don't want that life."

He could hardly hear her barely-there whisper and was obliged to lean closer. "Why not?" When she didn't answer, he nudged her shoulder. "Tell me. I might not be every woman's dream of a perfect husband, but I'm a good listener." As he uttered those words, he felt himself falling, tumbling, being buffeted about inside a funnel of darkness that sucked at him, ever-pulling him downward into the dregs of depression.

I don't want this life.

When Jane finally looked at him and met his gaze, the myriad of emotions in her jeweled eyes stopped the slide ever so slightly. "Because I've found myself presently fascinated by the second son of an earl. I can't leave him until he's well and truly away from his troll bridge, now can I?" She winked, but there was a sad little tilt to her lips. "He needs to be able to slay dragons before I can trust he'll be all right alone."

A rush of feeling filled his chest, and it smacked of pure, unadulterated joy. "I suppose not." He didn't mind that she thought he wasn't able to look after himself, for if he truly thought about it, those words might have rung true.

"Well then." She took a deep breath and let it out. "This seems a wonderfully quiet spot."

"Does it?" Finn hadn't noticed, for he'd been entirely focused on her and the fact that he'd soon lose her before he'd had the chance to appreciate what he'd found. He shook his head to clear all the fanciful notions bobbing around his mind. They'd covered a good area of the park while they'd talked, and his world had plummeted toward darkness. Oak trees lined this section of the path, and with their leaf-laden branches extended, shade covered the area. "Yes, I suppose this will do nicely." For what, he couldn't imagine; he'd been knocked off course.

By rote he guided the phaeton to the side of the pathway beneath the trees. The horses were content enough to graze on the lush green grasses. He threw the hand brake and wrapped the reins about that lever. As the hairs on his nape prickled, he used his hands to turn his body toward Jane's. She watched him, unconcealed excitement in her expression. "So, what question would you ask of me?"

Surely this can't be the end of this friendship, this... well, how could it be anything more?

"Tell me about your injury," she said without preamble.

He quirked an eyebrow. "I beg your pardon?"

"I'd like to know about your injury." Her sweet lips curved with a smile that had him reeling. "Why do you think it makes you lesser than other men?"

Heat crept up his neck and infused his cheeks. He tugged at the knot of his cravat, furthering loosening it. "That is not a conversation for an innocent lady." Or for any lady gently bred for that matter.

"What makes you assume I'm innocent?" A faint blush stained her cheeks. "Perhaps you should have inquired deeper into my past, Major."

He gawked. If she'd announced that she was London's most sought-after courtesan, he wouldn't feel more surprise than he did now. "Beg pardon?"

She looked at her hands in her lap. "Uh, I have a tendency to throw myself whole-heartedly into the moment, into everything I'm interested in, so I…" Her blush deepened, and it was one of the most beautiful things he'd ever seen. When she raised her head and met his gaze, pride and amusement shifted through her eyes. "I had relations with both of my fiancés, as I hinted at during one of our previous meetings. My father doesn't know, so kindly do not tell Worchester the next time you might meet."

Dear God. "I… I'm not sure what to think, for I'd honestly forgotten about that part of our conversations in the face of the random patches of feeling returning in my leg. I suppose I also chose to dwell on other happier things you've told me." How was that possible? She'd told him that in confidence with genuine emotion, and he'd been so wrapped up in himself and what he wasn't that it had slipped right out of his mind. "Forgive me. I'll do better."

For her. Because she meant… *something*.

Jane shook her head. "It doesn't matter."

"It does, and I'm sorry for being selfish." Disappointment sank like a heavy, cold stone into the pit of his belly.

"I suspect you've always been so, at least since you came back from the war. It's something you can work on."

"Yes." He regarded her with a wild sort of feeling that whipped about him. It was much like finding oneself stuck in a fairy story where magic abounded. How did she do it?

"Good." She inhaled deeply and let the breath out slowly. "Please say you don't think badly of me for being so scandalous, but I truly did adore those men, and in those moments, it was the most important thing in the world to show them I loved them, to be with them in that way."

"There's no need to explain." Lucky bastards, the both of them.

"Well." Her gaze fell again to her lap. "It's wonderous when one is in love, Finn. Or, at least I thought so. Perhaps it always feels that way." When her chin trembled, his heart did too. Never had he known anyone so honest or who wore her feelings on her sleeve as she did.

Teach me your secret.

"Also please know I don't give of myself *that way* lightly. It hasn't happened since."

"Stop." He put a finger beneath her chin and lifted her head until their gazes connected once more. "You don't owe me an explanation." Obviously, she was a woman grown who knew her own mind as well as what she wanted…

… And he couldn't give her any of that even if he might have wished it *before* she'd told him of the duke's interest.

"Are you, uh, still one for scandal?" *That* was the question he'd chosen to ask?

"Not anymore." She shrugged. "And I only did it twice since my mother died."

"Oh." He shoved a hand through his hair, upending the short tresses. "When you were young, I take it?"

"Yes, from a respiratory disease. I was eleven."

The feeling of being lost, so very lost, assailed him. It was different from the cloying darkness, but as confusing. He didn't understand how to process what she'd told him. And damn his injury that wouldn't let him feel anything carnally, for with her tear-luminous eyes and her obvious distress at the confession, he could have taken advantage if he hadn't been such a bloody gentleman.

"Do you wish to know of my injury?" The whispered question was yanked from him with all the ease she'd pulled all his secrets from him.

"Yes." She took possession of one of his hands.

"Very well." Finn nodded. "I took a ball to my spine. The field doctor said the bones could have been shattered, but I wouldn't know until I arrived in England." He rubbed his free hand along his jaw. "Once at the hospital in Bath, I was examined again and properly stitched up. My spine is intact, but the nerves twisted around it have been compromised if not cut. It all has resulted in paralysis."

Jane gave him a small, intimate smile. "Go on."

"All of that means I have no control over my bowels, resulting in the need to wear a cloth diaper like I'm a damned baby." He tried to pull his hand from hers, but she held on. "My valet must exercise my legs every day to keep the muscles limber, so they don't waste away. He must help me bathe myself morning and night. Beyond that, my prick doesn't work, so I can no longer… perform with a woman." He looked away, loath to let her see the failure and embarrassment that was no doubt reflected in his eyes.

"There's nothing to be ashamed of." She put a palm against his cheek and forced him to look at her. "You are alive, have been given a second chance. That's all."

"Oh, *this* is a second chance?" He scoffed. "This being reliant on everyone for nearly everything, even the basest of things?"

"I didn't mean—"

"Don't you understand?" His voice rose along with his ire. "Even if I put all of that aside, I cannot sexually pleasure a woman, so even if I found someone, fell in love with a woman, what is the damned point?" Did she not understand the enormity of that fate?

A tear fell to her cheek. "There are other ways to show a woman love, Finn."

"Bah." He wrenched from her touch that he both craved and feared. "No woman is that self-sacrificing nor patient."

"So you assume, but to the right woman, none of it will matter." She looked down the path, her gaze far away. "Love, true love, accepts someone for who they are, not who they used to be or who they can become."

What a poor deluded, naïve girl she was. "Pardon me if I choose not to believe you." Especially her, a woman who'd already given herself to two men. Perhaps had she been a virgin it wouldn't have made a difference, but now? No doubt she'd found him lacking. And why the bloody hell was he even thinking along those lines? There was nothing between them except friendship, and that was becoming quite trying at the moment.

"There you go, retreating beneath your bridge again, too afraid to stare the future in the face and see what might be possible because you can only see what you've lost." Jane shrugged. She tossed her reticule to the bench between them. "My brothers think you are a project that needs fixing."

"Why?" The change of subject rocked his mind. Or perhaps it was being in her company that set him at sixes and sevens. It was terrifying to like having her about when she'd all but admitted her path wouldn't run parallel to his.

Not in those words, of course.

Color blazed on her cheeks. Her freckles stood out in stark relief. "When I work at the clinic and find men who strike a chord with me, my brothers call them projects, for I give them the tools to fix their outlooks."

Something inside him broke. Too many emotions crashed into each other within his chest, threatened to break him apart from the onslaught. "I do *not* need fixing!"

"I never said you did." One of her red eyebrows rose. "You're the one who can't seem to grasp the concept." Compassion clouded her eyes. "There's nothing wrong with you that keeps you from being a kind, decent, productive man except your own damned stubbornness."

His chest tightened, for that was true also. He'd put barriers in his own way out of resentment and bitterness, and to keep from being hurt. "Then why do you want to know about my injury?"

"Are you so daft that you can't see what's right in front of you?" Her eyes widened. "I like you as you are, Major Storme. I'm curious, all right? I want to know what makes you… you." Then a frown tugged those lush lips downward. Confusion lay stamped over her face. "Why is this a bad thing?"

"Because I've never had a woman take such an interest in me, the *broken* me, before." He waved a hand as his heart beat wildly behind his ribcage. Might as well drive a wedge between them now, so when she finally left him for the duke it wouldn't hurt more than it already did. "Besides, you're too sunny and too deuced perpetually happy. I doubt you've ever known sadness or grief or trauma." As soon as the words fell from his mouth, he knew they weren't true. She'd told him so, and once again, he hadn't truly listened.

Selfish bastard.

"You're quite insane, you know." She turned toward him, eyes flashing green fire, anger lining her expression, and she fairly quivered with ire. "Have you suddenly forgotten my two engagements?" Her eyes reflected exasperation. "Shall I further inform you of my credentials in ill fortune so that I might reach your lofty level of wretchedness?"

"I didn't mean—"

"Oh, yes you did. Words wound as deeply as a knife or a ball from a rifle, and frankly, I'm weary of being on the receiving end of your bad moods."

"That wasn't what I—"

She shook her head when he once more attempted to interrupt. "I lost my grandmother at a time when I needed her most. My brother came back from war missing an arm, and that devastated me to my core, for I had to watch him pick up the shattered pieces of his life and begin anew. My other brother is a brilliant surgeon who adores his profession, but my father won't allow him to keep working the calling because he'll have to be an earl someday. It breaks my heart." She paused briefly for breath, her chest heaving.

"Jane, I—"

She shook her head so vehemently that the ribbon beneath her chin unknotted and her bonnet slipped off her head to the bench. "And every bloody day I'm in that clinic, I see men who are worse off than you, but they are truly grateful to be alive. Knowing I can't help them tears me up inside, but yes, I retain a sunny attitude, for I think that ultimately helps everyone. Not to mention I lost a babe years ago. That leaves a permanent scar on a woman's heart." Tears sparkled in her eyes. "So, please, argue with me again about how I *don't* understand."

Finn could do nothing except gawk at her. By God, she was magnificent in the storm of her own making, and he'd never seen anything more breathtaking. Before he could change his mind, he slipped his arms around her, pulled her as close as he dared, and claimed her lips in a kiss he'd wanted ever since he'd first met her. With little effort, he moved over her mouth seeking, introducing, exploring, and those two pieces of flesh were as plush and petal-soft as he'd imagined. He kept kissing her, familiarizing himself with the shape of those lips, her very taste until he wrenched away merely to have a look at her. When he peered into her eyes, he grinned.

"I apologize."

"For being an arse or the kiss?" Jane was as breathless as he, but her kiss-swollen lips curved in a smile. She slipped her hands up his chest to lock behind his neck. Clearly, she'd taken no issue at being so close to him.

"The first, for I'll never apologize for kissing you." He'd had no right, especially if she were well and truly promised to a duke, but he'd enjoyed it so much that he did it again. She was like heaven and every good thing in the world. Over and over, he drank from her, and when she made tiny sounds of pleasure at the back of her throat, he kissed her all the more, for in her arms like this, he could believe that nothing truly mattered regarding his physical limitations and that there was certainly a bright future ahead.

Finally, she pulled away. Her eyes had taken on a dreamy quality and a tendril of ruddy hair had escaped its pins. "Can we agree that you're capable of a great many things? The least of which is kissing. In that you are quite proficient."

"Yes." He caught her into his arms, but this time he merely held her. "Thank you for the reminder. I suspect I'm a nodcock most times."

She snorted. "You are, but I'll overlook it if you consent to see me again."

Too much more of that and people would assume they were courting. His heartbeat accelerated. "I'm promised to my mother all day tomorrow."

"Oh. How about the day after then?"

Muscles in his right leg twitched as if coming awake from a long slumber, but he couldn't move the limb. Or anything else below his waist. Did he want to court Jane despite the certain heartbreak that path would hold? He grinned and pressed his lips to her temple. "I can't think of a single reason why not."

He'd enjoy her company, for she kept the edges of the darkness at bay, but he couldn't promise either of them a future and refused to think that far ahead. No sense ruining the present. Yet the kernel of hope budding in his chest was a powerful thing.

At least she'd taught him that.

CHAPTER EIGHT

July 6, 1817

J ANE HID A yawn behind a hand as she glanced about the interior
of the clinic. With quick, efficient movements, she donned a
pinafore apron and tied the strings behind her back. She hadn't
slept well last night due to continuing thoughts of Finn and the
kisses they'd shared. What had pushed him to that pass, she didn't
know, but she wouldn't complain. It was as she'd thought; he was
an expert kisser.

Though it was Sunday, the clinic served a purpose in the
community. While a minor procedure currently occupied
Royce's time, Trey worked with a few patients who required
muscular exercise, so Jane wandered over to a group of three
men, one of whom was in a Bath chair much like Finn's.

"Good afternoon, gentlemen." She slipped into a straight-
backed wooden chair near them. "How are you?" Not familiar
with any of them, Jane bounced her gaze between them. "I'm
Lady Jane Marsden, and if you need cheering up, I can do that."

"How do you think we're doing, my lady?" A man with a
pinned-up sleeve asked. "We're here instead of doing what we
liked best."

"What would that be?" she asked though steeled herself to
hear the answer.

"Anything other than being a figure of pity," he replied.

"And there's not beer here," said another. He was missing a foot and had a crutch propped against one leg. "Even if there was, it ain't gonna put my foot back."

Laughter circled around the men, but it held a touch of bitterness more than mirth.

The man in the Bath chair snorted. He flicked his tired gaze to her. "That's all well and good, my lady, but sometimes a man doesn't want to be cheered."

She frowned. "Whyever not?" These men were harsher than Finn even if they shared the same attitude.

"That sort of thing can't alter reality. We're injured and always will be, so we need to talk to someone who understands. Not some little miss from the *ton* who hasn't any idea of what we've suffered and is only here to make herself feel good."

"But that's not true…" At the last second, she tamped the urge to roll her eyes heavenward. "And if talking with someone else doesn't work?" There were times when sitting with wounded soldiers felt a colossal waste of time.

The man without a foot looked her up and down with slow perusal that made her feel cheap and tawdry. "A good meal and a good fuck can make life better by increments, and that's the truth."

General ribald laughter circulated through the room. More men than the ones she sat with looked her way.

Heat flooded Jane's cheeks. "That was rude."

"It's the truth." He cocked an eyebrow. "Want to give it a go, my lady?"

"Absolutely not." She stood to leave, but the man in the Bath chair spoke.

"Except us that can't use our pricks," he said with a sage nod. There was no resentment in his expression, only resignation. "Then it doesn't matter."

The man missing an arm snorted. "I'll gladly take your share if she's giving," he said with a leer at Jane. "You can watch if that'll give you a thrill."

Oh, dear heavens. No, these men were *nothing* like Finn, but did he harbor the same thoughts? She turned to leave, the same time that a female nurse approached the man in the Bath chair.

"Enough vulgarity, Mr. Sumtner." The nurse, Miss Clark, had worked at the clinic for a year, and she'd been there the longest of all the female staff. Through Royce, Jane had discovered Miss Clark had spent a few years as a midwife, but when both of her brothers had come back from the war inured, she'd apparently shifted her focus into caring for wounded and disfigured soldiers, which made her a good fit for clinic work. "Let's get to it straightaway, shall we?" Miss Clark slipped behind the chair and wheeled him across the room and through a connecting door. Curious, Jane followed. The next area held six cots. The nurse pushed him over to one of them, and as the man maneuvered himself from the chair and onto the cot, she said, "You're due for bathing."

Jane raised her eyebrows. Could Finn get himself in and out of his chair without assistance? She'd never had cause to ask and neither had she seen him do it. "Would you like help, Miss Clark?"

"That's appreciated, Lady Jane, but if you'd rather not sully your hands…"

"It's fine." She wasn't opposed to lending her help when needed.

"Very well." Miss Clark nodded. With efficient movements borne of experience, she had Mr. Sumtner stripped of his clothing except for a diaper-like garment that wrapped about his privates and bum. Did Finn need to wear something similar? He'd alluded to it, but she hadn't been able to visualize such a garment. "There's a porcelain bowl with clean water, a rag, and a bar of soap in the corner. Please bring it over."

Jane did as she was told. By the time she'd returned with the requested items, Miss Clark had removed the protective garment, laying the former soldier bare as the day he was born. The fabric was soiled in both front and back, but neither the man nor the nurse was embarrassed or even concerned.

In fact, Mr. Sumtner did his level best at flirting. "Are you unattached, Miss Clark?" he asked as the nurse took the basin from Jane's hands. In its stead, she placed the soiled undergarment.

"There's a bucket by the door. Give it a good rinse then drop it in the hamper next to it. You'll find a fresh one in the cabinet near the washstand." As she wet and lathered the rag, she smiled sweetly at Mr. Sumtner. "You know that I am. When would I have the time to land a man?"

Oh, dear heavens, the smell! Only slightly familiar with a dirty baby nappie, for she'd never had reason to be, the stench of a grown man's excrement caused her to dry heave while the other two continued what was undoubtedly a familiar conversation. The mess in the garment was still warm and she could barely look at it as she scurried over the floor to the bucket. However, she was the only one reacting in such a way, and embarrassment fired deep in her cheeks.

I'm better than this, aren't I? She had no idea if she meant her reaction or the chore.

With no one to rescue her from the task, she plunged the soiled fabric into the water and swished it around until the worst of the mess had fallen away. Finn's words from the other day rang in her ears. *You'll have to get your hands dirty to make a considerable difference.* Had he meant in this type of situation? While she scrunched up her nose and squeezed the excess water from the garment, she shoved all thoughts and feelings away. Then she threw the fabric into the assigned bin, retrieved a fresh cloth, and returned to the soldier's cot.

Miss Clark glanced up at her with an encouraging smile. "Thank you." She gave one more swipe of the rag to the man's privates. It came away faintly soiled. "If you'd like to dress the area, I'll lift his hips."

"All right." Jane attempted to school her features into a mask of bland indifference as the nurse hefted the man's hips. She slipped the unfolded garment beneath his hairy buttocks.

"Go ahead and look your fill, my lady. I'm not ashamed," he joked while he gripped the sides of the cot to assist in moving his body so she could wrap the makeshift drawers about his thighs and equipage.

Her cheeks continued to burn, and she wouldn't look him in the eyes. "I'd rather not. Thank you." She took one of the pins Miss Clark handed her and did her best to close one side of the modified diaper, but her fingers fumbled so much with them both watching, she mucked it up.

"It's difficult your first time." Gently, the nurse batted her hands out of the way and then deftly manipulated the pin. "Fold over the side and stab all layers of cloth through." She did the same with the other side. "Twice a week, men like Mr. Sumtner come to the clinic for muscle exercises and a bath. It's oftentimes the only chance they have of cleaning the area, which is important for personal hygiene."

Jane merely nodded, for she'd been rendered speechless. The blinders fell from her eyes, for she realized how privileged members of the *ton* were to have valets and other servants that would assist in daily bathing and exercise. *What a terrible person I've been to think my silly talk of cheerful attitudes would help.* "I appreciate the tutelage." Why weren't laws passed in Parliament that would render aid to these men who'd given so much for King and country?

"Don't worry. The more experience you gain, the easier it will be." Miss Clark patted her hand and flashed her a tentative smile. "We could surely use another set of hands around here."

"So I gathered." She swallowed around the lump of tears in her throat. "I'll endeavor to volunteer more of my time." No matter how uncomfortable it made her.

"I'm glad to hear that."

"Me too, my lady." The soldier blew her a kiss. "Having a glimpse of those bosoms does wonders for my attitude." He winked.

Jane fled the room as Miss Clark said, "Time for your exercise, Mr. Sumtner, so let's get you dressed. How naughty you are to tease the lady."

Back in the main room, Trey happened to catch her eye as his group broke up.

"If you don't mind, little sis, could you check Mr. Wolmack's arm dressing? We've had a surge of new patients arrive in the last half hour, and I don't have time to do it."

"I'd be happy to." That she knew how to do and was familiar with, but it didn't mean she enjoyed the task. Once she'd gathered the correct supplies, she stopped at a chair where the soldier sat. "Let's see how progress had been."

The older man nodded. "It doesn't seem to heal properly."

"Tell me again how you injured yourself." Jane unwound the bandage currently on his forearm. The wound, though not oozing pus or blood, looked decidedly angry, and the certain smell that arose from it nearly had her emptying the contents of her stomach right there. She swallowed the hot saliva several times to ward off retching.

"I'm a bricklayer by trade. One of the buggers fell off a wall and hit me. Tore through my sleeve and left a big gash behind some three weeks ago. Haven't had the coin to see a doctor." He met her gaze. "Someone told me about this clinic. I'm leaving my father's watch for the surgeon here as payment." His eyes filled with tears. "Hoping it's enough."

Oh, dear God. When will the abject poverty and class separation stop? She nodded. His arm was hot to the touch, which meant infection. "You'll need to have Doctor Marsden take a look at this, and definitely will need a salve." Her stomach heaved and she stood abruptly. The supplies tumbled from her lap. "I'll let him know you're here."

Needing an escape, she'd barely told Royce about the man as she passed him in the short corridor that led to his exam room. Then she pushed against a door that dumped her into the alley behind the clinic. Without finesse or dignity, Jane cast up her accounts into a scraggly bush. She continued to heave until there was nothing left to give. Tears streamed down her face as she wiped her mouth with a portion of the apron's skirt.

Belatedly, she remembered she'd need to scrub her hands with the astringent soap kept on the premises before and after tending to patients, but instead, she stumbled to the few steps she'd tripped down to reach the alley and she sat hard upon them. Now she fully understood more of what Finn struggled with, and the reality of it was horrible.

She wept for the injustice of it all, for the plight of all those men inside the clinic, for every forgotten man that society had turned their collective backs upon and pretended not to see, and when she had no more tears, she sat on those steps and let her heart break.

I need to do better, to use my position in society to help these people. Only by her example—her brothers' work—would she draw the *ton's* attention to the problem. Until there was sweeping reform in the country, she could—would—make a difference one person at a time.

Finally, with a shuddering sigh, she stood and reentered the clinic and stopped to thoroughly wash her hands in one of the many basins.

When she returned to the main room, the man she'd helped was gone. Hopefully, Royce had taken him back to the exam area, for the both of them were nowhere in the common room, but as the baby fine hairs on her nape quivered, she scanned the room and gasped. Her heart leaped. Finn was there. He chatted with the man in the Bath chair that she and Miss Clark had bathed, and from the intensity of their expressions, they were engrossed in whatever the conversation was.

He never looked her way, and she didn't wish to disturb him, for he needed to socialize with others like him. All the same, silly pleasure welled within her chest. Had he come to see her or to visit the clinic for his injury? A new thought stole her happiness at seeing him. Had he injured himself again?

With half her attention on Finn, she drifted over to a battered wooden desk and slipped into the chair behind it. Various folders lay stacked in disarray containing the charts and notes of the current patients of the clinic. Quickly, she sorted them alphabetically and then pulled the two of the men she'd seen that afternoon. While she jotted down notes of what treatment they'd been given, she kept an eye on Finn. When he laughed at something the other man said, she unexpectedly lost a piece of her heart to him, for all that he'd experienced, for the fact he was here at all, for the miracle that he seemed to be helping the other man.

Across the room, Trey met her gaze and lifted an eyebrow in question then gestured with his head at Finn. Jane shrugged, but she smiled. Oh, she was smitten by the man, true enough. It wasn't a bad thing, but there was a definite challenge ahead.

Did he feel the same way about her? Outside of those kisses, it was difficult to discern. He kept his emotions close to his chest. Perhaps to him, she was only a fleeting interest, and if he'd been with a different lady in that phaeton, he would have no doubt kissed her too.

Cold disappointment circled through her midsection as she completed her task. When she looked up again, Finn was there, waiting in front of the desk. "Good afternoon, Major Storme," she managed to force out in a whisper.

"Good afternoon, Lady Jane."

"How did you know I was here?"

"I called at your home as requested, but finding you out, I asked the butler where you might be this time of day. So, I came over." He grinned, but she dropped her gaze, suddenly shy in his company after what she'd seen and thought. "What's wrong? Your eyes are red." He lowered his voice. "Have you been crying?"

"Yes." In the event he didn't hear her tiny answer, she nodded and kept her focus on her hands.

"Why?"

"I'd prefer not to say just now." How could she tell him that her respect for him soared without him interpreting it as pity?

"I see." Silence brewed between them while the clinic bustled with life around them. He cleared his throat. "My carriage is waiting outside. Would you allow me to take you home?"

"That would be lovely." Finally, she raised her gaze to his. Compassion and worry clouded his sapphire eyes, and her heart trembled. "Thank you."

"My pleasure." A tentative smile curved his sensuous mouth. "I'll even let you push me outside without complaint."

"And that will be *my* pleasure," she whispered as tears welled again in her eyes. It took a few minutes to remove the apron and hang it on a peg and then wash her hands again before she helped it outside.

At the curb where the shiny closed carriage waited, with the golden crest of the Hadleigh family—two swords and a spear encompassed by a swirling storm—the driver lifted him out of the Bath chair and into the carriage. While Finn scooted across the bench, Jane glimpsed the driver strap the chair to the rear of the vehicle with a set of leather straps and buckles before she climbed into the carriage. Her stomach plummeted, for London wasn't an easy place for the disabled to navigate. In that Finn was fortunate, but what of the rest of the men in Bath chairs? Or the men who couldn't afford even that?

A strangled sob escaped. She turned her face to the window as the carriage lurched into motion. No longer was her world bright and happy with a rainbow of colors. Shades of gray had intruded into the picture.

"I like the clinic." The rumbling tenor of Finn's voice broke into her musings. "I felt comfortable there, as if some of the men need my experience. They understand me and my unique struggles as well as the difficulties with acclimating to the civilian life."

Jane wiped at a tear on her cheek but didn't look at him.

"You're more than welcome to visit any time you wish. Trey could use the counseling help."

"I could see that. It was quite busy."

"I'll put in a good word for you with my brothers," she assured him in a flat tone. The enthusiasm for the day had paled. Suddenly, she hated her place in the world with its privilege and its shielding.

"Thank you." When she didn't respond, he sighed. "Jane, tell me what's bothering you." The worry in his voice broke through her thoughts and her reserve.

Briefly, she gave him an account of how she'd spent the last couple of hours. "I had no idea what your injury entailed, couldn't fathom what you'd meant when you tried to explain it to me yesterday, but now that I've seen..." Her words trailed away as she met his gaze.

He frowned. "No pity, remember?"

"I'm not pitying you." She moistened her lips. Her heartbeat accelerated when he watched the movement. "In fact, I'm quite in awe of you." A tear fell to one cheek then another. "And I'm definitely not worthy of being your friend... or whatever it is we are to each other," she couldn't help throwing in.

"Ah, Jane." Finn patted the bench next to him. "Come here."

She accepted the invitation with alacrity. The warmth of him seeped into her, but even that didn't sweep away the chill that had invaded her person. "I'm so sorry that I assumed a positive attitude and thought a sunny disposition could fix everything." Another few drops wetted her cheeks. "I was so stupid. No wonder you were angry at me."

"Hush." He turned his body and then gently wiped away the moisture from her skin. "There's no need for this self-recrimination."

"Oh, but there is. I've been content to sit in my ivory tower, never dirtying my hands with real work, and now that I've seen the disparity of our worlds, I'm compelled to do something about it."

"Then you belong to a small percentage of the *ton* who wishes to give back and improve conditions for the less fortunate. I'm proud of you." The delicate skin at the corners of his eyes crinkled with a grin. "Now that you know, I don't doubt you'll set the *beau monde* on fire."

A rush of pleasant sensation encompassed her from his praise. "Thank you for that." On impulse, she surged upward and pressed her lips to his in a brief kiss.

Finn pulled back and stared into her eyes. What the deuce was he looking for, and why did she hope that he found it? Then, with a groan, he gathered her into his arms and treated her to a series of long, drugging kisses that had her perilously close to forgetting her name… and everything else. The desire between them was a palatable entity. Heat swirled through her insides as awareness danced over her skin. She knew one thing with crystal clarity—she wanted him as a woman to a man.

All too soon, the carriage rocked to a stop, and she and Finn sprang apart staring at each other.

Jane patted escaped tendrils of her hair back into place. *Drat,* she'd misplaced her bonnet at the clinic. "Do you attend Lord Danbury's musicale evening in two nights? I'm going." She quickly moved to the opposite bench.

Heat and stark need clouded his eyes, the same feelings coursing through her veins. "I suppose I could be persuaded to locate my invitation. Why?"

She swallowed to encourage moisture into her suddenly dry throat. "I'd like to perhaps find a bit of scandal."

"With me?"

Any second the driver would open the carriage door. "Oh yes." She smiled as he fixed his loose cravat.

"Even though I'm not a man as able-bodied as the duke?"

Warmth touched her cheeks. "Yes." She nodded, for emphasis. "I like *you*, Finn. Sometimes a woman knows what—who— she wants." Would he know what she didn't say?

He cleared his throat as his eyes darkened. "Then let us pray we're afforded time alone when the event arrives."

"We'll make certain of it," she said in a low voice as the door swung open and the driver offered her a hand.

As she stepped to the curb in front of her townhouse, she thought she heard Finn whisper, "Bloody hell, I think I'm in trouble."

Oh yes you are, Major. And I intend to show you that you are still very much worthy of... everything.

What she'd do if that didn't happen, she didn't know. That was a worry for another day.

CHAPTER NINE

July 7, 1817

F INN SAT IN his closed carriage while contemplating the front
door of an ordinary, smallish townhouse in Piccadilly Circus.
The street had been quiet the whole time he'd sat there with a
soft rain beating against the window glass. The overcast skies lent
a gloomy atmosphere to everything, and quite frankly, it matched
his mood.

With a frown, he stared at the emerald ring he'd stuck on his
forefinger. The small gold band, made for a tiny, slender finger,
only went to his first knuckle, but it didn't belong to him. No, this
was the engagement ring meant for his best friend's girl, the one
he should have seen straightaway after he'd returned to London.
Yet here he was, eight months later with the ring in his possession
because he was a coward.

From the other bench, Rodgers frowned. "Best have this over
with, sir. You'll feel better for it."

"Perhaps." It certainly wouldn't weigh on him any longer.

A sharp rapping on the door preceded the panel being swung
open. His driver stood with his shoulders hunched into his
greatcoat, water dripping off the brim of his hat. "Will you need
your chair, Major? Or shall we continue on?"

"Yes, I'll need it. I've put off this call long enough, and my surgeon is coming to call later."

"Right then. I'll just unstrap it and bring it around."

"Thank you, Collins. We shan't be long." He turned up the collar of his own coat. Once the driver wheeled the Bath chair to the carriage, Finn slid to the edge of the bench. Rodgers hopped out of the vehicle and turned, easily picking him up into his arms and then he set him into the chair. "Thank you, Rodgers. I appreciate your support." Having his friend and valet about helped to lessen the indignities he suffered on a daily basis.

"I'd sooner cut off my own arm than abandon you." The valet went ahead up the short walkway.

Thank the good lord there weren't steps to the nondescript door. When Finn nodded, Rodgers rapped upon the panel. Once it swung open, he stood silently off to one side so that Finn was the focus.

An older woman stared first at Finn then flicked her cold gaze to Rodgers. "What do you want? We're not *that sort* of household."

Despite the curiosity to know what *sort* she referred to, Finn shoved the urge to ask from his mind. "Is Miss Waterson in? My name is Major Storme, and I've a need to give her a message that's long overdue." Nervous sweat trickled down his back, at least where he could feel it, and his palms were damp inside his gloves.

The woman's dark eyes narrowed. "One moment."

Finn jumped as the door slammed closed. He glanced over his shoulder at Rodgers, who shrugged. For long moments, he focused his gaze on the closed panel in front of him while the rain *tap tapped* on his top hat and dotted his coat.

Finally, the door opened again, and this time a younger woman stood blinking at him. Sandy-blonde hair was caught up in a sloppy bun. She wiped her hands on a pinafore apron that was already decorated with streaks and smudges from cooking.

"Look who the cat dragged by," she said by way of greeting. Annoyance and grief mingled in her brown eyes. "When Edward wrote me of his best friend, I didn't expect he'd become a coward who is only just coming to visit." She crossed her arms at her chest while looking him over, no doubt finding every flaw. "I received a letter from Edward's mother nigh onto eighteen months ago telling me of his death. Where have you been?"

This was the sweet woman his best friend had wished to wed? Yes, grief changed people, but this wasn't for the better. Her ire brought his own bubbling into his chest. "Not that it's any of your business, but I spent copious months in various rehabilitation and recuperation hospitals before I was released to my own devices."

"In his last letter to me, he asked me to be his wife. Edward also said that if anything were to happen to him, you would come by and take care of me." A tiny waver had entered her voice, the only testament to the grief that did indeed still plague her. "Yet where were you when I needed you?" she finally asked in a soft voice.

What the devil was this then? He gawked as his mind reeled. "While I did know of Edward's plan to find himself engaged to you, I had not been apprised of his wish that I take care of you." He shook his head. What a coil. "As this is our first meeting, I'm going to respectfully decline his premature offer." Why the deuce would his friend promise something like that without consulting him?

"Ha! Just as I thought. Men are all the same. When it comes time to do the responsible thing, they balk." She looked him over again. Shades of disgust colored her expression. "As if I would ever wish to find myself wed to an injured man. I have enough work already without taking care of a grown adult."

"To that end, why the hell would I wish to align myself with a shrew like you?"

Her eyebrows lifted. "Shrew? What do you know of my life as it is now? Every dream I had depended on wedding Edward. Now, what is left for me?"

"You could find someone else to marry. There's nothing stopping you."

"Except you were the second-chance plan, and now look at you."

"Ah, so your misfortune is to be my fault?" His cheeks heated with shame. Her words cut to the quick and sliced away at his confidence. "Of course, you're entitled to your opinion." Before the situation could grow more entangled, he plucked the ring from his gloved finger and held it out to her. "He wanted you to have this."

She snorted. "And what am I to do with a bauble? It certainly won't take care of me in old age and neither will it keep me warm at night."

"I understand that you're talking out of grief and loss, but it's a token of his affection, a reminder of him that you can wear always." Again, he offered the ring. The stone wasn't as brilliant in the overcast air.

"Edward couldn't manage to stay alive so that he could come home and wed me. Why would I wish to remember him? It's not as if my life will become any easier from wearing a useless engagement ring." Before Finn had a chance to say anything more, she stepped inside the house and slammed the door.

"At least pawn the ring if you don't wish it for a memento." That was the logical thing to do.

She turned up her nose at it. "I've washed my hands of both of you and am tired of the disappointment."

Or perhaps she enjoyed playing at being pathetic more, but that didn't matter, for her words had found their target. Hot guilt twisted through his chest. From everything his friend had told him, he and this woman had loved each other wholeheartedly. Perhaps it had been a blessing in disguise that Edward hadn't made it out of the war. Sentenced to a lifetime with such a woman would have devastated the jovial man that he'd known. With a shaking hand, he tucked the ring inside the pocket of his waistcoat. "Well then. That couldn't have gone more wrong if Drury Lane writers had concocted it."

"Put her from your mind, sir," Rodgers said as he assisted

Finn in turning the chair around. "A woman of her caliber and ungratefulness will only bring more trouble."

"Perhaps." But those words would haunt him for a long time and tie into the guilt and pain he already carried for not being able to save Edward on that damned battlefield. "Let's go home. I would appreciate a drink before my next appointment."

Why was life so bloody difficult... and disappointing?

FINN SIGHED WHEN his surgeon came into the drawing room. He set aside the notebook where he'd been steadily writing for the past couple of hours. The rain from the morning had persisted into the afternoon, so he'd decided to meet the man there where the doors to the terrace beyond had been thrown open to encourage the rain-scented summer breeze into the room. Wellington sat on the threshold watching a few birds, her tail twitching but far enough from the rain that she wouldn't get wet. "Thank you for coming, Doctor. I'm anxious for this examination."

"Oh? Why is that?" The man's red hair had been tamed with pomade and parted in the middle of his head. He'd rested a black medical bag on a small table near to Finn's position.

"I have some questions, for... things have happened I need advice on." Jane hadn't been far from his mind. How could she be? After the kisses they continued to share and the hints they'd both made regarding a possible assignation at the upcoming musicale tomorrow evening, he couldn't forget her. For the first time since his life-altering injury, he needed knowledge regarding sexual performance.

"Well, that's how we learn." The doctor came into his personal space. For the next several minutes, he performed the typical exam—feeling the muscles in Finn's legs, looking over his limbs for any sign of sores or atrophy, then he bent him over in the chair to run his fingers over the scar on Finn's spine. "You are consistently doing the leg and foot exercises I prescribed?"

"I am. My valet assists."

"And you've taken to getting outside to breathe relatively clean air into your lungs?"

"I have."

"Good. Building up self-reliance is helpful in these cases as well." He glanced at Finn with a nod. "Everything seems in order. No changes since my examination three months ago."

"That's good." He slipped a linen shirt over his head, shoved his arms through the sleeves, and smoothed it over his torso.

"Indeed." The doctor wrote a few notes into a leather folio. "Do you need a new prescription of laudanum?"

"Not just yet."

"Oh? Have the nightmares subsided?"

"They haunt me but are not as relentless nor every night as they were before. When they become unbearable, I use the medication." He laid that firmly on Jane's doorstep. Being able to see her, spend time in her company was as healing as sitting in the sun.

"I'm glad to hear that." Something about the doctor, his mannerisms, seemed familiar. He took a seat near to Finn's chair. "If you don't mind, I have a few questions before we move on to yours."

"Please, go ahead." Out of all the surgeons he'd had since leaving Waterloo, Doctor Marsden had been the most attentive and thorough.

"Have you been socializing? That's good for mental health," the doctor began.

"I have." Had it only been over a week since he'd met Jane? Damn, but it felt as if he'd known her longer than that. "Though I can't say that I've stayed at any event to its end."

"Understandable. The *ton* is exhausting." He made another note and then leaned back in his chair, resting an ankle on a knee.

"Do you imbibe in alcohol or spirts while out?"

"Only within reason." Finn frowned. "I had a snifter of brandy late this morning." Why did the doctor wish to know?

"Excellent. Mixing drinking with laudanum is never a brilliant idea."

"I'm aware of the dangers, but I'm careful."

"Ah." Another bob of the doctor's head. "Are you prone to bouts of depression? Having laudanum around if so is equally dangerous."

"Depression never goes away. I'm slowly learning how to keep it at bay." Thanks to Jane's influence. "But on the days when that doesn't work, I suffer through and hope for the best. Having the cat around during those times also helps keep me grounded."

"I see." The doctor flicked his gaze to Finn's face, searching for God only knew what. "If it grows worse, I'll need to know."

"Understood. I've taken up fiction writing to help counter or even funnel those feelings. It's a new hobby yet, but I'm cautiously optimistic."

"That's good. It also exercises the brain." He tapped his chin with a forefinger. "Now then, to change the subject, you're a relatively young man. Have you considered finding a woman and settling down?"

Finn narrowed his eyes. "That goes beyond professional curiosity, don't you think, Doctor?"

"I merely meant that you shouldn't let your injury hold you back from enjoying a full life." He smiled, but the gesture was tight. "Have you become interested in a lady? That could change your mindset."

How the devil did he know *what* his mindset was? "Actually, I have. We've spent some time together."

"That's encouraging."

For long moments, silence brewed between them. Finn glanced at the terrace. Wellington had stretched out a long arm so that the tip of her paw was in the rain. Anxiety circled through his chest, and he held out hope that the answer to his next question was favorable.

"Since there *is* a female in my life, my thoughts have turned to the future."

The doctor nodded. "Also understandable."

Finn cleared his throat. "Will I be able to have carnal relations should things advance that far?" And if everything between him and Jane continued as it was, there was the strong possibility they'd soon hit that milestone.

The doctor's red eyebrows soared into his hairline. "You have advanced that far?"

"There's always the hope."

"I see." A certain frostiness had entered the other man's eyes. "Do you plan to romance a woman or merely seduce her?"

Was romance—courtship even—what he intended, or did he merely want to discover if he could experience desire? To feel like a man again?

"I'm not sure, but I do want to know if sexually pleasing a woman is possible in my condition."

The doctor flipped through a few papers in the leather folio until he came to a drawing of the spine. "That's difficult to say. It depends on many factors." He tapped a forefinger on the drawing and held it up so Finn could see it. "Your injury is between the tenth and eleventh thoracic vertebrae, and a complete injury at that. Do you experience a psychogenic erection? This means your shaft hardens by mental stimulation like thoughts or seeing something arousing."

"Unfortunately, no." Try as he might, thinking about Jane or her tempting charms produced no reaction below his waist.

"That's consistent with your injury location. What about a reflexogenic erection? These types come about by being stroked, caressed or teased with fabrics, or by self-fulfillment."

"Yes, sometimes, though I haven't taken myself in hand in a long while due to frustration." Heat infused his cheeks from embarrassment. Had he failed even in this?

"Why is that?"

Finn shrugged as if it didn't matter. "The erection or reaction doesn't last long. Perhaps a minute if I'm fortunate, but usually less than that."

Never had he cared to inquire about such intimacy before because there wasn't a reason. Now there was. Damn but he wanted Jane, wanted to claim her, show he wasn't merely a good friend, but an excellent lover too.

"Ah." The doctor scribbled another few lines of notes on the diagram. "Unfortunately, the action of intercourse as you once knew it might not be possible. If you cannot maintain an erection for longer, there's not time to have your shaft penetrate a woman, let alone maintain shape for thrusting."

"That's what I was afraid of." His hopeful spirits plummeted and left behind an aching empty void in his chest. Once he told Jane this, would she make her excuses and leave?

"This doesn't mean you shouldn't let yourself become intimate in other ways. Sometimes simply remembering what those sensations felt like or watching a woman fondle you is its own reward."

Finn snorted. "So says a man with equipage that works." It was a bitter pill to swallow.

A ghost of a smile touched the doctor's lips, and again, a hint of recognition toyed with Finn's mind. "Should you wish to begin a physical relationship, be certain to talk about it with your lady. Also, void your bladder before the event, and don't be embarrassed if your first time out or so doesn't go well. Remember, these things aren't always about the physical to find fulfillment."

The longer Finn stared at his doctor, the more the pieces clicked into place. "Oh, good God. What a bloody idiot I've been." He shoved a hand through his hair. "You're Doctor *Marsden* and have red hair."

"Yes, what of it?" Confusion lined the other man's face.

"You're Lady Jane's brother." Both relief and anxiety clogged his chest. *Bloody hell.* And he'd just expressed an interest in beginning a carnal relationship with her.

"Honestly, I'm surprised you didn't draw that conclusion

sooner." The doctor shrugged as a sheepish smile sneaked across his face. "It wasn't as if we were keeping secrets."

"Of course not, but either of you could have mentioned it in passing." Though, to be fair, it wasn't exactly a subject of conversation, not when he was preoccupied with how lush Jane's lips were or how much he enjoyed holding her.

Doctor Marsden closed his folio, laid it in his lap, and folded his hands atop it. "Now that you know, let me speak with you as an older brother to his little sister's potential suitor."

Oh, God.

"While I don't take issue with Jane finding interest in you as a man who is in a Bath chair, I don't wish to see her hurt." His eyes, so much like hers, held a hard edge. "She's already seen a lifetime of heartbreak. Please don't add to that."

While annoyance from the conversation sat like a rock in his chest, Finn nodded. If he had a sister who'd had Jane's history, he'd show concern too. Bloody hell, there was a good chance this man didn't know of her... scandal and subsequent failed pregnancy. He rubbed a hand along his jaw, extremely conscious he wasn't a social equal to this man, this earl's heir, especially while not wearing breeches or trousers. "I'm not a rake if that's what you assume."

"I assume you're randy, plain and simple." A warning glint appeared in the doctor's eye. "Jane is special, the kind of woman that isn't found often. I'd like to see her happy, not some man's mistress or lover who's a friend until someone better comes along." Doctor Marsden held his gaze. "Or until his demons occupy his full attention."

Finn frowned. Was it so easy to read him? "You think I'm not good enough for her."

The other man shrugged. "You tell me. We both know what your prognosis is. If a relationship progresses between you and Jane, can you give her what she'll need for a fulfilled life?"

Could he? Hadn't he asked himself the same question every damned day since he'd met her? But again, he couldn't find fault with this man, for Jane was indeed quite unique. "I rather think that's between her and I." He carefully mulled over his next words before he spoke them. "Perhaps we won't progress into the physical, for what we currently have is enjoyable on its own." The muscles in his shoulders and neck tensed.

Wellington wandered over to his location, no doubt alerted to trouble by the tone of his voice. She took up guard like a sentinel by his right wheel, her front paws lined up perfectly and her tail curled elegantly around them.

He couldn't help his smile. At least some living thing in the room believed in him. "However, I ask that you let things alone and leave her to make her own choices."

Please, God, let her choose to move forward with me despite the challenges.

For long moments, the doctor stared at him. "Father wishes her to marry the Duke of Ballantrae."

"I am aware." If he clenched his jaw any harder, his teeth would crack. Wellington eyed him askance. "But as of yet, she hasn't shown an interest in the duke, and neither has he asked for her hand."

A half-smile tugged at one corner of the other man's mouth. "This is so."

"Is that a match you wish for her to make?"

"It would certainly advance her standing in society and she'd be well cared for..."

"That doesn't answer my question, Doctor."

"No, I suppose it doesn't." He heaved out a breath. "In my personal opinion—which remains confidential between the two of us—I don't feel the duke will encourage her unique... talents. Her personality isn't something that should be eclipsed or forgotten beneath someone else who has a larger part to play."

"Agreed." Finn fought off the urge to grin. If her oldest brother didn't want to see her matched to the duke, then he had a chance with her. Perhaps if push came to shove and they did go far enough in their relationship where he'd might come up to scratch, the doctor would give support. "Before you go, I have been experiencing strange symptoms of late." Briefly, he mentioned the weird sensations through his leg as well as the traces of feeling.

"Now that *is* interesting." The doctor opened his folio and scribbled another set of notes. "Perhaps being more active of late is stimulating or waking up those nerves." He glanced at Finn with speculation in his eyes. "It's possible the field doctor as well as the first surgeon you saw in England made an incorrect diagnosis in stating your injury was complete."

"How so?" A frisson of excitement danced over his skin.

"When someone receives a ghastly injury to the spinal cord, inflammation sets in. It would mask the findings, leading a harried surgeon to list your injury as complete instead of the more likely incomplete." When Finn frowned, he rushed on while writing notes. "Think of it as the body's way of trying to protect itself from further trauma." He met Finn's gaze. "It takes a good amount of time for said inflammation to reduce itself, for every man's body and healing timetable is different. Once that occurs, without the pressure, nerves that have healed but were repressed by swelling are encouraged to work again, especially with additional movement or stimulation of the body."

"Meaning?" Finn nearly held his breath. Would a reverse of his prognosis happen? "Will I retain full use of my body?"

"Do you have the same tingling and patches of feeling in your other leg?"

"No."

"In your genital region?"

"I do not."

The doctor shrugged. "It's difficult to say, but what you're experiencing is encouraging. From a medical standpoint, there is a *small* possibility that you *might* regain some use of your right leg. The rest of you is questionable. But at least there is the hope of improvement."

It was more than he had this morning. "I'm grateful for whatever happens." Did he mean with his body or in a relationship with Jane? At this point, he couldn't say.

"I am as well." He stood and moved to the table where he put the folio into his bag. "I'll see you again in three months—professionally. Personally, I'll call sooner if you play with my sister's affections." The verist hint of a warning rang in his voice.

"What if she does the same with me? I'm the more vulnerable one here."

The doctor's expression softened. "It's all a risk, Phineas. Only you can say if it's worth it as long as you both go into this with your eyes wide open instead of thinking a happily ever after depends on your ability to perform in bed."

"I understand." It was a large hurdle to overcome, for it was his ego that would end up wounded if such a thing finished with disaster.

"Keep an eye on the leg as well as how your shaft behaves as time goes on." Doctor Marsden took his bag in hand. He gathered his top hat and his gloves as he headed to the door. "If there are any changes—good or bad—send me a summons. I wish you luck, Major Storme, in all your... endeavors."

"Thank you. I appreciate that." Finn watched the other man go, then he glanced at Wellington. "Let's hope I have the courage to proceed, girl, for that way there be monsters."

Her only response was a cheerful, "Meow!"

CHAPTER TEN

July 8, 1817

J ANE'S HEART BEAT in double time as she attempted to sit demurely in the large drawing room of Lord Danbury's townhouse. She and the other guests had already been treated to four musicians of various talents, but the last young lady had set her teeth on edge with several missed notes, whether from nerves or inexperience, she couldn't say.

As of yet, she hadn't seen Finn, nor his mother, and that left her with cold disappointment circling through her insides. As soon as an intermission was announced and light refreshments offered in the parlor, she left the pretty, gilt-painted chair and bolted from the room…

And ran headlong into the warm body of the Duke of Ballantrae. "Please pardon me, Your Grace," she said in a rush. Oh, she didn't have time for such a delay.

"How fortuitous to see you, Lady Jane." He grasped her shoulder and hand in order to steady her. "I arrived late and wasn't able to secure a seat next to you."

"Yes, it's rather crowded this evening," she responded with a vague wave of her hand. Surreptitiously, she attempted to peek around the duke's shoulders, but she still didn't catch a glimpse of Finn. Surely, he'd not begged off for the evening without telling her.

"Could I escort you to the refreshment table? We are afforded a half hour before the second half of the evening's entertainment begins." He held out his crooked arm, clearly expecting her to accept.

"Of course," she said in a small voice while she racked her brain for a valid excuse. Listening to the musical abilities of young ladies wasn't exactly the entertainment she'd hoped to enjoy tonight. Guests milled through the corridor, rendering her progress with the duke slow, which only served to heighten her frustration. "Have you had the opportunity to speak with anyone this evening?"

"A few acquaintances. Some of my time is spent avoiding the braver debutantes. One of them had the audacity to proposition me." Shock threaded through his tone. "Veiled, of course, but she wanted to meet me in a room little used for a bit of scandal. No doubt one of her friends would 'drop by' and catch us in a compromising position, thus securing her future." He shook his head. "As if I'm that naïve."

"Lucky girl," Jane murmured, for that's exactly what she wanted to do with Finn. Where was he? Then she cleared her throat and attended to the duke's statement. "You're absolutely right in avoiding that pitfall."

As they gained the refreshment tables set up in the parlor on the same floor, the duke handed her a glass of watered-down lemonade. "On the way in, I spoke briefly with a Major Storme."

Jane choked on the sip she'd taken. "Oh?" When she reached for a linen serviette, he handed her one. Their fingers brushed, but there was absolutely no reaction sparking between them.

"Quite a fascinating man. I'd rather like to pick his brain and hear his thoughts on the Battle of Waterloo. There's so much we civilians weren't privy to, I'll wager."

"Yes." She couldn't think of a single erudite thing to say, for as soon as she heard that he was, indeed, in the house, every nerve in her body felt strung too tight. "Uh, where did you see him? I must have missed his arrival." And then she *knew*. If he were truly after a clandestine assignation with her this evening, he certainly wouldn't go to the trouble of having a footman carry him—as well as his Bath chair—up the stairs. More to the point, he couldn't easily sneak out to an unknown location with the contraption.

"We'd come in together so chatted briefly in the entry hall. He must have an interest in music, for anticipation was fairly stamped on his face."

"Oh." She fought off the heat in her cheeks. It wasn't the event he looked forward to, it was spending time with her. Another little piece of her heart flew into his keeping.

The duke sipped his own lemonade. A slight smile curved his rather thin lips while indulgence sparkled in his blue eyes—too light and not the rich sapphire of Finn's. His golden hair gleamed in the candlelight, and every inch of his expertly tailored clothing fit his body like the proverbial glove, but somehow, she preferred midnight hair in disarray and a cravat always hopelessly loosened. "I wondered if I might call upon you soon."

Yes, in theory she should be properly grateful he'd deigned to speak with her tonight or that he'd even shown an interest in the future, but...

He simply wasn't as intriguing or exhilarating as being in Finn's company was.

When she realized the duke stared at her, she took another gulp of the lemonade. "Um, you may if you wish." Though whether she'd be at home was another matter entirely.

"Good." He nodded.

"Ballantrae!" Someone hailed him from across the room.

He lifted a hand. "If you'll excuse me? I must speak with Alderson a moment."

"Enjoy the remainder of your evening." She didn't offer anything else, for she didn't wish to encourage him. After setting her empty glass at the end of the table, Jane left the parlor. Was Finn waiting for her? As she strolled casually toward the staircase, she smoothed her gloved palms along the front of her peach silk gown. The sheer lavender overskirt shimmered with tiny clear beads. With a quick glance around and confirming that no one paid her the slightest attention, she sneaked down the polished wooden stairs. "Where are you?" she whispered to herself.

Thankfully, the corridor was empty. Four closed doors drew her focus. Which one? As silently as the heels of her slippers would allow, she crept through the hall, and as her gaze fell upon the edge of the rug in front of one of the doors, she smiled. It was mussed and rumpled as if a wheeled object had made a sudden turn into that room.

He'd been in a hurry to hide.

Her pulse raced as she pressed the latch. Excitement tingled down her spine while she pushed open the door. "Finn?" Dimly lit, it took her eyes the space of a few heartbeats to acclimate. "Are you here?"

"Thank you for finally joining me, my lady." Sarcasm hung heavy on the response. "I began to fear you'd left me for a fool."

"Oh, hush." Before she could change her mind, Jane softly closed the door and made certain to turn the key in the lock. "Don't ruin our night by being horrid." But his concern was valid. No one enjoyed being left to the wolves of society, per se. When she faced into the room, her ability to breathe left her at the sight of him.

The requisite dark evening clothes were stunning on him, but the silver satin waistcoat drew her focus to his flat abdomen. A sapphire pin in the snowy folds of his cravat winked in the light from a fully lit candelabra that rested on the fireplace mantle. He waited in his Bath chair near the darkened hearth, his midnight hair tamed this evening, but the slight grin that curved his sensuous mouth held wicked promise.

"I've never seen a man so… stunning," she finally said into silence when the capacity for speaking returned. "You could have your pick of women, yet you're here. For me." Her swallow was audible as she approached him with hesitant steps. "Why?"

He snorted. "Most women don't look twice at me once they see the chair." His eyes glittered. "I'm merely waiting for your common sense to return. Then you'll see how much better you can do as well."

"Do stop. I've chosen to live in the present." She refused to think about her father's wishes or those of the duke. Anything that happened tonight was a gift to herself, and she didn't care to hear more nonsense. Perhaps ignoring duty was folly, but so was not chasing happiness. Leaning down, she bussed his cheek. Oh, dear heavens, he smelled so good! That spicy citrus and sage scent wrapped around her like an invisible thread pulling her closer to him. "There is nothing shameful or wrong with you, Major."

"You're a liar, but I'll let it pass this one time." Finn caught her gloved hand. He must have taken his off prior to her arrival. "That gown suits you. It looks like the clouds at sunset."

Inordinately pleased with the compliment, heat rose in her cheeks. "Shall I twirl for you? Every woman wishes for an excuse when wearing a particularly wonderful gown."

"Absolutely you should." He released her hand, his eyes dark with expectation and desire. "Let me see the full effect."

"Not that you can in such dim light." She moved away from him a few steps.

"I can imagine." He gestured a hand in a circular motion. "Go on."

Jane twirled around and around until her skirts flared. When she came to a halt, she giggled and walked drunkenly toward his chair. "What do you think?" It had been such a silly thing to do, but if he enjoyed it, the stunt was well worth it.

"I think that if you don't come here, I'll go out of my mind." Once more he grabbed her hand and tugged her close until she tumbled into his lap. His arms came around her, snug and sure.

Tingles played along Jane's spine. She looked into his face, brushed a lock of hair from his forehead as her heartbeat accelerated into a gallop. "Are you quite certain you wish to do this?" Her question sounded breathless. "I promise I won't be out of sorts if you cry off."

He held her gaze with his. "Honestly, I've never wanted anything—anyone—more." There was nothing except need and desire in his dark sapphire depths.

"I believe you." In a twinkling she'd removed her gloves. They dropped to the polished hardwood with nary a whisper. "I want you, too." Though she didn't know how it would work, she threw caution to wind and slipped her arms up his chest to furrow her fingers into his hair. "Oh, you feel so good."

"Mmm." Finn caressed a hand down her back. His other sneaked beneath her skirting to glide along her thigh. "So do you." He kissed her, gently and hesitantly, almost as if he were unsure about his reception. "It's been a few years since I've done this, and certainly not since my injury—"

"Shh." Jane nipped his bottom lip and giggled again when he groaned. "We'll discover how it will happen together."

"You won't have the freedom to make much noise in the event you're a screamer. The last thing we need is to have an erstwhile butler and an angry host bursting through that door."

She snorted, but the threat of being found out added a touch of danger to the meeting. "When lost in the moment, I do forget myself." With a wink, she slid from his lap only to come back and straddle him. Her skirting pooled between them. "If discovery is imminent, we shouldn't dawdle."

"I guess I have my orders." Finn wrapped his arms around her and fit his lips to hers. The longer he moved over her mouth, the closer she pressed her body against his chest.

Following the course of the other kisses they'd shared during the week, the thrill and excitement swept her away. His skill sent her into the heights of fantasy, but it was she who first sought out his tongue to deepen their connection. As silk twined with satin, need circled through her insides like a hungry beast.

His groan resonated through her chest. He broke the kiss but trailed his lips along the column of her throat, followed the rounded neckline of her bodice, licking and nipping the top slopes of her breasts as he went. "From the moment I saw you I've wanted to taste you, feel your skin."

"Nothing's stopping you, Major." The breathy whisper was uttered against the underside of his jaw. She spent a few seconds exploring the area, and when she teased a place near his ear, he gasped and fumbled with the few buttons at the back of her gown. "Haven't you learned by now that that if you want something, you must take it in that moment? Life moves so quickly you might miss an opportunity if you tarry."

"Message received, my lady." With a wicked glint in his eye, he drew the loosened bodice of the dress, along with the petticoat down, baring her breasts. "Gorgeous." He took the globes in his hands, smashed them together and then brushed the pads of his thumbs over the nipples.

"Oooh." Jane threw her head back. Wild sensation coursed down her spine and zipped between her breasts like lightning. "I'd forgotten how nice that feels."

He didn't answer with words. Every pull of his mouth, every tiny bit of suction, each swipe of his tongue, every nip from his teeth on those straining buds had her body shaking with need and longing. When he pressed fine kisses over the curves of one breast, rolling the other nipple between his thumb and forefinger, she uttered a soft cry. Urgency twisted low in her belly to collide with the anticipation, and she rocked her hips against his.

Not wanting him to have all the fun, Jane made quick work of the buttons on his jacket and waistcoat. Once those gaped open, she tugged his shirt tail from his trousers. "Oh, yes." With a sigh and a shudder from what he did to her, she pushed her hands beneath his shirt and roved her fingers over the expanse of his chest. "I've dreamed about what you might look like, feel like." Would that she was able to completely disrobe him, for the contours and dips of his muscles she encountered added another layer to the rampant desire slowly replacing her blood.

The second she circled one of his flat nipples with her fingertip, he hissed out a breath. Finn's eyes popped open, clouded with surprise, and when that nub was hard, she gently pinched it. He uttered a sound between a moan and a growl.

Before she could inquire, he held her head in both hands and kissed her with an intensity she hadn't encountered with him yet. Her fingers stilled on his chest, her fingers curling in the mat of hair there, for she couldn't remember her name let alone what she'd been doing while he drank from her as if she held the last drop of water on Earth.

Finally, she wrenched away in order to draw breath, removing her hands from beneath his clothing. Her heartbeat hammered behind her ribs. "How are you doing here?" She slid a hand between them to rub along his shaft, but there was a suspicious lack of arousal.

"Not well." This time he did growl. "Perhaps with more intensity, things will change." He glanced over the room. "There." As he wheeled them behind a sofa with a high back, she clung to his shoulders. "Prepare yourself." A slim table ran along the rear of that piece of furniture, its high polish visible in the dim light. Finn halted, grasped her about the waist, and then lifted her off his lap, depositing her bum onto the table. A small statuette and a potted plant tumbled to the floor, their fall muffled by the thick Aubusson carpet.

"I'm impressed. You picked me up as if I weighed nothing."

"You don't. Is that such a problem?" Finn wheeled himself closer. He delved his hands beneath her skirting, shoving the fabric up and bunching it at her waist. As she leaned backward, her hands on the wooden frame of the sofa, he slid her forward on the table. She rested her feet on his shoulders, and while he spread her thighs open, he buried his head between them.

"Merciful heavens," she breathed while her world tilted. Never in her wildest imaginings did she think he would do... that. Neither of her fiancés had ever treated her to such exquisite torture. It was rather like she'd died and was now floating, flying... "I... I..." *Devil take it.* Thinking and talking took too much effort, and she needed every drop of strength as he licked and nibbled his way over her sensitive flesh. The second he teased that all-important nubbin with the tip of his tongue, she temporarily lost her mind. Pleasure coursed through her entire being. Her breathing became labored and ragged. She dug her fingernails into the wooden sofa frame. And when he sucked that swollen button into his mouth…

"Finn!" Though her exclamation was muted, it didn't seem enough. He either didn't hear her or didn't care, for he renewed his efforts. The man was talented, she'd give him that, as well as efficient, thorough… magical. All too soon her body shook. Tingles fell down her spine. Trembles racked her thighs where he held her steady. The circling pressure inside broke.

"Oh. Oh. *Oh!*" Jane bit down on her bottom lip to keep from shouting to the world as she fell into bliss. The release came hard and fast, battering her in waves of heated pleasure. She couldn't catch her breath while flutters filled her channel; couldn't remain anchored on her hands as her body went pliant. The surprise of it all confounded her mind.

As she slid from the table, nearly a boneless mass, Finn pulled away and caught her, held her until her feet found purchase on the floor.

"All right?" His grin was a cheeky affair as he tugged a handkerchief from an interior pocket of his jacket and wiped his face.

"Not yet, but I will be." She shivered with residual tremors. "Turnabout is fair play though."

"Oh? You think so?" Desire glittered in his eyes, and he wheeled backward, away from the table and the spilled dirt from the fallen plant.

"I do." Still in a daze from how she'd come apart so easily in his care, Jane kneeled on the floor. She batted his hands away when he would have gone for the buttons of his frontfalls. "Let me." Her fingers trembled and she fumbled the task, but eventually she opened his trousers. "May I?" she asked as she paused at the towel beneath.

"Yes, but I—"

"I'm not put off by you, Finn," she whispered and undid the pins on each side of the towel. A quick glance into his eyes revealed his unease. "Relax and let me give you the same pleasure that you gave me."

"I've looked forward to this since I met you." He cupped her cheek, drew the pad of his thumb along her lower lip. "Thank you."

She dipped her head. Heat surged into her cheeks and her heart skipped a beat from the gratitude she'd seen in those depths. He shouldn't need to thank anyone for showing him kindness and respect or even having desire for him. Once his shaft was freed from the fabric, she gently fondled him, stroked her fingers up and down his silky length, reveled in the intimate heat of his length.

Slowly, ever so slowly, his member hardened from her touch. Jane cupped his stones, squeezed each one and then wrapped her fingers around the growing appendage. When she thought it might behoove her to climb into his lap and ride him, the tricky rod went limp. "Well, we can't have that, can we?" Not overly concerned, she renewed her efforts with a bit more friction. Once more his member stiffened. She leaned into him, wetting her lips in anticipation of taking him into her mouth.

"Stop." Emotion graveled the command. When she glanced up at him, acute embarrassment lined his face. "Not now, is what I meant."

"All right." Jane grabbed one of his hands. "Stroke yourself while I get into position. The hope is to not lose rigidity."

Finn snorted but did as she asked.

She put her lips to his ear while gathering up her skirting. "I can't wait to feel you inside me, impaling me until I want to scream your name." At his sharply inhaled breath, she grinned and climbed into his lap, once more straddling his lap.

"Quickly," he urged. When he grabbed her hips, Jane lifted onto her knees, took him in hand to make certain he was hard enough for the task, and then attempted to lower herself upon him. The head of his member barely cleared her opening before the erection lost much of its stamina. "Damn it."

A trace of cold disappointment coiled through her insides. "Don't fret. We'll simply make you stiff again." She delved a hand between their bodies.

"Stop it, Jane. For all that's holy, leave off. It's embarrassing enough." Anger echoed in his stilted, whispered words. "The fact is I'm not able to have relations."

"That's not true. We can—" A squeak escaped her when he dumped her unceremoniously off his lap. She stumbled and landed on her arse in front of him, her legs splayed, her breasts hanging ignobly out of her gown. Her ardor quickly cooled. "Finn, how rude."

"You should go." His face, half in shadow, was a fearsome mask of anger and self-loathing.

"Why?" Her heart squeezed. She scrambled to her feet. Perhaps they could salvage the evening. "What you did already was amazing. Let us not waste the momentum."

"Don't you understand?" He lifted his stricken gaze to hers. "Intercourse with me isn't possible. I'll never know what it feels like to find release again."

"That's not true." When it became apparent that he wasn't merely stalling for time, Jane hiked her bodice back into place. "We can try again."

He rolled his eyes. "It's all right if you wish to show or voice your disgust with me. I had promised you a night of passion, and you received hardly that."

"Truly, I'm not disgusted." She turned her back. The night had lost its charm. "Please do up the buttons lest we give away our assignation."

"Fine." Annoyance propelled the word. He did as she asked, but his touch didn't linger like a lover's would. "But you *are* disappointed in this evening."

For a few seconds she remained silent. "Perhaps a tiny bit." She faced him. "I wanted to give you the same pleasure, and I think that if I had continued you could have—"

"Do shut up. It's hopeless." Finn held up a hand. In the candlelight, despair clouded his eyes. "This, you and I, was a rubbish idea." He efficiently re-pinned his towel and then methodically set his clothing to rights, but he wouldn't look at her. Angry red color had seeped above his collar and highlighted his cheekbones. By increments, he withdrew into himself, putting up an invisible barrier between them, much like he'd done at their first meeting. "Go back to the drawing room and finish the musicale."

"I'd like to stay with you, perhaps talk—"

"No!" Anger propelled the word into the darkened air. "There is nothing to say except I'm a failure at even the basest of carnal functions. I couldn't do what was expected of me, couldn't feel anything." His Adam's apple bobbed with a heavy swallow. "Return to the drawing room... *please*. I'll wait here for a while before calling for my carriage. No one will know we've been together." His tone was flat, a monotone, devoid of all the personality and life he'd had at the start of the evening.

Why can't you understand I merely wish to be with you, regardless? "But Finn—"

"Damn it, Jane, don't make this worse than it already is. I couldn't maintain an erection, couldn't couple with you, so what else is there for me during intimacy?" He avoided her gaze, but the loathing and despondency in his voice tugged at her heart. "We should never have come here, tried—"

"Don't be an arse. It was only a first attempt. These things don't always go off perfectly, even in the best of circumstances." Annoyance bled into her tones, for he couldn't quit after a failure. "Next time we'll try something else." Panic pinged through her chest. Was this the end of their relationship?

"Are you that daft?" Finally, he dragged his gaze to hers. The darkness in his eyes was a clear indication of his already being lost from her. "Another time will yield the same results." He waved a hand. "Find Ballantrae. At least he's deserving of you, and he has a working prick."

Tears stung her eyes. Why couldn't he understand that she didn't want anyone else except him, regardless of the obstacles? "Finn, listen to me—"

"Go." His chin trembled, but he swallowed, obviously struggling to conquer the emotions that battered him. "You and I are done, my lady." He turned his chair away from her. "I'm sorry."

"Finn, please…"

"Damn it, go!" The command echoed through the silent room.

She had no recourse except to cross the room, retrieving her gloves while she went as moisture welled in her eyes. At the door, Jane glanced over her shoulder. He had his hands pressed to his ears as if attempting to block out noise where there was none, at least none she could hear. "This isn't our last meeting, Phineas Storme," she whispered as she fumbled with the key in the lock. A quick wrench of the latch, a tug on the panel swung it open, and she darted through the opened space.

Once into the empty corridor, she pressed the heel of a hand against her mouth to stifle the sob that welled in her throat. How had things gone so terribly wrong when there'd been such promise in the evening?

CHAPTER ELEVEN

July 9, 1817

T HE LONGCASE CLOCK on the floor below struck midnight, and the everlasting chimes resonated throughout the house, reaching into the depths of Finn's rooms. Those tones were much like a death knell, constantly tolling, telling him his time on this mortal coil was finished, and that perhaps he'd already overstayed his welcome.

He'd arrived home an hour ago, but the acute mortification, anger, and self-loathing that had held him captive at that society event churned through his chest. His head ached from the barrage of voices telling him he wasn't good enough, was an embarrassment to his friends and family, would always be a burden, that no woman would want him in his current condition.

Damned depression. Too tired and heartsick to fight it, he let it have its way with him. Devil take the consequences.

When he'd imagined this evening, it had ended much differently than the reality. He'd pictured Jane draped across his chest, languid and limp and sated from carnal play, replete from his skill. Instead, though he'd brought her to release with his mouth, when it had come time to claim her body, his bloody prick had turned traitorous. Or perhaps he hadn't believed his limitations were as real as the doctors had warned, assumed he could overcome them if he'd thought positively, tried hard enough, wanted that climax more than anything.

He snorted. Getting *hard* and staying that way was exactly the problem.

Now, it was glaringly obvious he couldn't have intercourse with anyone; to say nothing of being able to penetrate a woman. The magnitude of that hit him in the chest with all the force of a blow. The pain of it made him double over in his Bath chair. He'd failed at the one thing in which a man was supposed to excel. Not to mention he'd disappointed the woman he'd wished to impress with his prowess. A flutter around his heart stole his breath and he rubbed his fingers over the spot. To see that frustration in her beautiful eyes, suffer through her futile efforts to stimulate his shaft, feel hope die when he knew anything further she wanted to do would have the same results...

God, it had been too much.

As the darkness of depression had crept over him in that parlor, he'd made sure to drive a wedge between him and Jane. He'd ended the relationship before the dismal reality of who he truly was could set in with her; before they could grow closer... before she had just cause to regret her choice or resent him... or mourn for him. Now, the last thing he needed to do was rid the world of his presence so he wouldn't hurt anyone else with his inability to remain whole.

Like a man should be in all aspects of life.

From the bed, Wellington glanced at him with unblinking blue eyes. She meowed as if to inquire why he was acting like such a nodcock.

Finn shook his head. "Don't try to talk me out of this, girl. My mind is made up."

The cat meowed again. She sprang from the ball she'd coiled herself in and stood at the edge of the bed, whiskers quivering as she stared.

"No, I'm *not* being unreasonable. Nor am I giving up like a coward."

Yet wasn't that exactly what he was? He'd failed to save his best friend from Waterloo, because like a coward he'd left the battlefield before he could yell for Edward to retreat. And he'd been too much a coward to tell Edward's woman of his death and his wish to marry her. That had ended in disaster and grief that had never been dealt with. Perhaps, after everything, he was a coward toward Jane for not talking about what haunted him, about what he couldn't do.

"It can't be helped." That time had passed. No amount of conversation would fix what ailed him.

Wellington meowed.

He narrowed his eyes on her. "Why would you think it's my mind playing tricks?"

Of course, she didn't really think anything. It was nothing but his consciousness reminding him that he was, indeed, acting like the arse Jane had likened him to. He tapped a forefinger against the notebook in his lap. *Ah, God, Jane.* The ache in his chest renewed. She'd been so beautiful and magnificent when she'd found release, so happy from his compliments on her dress, so lighthearted as she'd twirled to show it to the best advantage. For a short time, only the two of them had existed in a bubble... until his body had ruined everything. "I'll miss you," he whispered. Though they'd known each other for the span of a week, she'd managed to crawl beneath his skin, swept the cobwebs from his heart in preparation for setting up housekeeping. "I refuse to trap her into a prison sentence."

Wellington meowed.

He looked at the cat who perched on the edge of the bed. "She really was like sunshine, but I'm too twisted and damaged for a woman of her caliber." *Would* she mourn for him? He clenched his teeth against the ache in his chest. Another reason for him to make his exit from the world. They were only friends, perhaps would have been lovers had this evening not failed, but he hoped she wouldn't spend too long in tears. He wasn't worth them. "She has to know Ballantrae is so much better for her than

I ever could be." Was she even now finding solace in the duke's arms? He grunted. She certainly would once word of his death circulated.

The feline batted a paw in his direction as if to disabuse him of the notion.

"I'm sorry you never had the chance to meet her. I think you would have liked the lady." In a fit of pique, he ripped a partial page from the notebook. "Perhaps I'll will you to her." Would that be cruel on his part? She'd always remember him when she looked at the cat, but oh how that would annoy the duke. He snorted. "Yes, perhaps I will."

Mother, the family will be better off without me. I can no longer bear the disappointment or the burden you must feel. Please see that Wellington goes to Lady Jane Marsden, the Earl of Worchester's daughter. Please don't mourn long. I'm not worth it.

"No backing out now, old girl," he told the cat. After setting the notebook containing his unfinished book on the bedside table, he laid the note on top along with the pencil. At least the pain in his chest would cease once this was over and done with. Heavy sadness pressed in on him. He'd been accepting enough of his injury before he'd come back to London, but once he'd met Jane, everything changed. He'd wanted to be better, more—enough. Because of her. For her.

But I failed.

Wellington uttered a very loud, very long meow. Her tail twitched, usually a harbinger of rash action.

"Do hush." However, beneath the pain of loss, the heat of anger and embarrassment, cold fear had taken up residence in his chest. He hadn't felt that since Waterloo. It closed icy fingers around his heart and squeezed. What if he didn't wish to go? What if things weren't as bad as he assumed in this moment? "No, my mind is made up." Or so depression wished for him to believe. Why should he not? Wasn't it always right? He swallowed around the wad of panic in his throat.

Finn shoved aside all thoughts. *This is the only way.* He wheeled himself closer to the nightstand. The brown bottle of laudanum rested on the side farthest away from his location and closer to his pillows for easy reach if nightmares plagued him. The stopper lay beside it in the small box the set had come in. No amount of reaching could help him to grasp that bottle now. "Bugger it."

Lifting his body by balancing his hands on the armrests of the chair, he scooted himself to the edge of the seat. This time when he leaned forward and reached over the nightstand, his fingertips brushed the bottle. "Almost have it." If he strained a bit more, he could grasp it.

With a firm meow, Wellington leaped from the bed to land hard on his shoulder. The added weight of the cat destroyed his delicate balancing act.

"Damn it." He tipped out of his chair, falling, but on the way down, his temple cracked against the corner of the nightstand. Brilliant white stars erupted behind his eyes as pain exploded through his head. As he hit the floor, darkness closed in on him and the voices of depression laughed even as he lost consciousness.

Failed again.

July 15, 1817

FINN CAME AWAKE to the sound of rain drumming against his windows. His head ached like the devil and when he lifted a hand to examine it, a length of cloth bandage was wrapped about it, covering most of his forehead and left temple. The insistent sound of purring came from the direction of the foot of his bed, and when he slightly moved his head and glanced there, Wellington lay curled in a tight ball with her nose tucked beneath her tail, asleep. Beyond her, his Bath chair awaited.

When he turned his head back, the sight of his writing note-book on his nightstand brought memories rushing through his mind. A groan escaped him. His hastily scrawled note as well as the laudanum bottle were conspicuously missing, but a look across the room showed them resting on the bureau top.

Immediately, fabric rustled at the open doorway. His mother swept in, a bright splash of royal blue color in the gloomy room. She bustled over and sat in the straight-backed wooden chair someone had put close to his bed. "I'm glad to see you awake and alert."

Finn pulled himself up into a sitting position. He propped a few pillows behind his back. The scrape of the sheet over his bare chest gave him pause, and he frowned. "Why am I naked?" Well, naked as much as still having the towel wrapped about his privates would allow. His throat was scratchy from disuse. "How long have I been out?"

"Almost three days. When we found you, you were covered in blood from your head wound. That necessitated changing your clothing," his mother said in a soft voice as she swept her gaze over his person.

"How did you know I was in peril?" A growl from his stom-ach betrayed his need for food.

"Wellington kept making an awful racket until Rodgers came in." She shrugged. "He found you on the floor, lying on your stomach. Your cat was sitting, paws tucked beneath her, squarely on your back, as calm as you please, no doubt telling him it was about time he answered her calls." She dabbed at the corner of her eye with a lace-edged handkerchief. "Yesterday evening, you woke briefly."

Finn glanced at his cat, who remained asleep. "I dreamed Drew was here."

"That must have been when you woke, disoriented. You'd sat up, glanced at your brother—who had just arrived—and then went promptly back to sleep. Rodgers laid you down and tucked you in."

Cold sweat formed on his back. "*Why* is Drew here?"

"He's the head of the family. I wrote to him the morning after Rodgers found you because I needed him to take things in hand." She eyed him as if he'd suddenly vanish into thin air. "*After* we found your note."

"Ah."

"How could you, Phineas?" Tears welled in his mother's eyes. "Do you think we're such monsters that we don't want you here or that we don't love you still?"

Hot guilt crashed into his chest. "Drew doesn't." The fact his older brother was even beneath the same roof as him brough out gooseflesh.

"If he didn't, he wouldn't have come."

I highly doubt that. He snorted. "Did you, ah, inform Lady Jane of my injury?" Shame twisted through his chest. Now that he'd failed at the suicide attempt, he felt... relief. Did that mean he hadn't wished to end it all to begin with?

"I sent a brief note the same time I sent word to Andrew. I also sent notification to your surgeon. He came immediately and looked at your wound. Said it wasn't deep and that head injuries always bled profusely. No doubt it's already scabbing over."

"Oh, God." If Doctor Marsden knew he'd attempted to kill himself, he'd never approve of a courtship. He caught his breath. Did he wish for such? More to the point, did Jane want to wash her hands of him now?

Speculation lit his mother's eyes. "Is Lady Jane important to you?"

Yes, she's as vital to me as breathing, as sunshine. "She's a friend, which is why I wanted her to care for Wellington." He ignored the heat creeping up the back of his neck. His stomach growled again. "Might I have tea?"

"Of course." His mother rose. "We shall talk later, but I trust you'll not frighten me like that again?"

"I hope not to." Once she'd left, he looked at his cat, nudged her with a toe until she awoke. She slowly lifted her head. "Thank you, old girl. You saved me from making a horrible mistake."

She meowed and went back to sleep.

A scratching on the door frame preceded the butler's arrival. "A parcel has arrived for you, Major Storme." He brought a small box into the room. Wrapped in brown paper and tied with a length of twine, it gave off a mysterious air.

Finn frowned. "From whom?"

"The courier didn't say. Only that this was to be given into your hands personally once you were awake." He placed the box into Finn's hands. "I'll check the status of your tea." The man closed the door after himself.

"Thank you." Baffled, he pulled the string, which Wellington promptly claimed, and tore through the wrapping. Inside the box, a notecard waited. "What's this?" With trembling fingers, he opened the note.

Finn,

My world nearly crumbled when Royce told me of your injury and your intent following that wonderful evening. Despite the fact you've acted like the world's greatest nodcock, I'm determined to pursue what's between us. This crisis has only shown me how much I've come to enjoy our time together. Quite frankly, I refuse to let death, or your personal demons, take you from me.

Enclosed, please find a couple of items that might aid your... problems. One is what they call a cock ring with an extension sheath. The other is a wooden phallus... for other uses. If you're wondering how I came upon them, let me set your mind at ease. Quite simply, I asked my brothers for assistance. After a long and truthful discussion with Royce, he put forth the idea of possibly employing this device. After testing, I'm to report back to him so that he might pass along the information to other men in your position.

Jane

Oh, the embarrassment! Now his surgeon had been appraised

of what Finn was doing with Royce's sister. "Bloody hell." He rather thought the woman was a tiny bit magical. The fact she harbored no ill-will—hopefully—and still wished to be with him left him gasping with shock. A kernel of hope began to bloom deep inside his soul. Was it possible to grasp happiness in life even though he was paralyzed?

He didn't have time to properly examine the contraptions in the box, for the sound of the latch being pressed captured Finn's attention. Perhaps it was tea already. But when the wooden panel swung open, his brother Drew stood on the threshold. The customary scowl slashed across the older man's face, but he was dressed with the usual sophistication, which befit an earl. Finn frowned at the interruption. Even more so when Wellington growled and then took her string, jumped from the bed, and hid beneath it.

Drew cleared his throat. "Ah, good morning." For the first time since Finn had known his brother, he seemed ill at ease.

"What are you doing here?" He wished Drew would leave so he could investigate the contents of the package.

"What's in the box?" Drew countered. When he craned his neck to see, Finn threw the bedclothes over it.

"Nothing that concerns you." He continued frowning. "What are you doing in London? I thought you'd recently married. Don't you have a wife to keep you busy, or can she not stomach who you are like the rest of us?" God, that wasn't well done of him, but he couldn't help needling his brother.

Drew narrowed his eyes. "I came because you nearly killed yourself."

Finn snorted. Which meant his brother was here to attempt to bully him out of the notion of trying again. "I was never near death. I simply fell out of my chair and hit my head."

"But the note you left?"

"Written prematurely in a fit of pique." He shrugged as heat crept up the back of his neck. "However, that crisis point has passed."

"How?" Concern creased his brother's brow. Confusion clouded his blue-gray eyes. "How the devil can you flip between such an intense emotion like depression and then act completely different not four days later?"

"I suppose I've found something that distracts me or makes those other emotions less important. Perhaps I've found… hope." Finn cocked his head to one side as he regarded Drew. That change was firmly laid at Jane's doorstep. "Don't misunderstand me. When my depression comes to call, there's every chance I won't be able to pull myself out of that dark place, especially not alone."

"That settles it. I'm staying here." Drew's voice was gruff from emotion.

"No." Finn held up a hand. "That's not the answer. Hell, you seethe with anger even now. Your anger feeds mine, and I don't want that beast to grow within me."

"But—"

"Stop." He grew silent for the space of a few heartbeats. How to explain when he wasn't certain himself? "No one outside of me can remove what I'm feeling, and no one's advice can help how I navigate my way through." It was a personal journey. As he rubbed his fingers along his whisker-covered chin, he nodded. "Neither can I pretend the things that happened to me while on those battlefields didn't. It is life."

Drew's eyes widened slightly. "How do you conquer those emotions without them consuming you?"

"It's a constant battle. On the days when I'm feeling weaker, then the darkness wins, and my thoughts follow suit." He shrugged. Damn, but he wished he had a shirt on. His brother's stare unnerved him. "Having people about with sunny dispositions and determination of their own helps." Regret wormed its way into his chest. He'd taken Jane's brand of happiness for grated, and he sorely needed her in his life. A low chuckle escaped him. "Of course, my favorite people to spend time with are those who have their own struggles but have come out the victor, for that gives me hope."

"I see." Drew gawked at him.

Did his brother struggle with his own demons in the attempt to grow? "There is one caveat."

"Oh?"

"For myself, I must want that change, I need to keep moving toward being a better man despite what happened to me." It was as if Jane sat beside him, encouraging him to finally see. "Going to war showed me that life is short, and I did things merely to survive, but coming home has shown me that life has the potential to be long, and..." He swallowed audibly. "I'd like to be around for some of it, to enjoy the time I have left. Only I can make certain of that." And he wanted to do that with Jane, to explore what might come if he tried his hand at courting her, perhaps stealing her away from the duke.

Drew finally nodded. "Well then, if you don't require my assistance..."

"I do not."

"You're well? Promise me you won't attempt this again." He looked as if he'd say more, but nothing came of it.

"I *am* well, but I can make you no promises. Depression is a formidable opponent." When his brother remained silent, he grinned. "My turn to ask questions. Why the devil did you marry so quickly, and to a woman you didn't know?"

"To fulfil my duty to the title."

"Ah. Mother threatened you with writing to William, didn't she?" Damn, how long had it been since he'd seen his cousins? More years than he wanted to remember. Would they come to London once the news of Drew's marriage filtered through the *ton*?

"Partly."

Finn couldn't help another frown. Drew remained an enigma. "Will you tell me about her? She must have an incredibly strong will if she married you, and..." He held up a forefinger when Drew's chest swelled with anger, straining the buttons on his waistcoat. "And you're standing here, not berating me for a shortcoming, but asking me how you might overcome yours." That was groundbreaking. Perhaps there was much they both needed to learn.

"Such gammon. And no, I will not." A flush appeared above his collar.

How interesting. Could it be that Drew loved his wife? "Still the arse," Finn said with a shake of his head.

"You would know." Drew shifted his weight from foot to foot. "I won't take more of your time, but mind you remain in bed to rest. I don't want any more frantic letters from Mother."

A genuine chuckle escaped him. "Oh, I intend to stay in bed, at least for some of the time." Heat filled his face, for if he was lucky, he might convince Jane to join him.

With a shake of his head, Drew left the room.

Once Finn delved back into the box, he took up the note again, seeing for the first time a postscript he'd missed before.

P.S. If you're feeling confident and randy, send for me. I would be delighted to help… for the sake of science and medicine, as well as your mental health. Otherwise, I'll call in a few days.

"Dear God." His whole face filled with heat. Why would she want to do this? He was nothing and having her in his bed would change nothing regarding his physical prowess. However… he glanced into the box again, touched a fingertip to the sheath of thin, pliant leather. She'd made an effort to help, and that was the start of a new beginning.

Perhaps he wasn't an unfortunate as he'd first thought.

CHAPTER TWELVE

July 18, 1817

J ANE TRIED TO keep her breathing even as she walked through
Mayfair on her way to call upon Finn. It had been over a week
since she'd last seen him, over a week since that evening when
he'd sent her flying, over a week since he'd made the decision to
remove himself from this world—and her.

Coming to terms with the crisis had taken her more than a
few days. Yes, she was upset about it and with him, but it had
solidified her feelings for the major. Before, she'd been confused
by him, and though she'd known exactly what she'd wanted from
him, realizing she had almost lost him had changed everything.
Now, beyond a doubt, she acknowledged that she was more than
enamored with Finn, wanted to help him live a full, happy life.
And if he couldn't find that contentment in her, then she'd wish
him well and walk away.

*Please, Finn, come to your senses and realize I want you just the
way you are.*

In her time away from him, she'd changed the trajectory of
her life. No longer was she an earl's daughter who'd let life
happen to her, pampered and spoiled in the *ton*. Every weekday
morning, she worked at her brothers' clinic, and this time she
grabbed opportunity with both hands, making certain they were

well and truly dirtied in the process. She'd thrown herself wholeheartedly into each task, and only occasionally did she speak her message of a positive outlook or that merely a change of thinking could transform the patients' lives.

Now, she knew better, and it was all because of Finn. Healing through trauma, both physical and mental, took time and patience and determination, not empty platitudes, but that wouldn't stop *her* from giving out sunshine to those who wanted it.

The one thing that had marred her new direction was the fact that the Duke of Ballantrae had called upon her twice during the week. He'd been everything lovely and polite that a lofty member of the *ton* should be, but though they'd enjoyed numerous conversations on a variety of topics, and he was quite an intelligent debater, there was simply no thrilling spark between them. Mutual respect and admiration, surely, yet the thought of spending a lifetime beside him didn't release a horde of butterflies in her belly like what happened when she let herself dream about a potential future with the major. The duke had left each time disappointed that she hadn't committed to any sort of future outing with him.

A horse's whinny on the street yanked her from her musings as she stood on the pavement in front of the Hadleigh townhouse. Knots of anxiety pulled in her stomach. Jane lifted her face to the summer sun and let its warmth sink into her person before squaring her shoulders and releasing the latch on the wrought iron gate. The time to confront Finn had come, and she wished to forge a new path with him. She'd steered him wrong before, and for that, she wanted his forgiveness.

Gathering courage around her like a garment, Jane moved up the short walkway. She rapped on the door and died a thousand deaths as she waited. What if Finn didn't wish to see her? His words that night had certainly sounded final, and there'd been no response to the rather scandalous gift she'd sent once it was clear he was on the mend.

Soon enough, the door opened and the Hadleigh butler stared down his hawkish nose at her. "Lady Hadleigh is out of pocket just now."

"I'm here to see Major Storme."

"I was given strict instructions by Her Ladyship not to let anyone disturb his peace." He looked her up and down, judgment unconcealed in his expression.

She tamped on the urge to sigh in frustration. Could he tell by looking what she and Finn had done that evening? Or that the outcome of said night precipitated his fall? "I promise I'm not here to further harm him. Please inform the major that Lady Jane Marsden is here to visit." Fumbling in her reticule, she handed the graying man a calling card.

"Very well. Follow me." He stood back from the door so she could enter the house. After, he closed the door and led her through the corridor to the drawing room. "Please, wait here. If the major wishes to see you, I shall let you know."

"Thank you." When she was left alone, she rolled her eyes to the ceiling. A pox on servants who thought they knew best. Of course, they would all be over-protective of someone they considered family, but she wasn't the enemy or a threat.

A quarter of an hour later, Finn wheeled himself into the room. She rose from her spot on a low sofa, smoothing her hands down the front of her sage green silk gown shot with gold thread. It was a trifle too elegant to make a social call, but she'd wished to look her best. Her heart hammered behind her ribcage while she devoured him with her greedy gaze. "You're looking well."

He snorted. "You mean for a man who tried to kill himself a week ago?"

"That's not what I…" Her words trailed to a halt when she caught the half grin that quirked his lips, and as he came closer, amusement twinkled in his sapphire depths. "Oh, you." A wave of relief smacked into her to know he hadn't suffered any ill effects, at least not visually. "How are you feeling?" A jagged scab decorated his left temple, the only testament to his misadventure.

He halted his chair in front of her. "Better." His gaze dropped to his lap.

Gooseflesh popped along her skin. Quick tears welled in her eyes. "Oh, drat, I'd really hoped I wouldn't make a showing as a watering pot today." When she would have turned away, Finn caught her hand.

"I'm sorry to have upset you," he said in a low voice full of emotion that had a thrill tripping down her spine. "I wasn't in my right mind at the time. Such is the case when I'm not vigilant enough and depression throws its weight around."

"I can only imagine." A few tears fell to her cheeks. "Devil take you, Finn. Why did you think there was no one in the world who cared for you? You're never alone, and I certainly don't want you to suffer by yourself." She sniffed, and when she wanted a handkerchief, she realized she'd left her reticule on the sofa.

He pulled a pristine square of fabric from his interior jacket pocket. "Here."

"Thank you." To blow her nose, she had to release his hand. "I was sad to think of life continuing without you in it." Another few tears fell and Jane mopped at her cheeks. She stumbled close to him and looked him in the eye. "Even if you don't realize it yet, you've made an impression on me in the short time we've known each other, and," she swallowed. "I would have missed you."

"I know that now." The hoarseness in his voice and the moisture in his own eyes spoke of more than what he said. "It was a mistake, and if it hadn't been for Wellington—"

"The duke?" She frowned. Perhaps his faculties still weren't right.

A rusty chuckle escaped him. "My cat. She jumped on my shoulder and saved me." He heaved a sigh. "It's a long story."

"I'd like to hear it some time." Such gratitude filled her being that she came into his personal space and swiftly hugged him. "Please don't ever think you should give up on life again."

He nodded, and his Adam's apple bobbed with a hard swallow, but he said nothing.

"Talk to me if you're feeling that way. I'm not going any-where."

"I'm coming to believe that."

"And I should apologize to you." She pulled away and dabbed at her eyes.

Confusion creased his face. "Whyever for? I'm the one who mucked everything up."

"I shouldn't have told you that your attitude could fix your thoughts. Being constantly positive and happy isn't sustainable and won't help in some situations." Quickly, she told him how she'd spent her time in the last week. "So, I'm learning how to help men like you in other ways. Never again will I make the same mistake as I did with you, for it probably contributed to what happened—"

"Jane." Again, he caught her hand, his grip tight, and oh how she wished she weren't wearing gloves. "Never stop being a little bit of sunshine, because it's desperately needed in the world... in *my* world." He pulled her down and brushed his lips against hers. When he let her go, his own tears fell. What was more, he didn't seem discomfited by them. "I was at a low point, embarrassed at my showing that night. I hated you saw me as weak, ineffectual."

"You're never that." She shoved the handkerchief into his hand. "None of it changes the way I feel about you; it never will. Only you have that power."

He nodded. "Thank you."

A weight lifted from her shoulders. Jane offered him a small smile. "Did you receive the parcel I sent?"

"Yes." A flush rose up his neck and into his cheeks. "Does that mean you..." How adorable he was that he couldn't finish the sentence.

"Yes. When the time is right." She couldn't wait to show him how it could be, help to build his confidence so he'd know there was more to intimacy than his being able to perform.

The grin Finn flashed sent tingles down her spine and dancing through her lower belly. "Would you like to move onto the terrace? We shouldn't waste the beautiful weather. Who knows when it'll rain again."

Jane nodded. "I'd like that above all things." It was time to slow their relationship to enjoy his company, know the man he was, instead of trying to rush into something he wasn't ready for. She moved across the room and threw open the French doors ahead of him. Once he'd wheeled himself through the opening and out onto the flagstones of the terrace, she followed...

And then immediately shrieked when two black beetles landed on her arm.

A genuine bark of laughter escaped him. "Do you require assistance?"

"No. Yes." Quickly, she shook her arm until the interlopers flew away. As a bee circled close to investigate, she squealed and danced about until it moved on. She gave into a whole-body shiver. "I detest bugs of all kinds." Did he think her a silly widgeon? "When we were younger, Royce used to chase me around in the country with all manner of bugs and small rodents, each one more ghastly than the last. It was terrible."

"Poor thing." Finn patted his knee. "Come here."

She glanced into the drawing room, but no one had come running from her sound of alarm. Craving his comfort and touch, Jane sat on his lap, her legs nestled with his, her skirting draped over his chair. The warmth of him, the spicy citrus scent of him both accelerated her heartbeat and brought her a sense of contentment.

"I'll protect you from every insect threat," he whispered against the shell of her ear as he wrapped his arms around her. "I'll put them on notice if you wish."

"Yes, please." Oh, it was so good to be with him again and know that he was alive. "How did your visit go with your brother?"

"How did you know about that?"

"Royce told me. You mother mentioned it in passing when he

examined you." Had she overstepped again? "If you'd rather not speak of..."

Finn tightened his fingers at her ribcage, which cut off her words. "I want to." He nuzzled his nose into her hair. "It was better than I expected."

"Really?" She drew back enough to look into his face. "Did you talk?"

"A bit. He's... changed."

Her concentration was nearly shattered when Finn nibbled at a spot beneath her jaw. Frissons of need circled through her insides. "Oh, how?" If her words were a touch breathless, it was entirely his fault.

"I think he's fallen in love with his wife." Marvel wove through his tones.

"But, that's a good development."

"It is." One by one, Finn plucked a few combs and pins from her hair, handing them to her as he went. Two remained that kept the front portion of her tresses up. The rest of the locks tumbled down her back and shoulders. When she glanced at him, jealousy and bitterness vied for attention in his eyes. "Mother told me he left abruptly for Derbyshire to be with Sarah. Said he needed to make things right between them, but that he'd come back to Town to attend Ballantrae's ball later."

"I'm glad for him. Love is worth every obstacle one needs to meet."

He snorted. "Do not forget we are *all* scheduled to attend said event." The muscles in his arms tensed. "No doubt your father will want you to do the pretty with the duke. Once more I'll lose you, and this time not from difficulties of my own making. If Worchester discovers you're wasting time with me—"

"Do hush." Jane listened with half an ear as she played with the heart pendant, sliding it up and down the golden chain. Grandmother's words rang in her ears. Was Finn worth incurring her father's ire? Would a life with the major fulfil her, give her everything she'd ever dreamed of even if they couldn't enjoy a typical, physical relationship? If he couldn't give her children? "I shall handle my father in good time."

"Yet you didn't deny you'd spent time with Ballantrae," he said in a small voice.

"I cannot give him the cut direct without cause." Thoughts and "what-ifs" spun through her mind like couples at a waltz. Did having offspring or not make her better or worse than others of her rank? Would it hurt her father terribly if she didn't reproduce due to Finn's injury? *If* by some miracle, she wed him? "You frightened me that night, Finn," she admitted in a hushed tone. "I was nearly in the depths of despair when you ordered me away." Would he always fight with his demons and be rendered unstable? What sort of a future was that?

"You would have come out right in the end." He twirled a lock of her hair about his finger where it curled naturally. "You have the duke, after all."

Did it make a difference that she didn't want the duke? "What folderal you speak. Ballantrae doesn't compare to you." Yet, was she a fool if she didn't make the right choice, the safe choice, the logical choice?

The *expected* choice?

"I'm broken, Jane." He cupped her cheek, tilted her head until their gazes met. "Best you learn this now, even though you tarry with me and hope there might be a future between us." He shrugged. "I can see it in your eyes, fairly hear you thinking over what you should do."

It was uncanny how well he knew her. "We're all broken to some extent." She worried her bottom lip with her teeth. "That doesn't mean our pieces aren't beautiful in the mess they make when glittering upon the floor."

He caught her earlobe between his lips and teased it with the tip of his tongue. "You're relentless, my lady."

"No, I'm determined to live on my terms instead of someone else's." She shivered from his attentions. Any moment someone could come upon them from the house, or a neighbor could step out on their own terrace and witness the scandal they flirted with.

"Why?"

"I wish to be with you in whatever capacity you'll allow. If that is only friendship, then so be it." Did that make her sound desperate? She rather thought it did.

"That sort of thinking is dangerous." Finn slipped a hand beneath her hair and stroked his fingers along her nape.

Butterflies pirouetted through her belly. "Why, because I might pull you with me into a different way of thinking?"

A small grin curved his lips, and she stared at his mouth, wanting, desiring, needing his kiss to assure her everything would indeed come out right. "I might pull you backward instead."

"Then you'll have company in the darkness, and isn't that better than nothing?" Her hand trembled as she fiddled with his cravat. *Something* kept niggling at her mind. Apparently, she wasn't finished talking about his near brush with death. "When I heard the news, I was hurt."

"Why?" He tangled his fingers in her hair and tilted her head backward.

"I felt I wasn't enough to keep you in this world, that I didn't do enough for you." Despite her vow not to cry in front of him again, a sob escaped, as did a few tears. "My brothers wouldn't let me come see you, thought it would be detrimental for us both in the event you suffered a relapse and finished…"

"You care for me that much?" He released her hair and caught one of the tears on her cheek with his thumb.

"Of course, you great lummox." Jane playfully smacked his arm. She sniffed. "Can't you see that?"

"I… It's never occurred to me before that a woman would." Wonder lingered in his voice.

"Perhaps you should start thinking along those lines." She scratched at her head. Finn batted her hand away. With an unintelligible murmur, he massaged her scalp, his fingers as talented in that task as when they'd last been together.

"Mmm." Sensations of soothing pleasure shivered through

her. She shuddered from the decadence... of the remembrance. "Many people care for you, but you've convinced yourself they don't. I'm going to show you that you're wrong, regarding everything."

"But—"

"No restrictions, excuses or requirements." She couldn't concentrate on her words; his hands wove too much magic. "The man you are is amazing, even if you don't believe me. I only wish for you to be happy." In the grand scheme, perhaps physical intimacy wasn't important. His healing was.

For a long time, they sat in silence. Eventually, he ceased his ministrations, and she laid her head on his shoulder. The cheerful chirps and squeaks of birds in the trees filled the air. A summer breeze wafted through the garden, stirring leaves, branches, and ornamental grasses.

Eventually, he spoke, and his voice rumbled through her chest. "Tell me something about yourself no one else knows."

A soft smile curved her lips. "I'm terrified of the dark."

"What's this? But you're fearless and confident." Admiration rang in his tones.

Jane snorted. "In some things." A sigh escaped. "My cousin was a tyrant when we grew up. He locked me in a cupboard once. For hours I was trapped until the housekeeper found me. Another time he left me in a wooded area where we'd played on my father's country estate. It was nighttime and we chased fireflies." She shivered. "My brothers were sent to retrieve me. By that time, I was nearly incoherent from fright. Another time, my cousin tricked me into coming up into the attics. He locked me in there for hours. I still have nightmares."

"How vile." Finn rubbed a hand up and down her back, the motion both soothing and arousing.

"I must have a candle burning until I fall asleep or have someone with me if I'm out at night. It's a failure on my part, I know, but I can't seem to overcome it."

"Shh." He held her close, and she reveled in the strong bands of his arms around her. For the first time in a long while, she felt safe. "I might be chairbound, but I'll protect you from the dark—and the bugs—as best I can... if you'll let me." A tiny shard of doubt echoed in his voice at tugged at her heart.

It was progress, and she was ecstatic. But she kept those emotions to herself lest they scare him away. "I will indeed."

"Good." He pressed his lips to her temple. "Also..."

"Yes?"

"I'd like to begin assisting at your brothers' clinic two days a week. That is if Royce doesn't mind. I... I think it will benefit the men there as well as me. To talk when I'm feeling... vulnerable and don't want to burden you, though you've helped tremendously."

"Oh, Finn." As much as she wanted to cheer with glee, she quelled the urge. "I shall ask him." She nestled more snugly into him. "You're growing."

"So are you." If only he knew. "Writing helps me too."

"I envy you that."

He snickered. "Don't, for it's a pain in the arse most times. Characters do what they want, plots don't come together, and heaven help me if their names don't suit their personalities." He chuckled. "Perhaps I'll show you what I've written soon."

"Oh, yes, please."

"Phineas, why are you outside?"

Dear heavens, his mother had returned! With her heart thudding hard, Jane slid off Finn's lap as the countess appeared in the doorway. As quickly as she could, she hastily pinned up her hair, haphazardly shoving combs into the mass. "Good afternoon, Lady Hadleigh."

"Who are you?" The glance she bounced between her and Finn held a speculative edge.

"Lady Jane Marsden. A friend of Finn's." For the moment, it was the truth.

"Ah, yes. The friend who nearly inherited Wellington." The graceful lady nodded. "Phineas talked about you in his sleep after that terrible ordeal." Her grin was that of a cat's after it ate the proverbial canary.

"Mother!" Embarrassment rang in Finn's strangled outburst.

Heat fired in Jane's cheeks. "All good, I hope?" How curious, indeed.

"He said you felt like sunshine and smelled like summer." One of her dark eyebrows lifted. "I assume that's good." Her grin widened. "Thank you for befriending my son. I'm grateful for it, for he needs someone."

"My pleasure." She glanced at him. Her heart squeezed when he peered back with a mixture of amusement and dread in his eyes. "He's a wonderful man."

The countess nodded. "The both of you, come inside and take tea with me. I have some questions for you, Lady Jane. Oh, and Phineas, I heard back from your cousin William. He says he'd like to come to Town soon, and he's bringing his sister Isabel. I thought you might wish to know since you probably haven't made plans." She returned to the drawing room, imperious as a duchess in the assumption they would follow.

Finn groaned softly. "You're in the soup now. Mother is like a dog with a bone. She'll discover what's happened soon enough."

"Not necessarily." But she couldn't help a grin. "If your mother likes me, you're the one in trouble." She giggled. "Hmm, I wonder how much I shall reveal…"

"Oh, God."

She slanted a look at him. "Who is Isabel to you?"

"A cousin whom I've rarely seen over the years. As children, we used to be good friends."

"Should I worry there's another woman wanting your affections?"

He snorted. "Absolutely not."

"Good." When she moved to return to the house, he followed.

Perhaps there was hope indeed she and Finn could have a future. It was too soon to tell, but it was more than she'd had this morning.

CHAPTER THIRTEEN

July 20, 1817

FINN GENTLY MOVED Wellington's back feet from his notebook as he scribbled line after line in his story. The cat sat on one side of the small secretary where he sat to catch the afternoon light, but progress was slow, for the feline thought the whole of his attention should be on her.

"Truly, Wellington, why are you striving for over-the-top annoying today?" He sighed as she flicked her tail, much like a gray-blue snake, over his paper and ran the risk of collecting drops of undried ink on her fur. "I must advance this story or else I'll lose the momentum."

It had been two days since Jane's visit, and since then, his muse had returned with renewed vigor that had him hard-pressed to keep up with. Wellington, of course, didn't like that. He'd thrown himself into the book to stay busy and make certain his mind was occupied, for he'd enjoyed his time with Jane on the terrace more than he'd probably should.

Neither of them had discussed future plans or physical intimacy, but it didn't matter. Having her in his life at all was a boon he was loathe to let go. Though he'd wanted nothing more than to kiss her, hold her, tell her how grateful he was she hadn't shunned him, he'd hesitated. Yes, she'd confessed her feelings for him, but he didn't want to harm their friendship—or budding romance—by rushing his fences or embarrassing himself again.

If the connection binding them was strong, the next progression would happen naturally without interference from him. At least, that's what he'd chosen to believe, for anything else was terrifying to contemplate.

He sat back in his Bath chair and contemplated his cat. "Wellington, I think I might be falling in love with the lady. And I said *might*. Such a thing hasn't happened to me before, so I have no way of knowing." Why he'd said it aloud, he didn't know, let alone spill the secret to his feline companion. "But it's folly of the first order."

Wellington meowed. She blinked but her light blue eyes remained fixed on his face.

"Why?" He set his pen into its holder and then stroked a hand along the cat's sleek side. "As much as I adore her, I don't want to consign her to a life with me that's not whole."

The cat bumped his hand with her head.

"I can't give her everything a man should. Hell, I don't even know what I want for my own life at the moment." For years, he assumed he would take up the reins of running Hadleigh Hall in Derbyshire, but now he wanted a more fulfilling role for himself. After being at the Marsden clinic, seeing the real need of men like him, he rather thought his mission in life was to give of himself in order to help others through their own darkness. Too damn bad such a position wouldn't come with enough coin to keep a household running, if at all. To say nothing of the fact that Jane was an earl's daughter and used to a certain way of life, a position in society. His chest tightened. "No, try as I might, I don't see any of it ending well."

The honorable thing to do was tell her he wished to keep their relationship a friendship. If he were a true gentleman, he'd encourage her to accept Ballantrae's suit, wish her well and happy even if such a development would shred his heart.

He snorted, and Wellington meowed. "I rather think I'm not

one-hundred percent a gentleman, girl." For if he were truly honest with himself, he wanted Jane in every facet life would give. That invisible connection that bound them together hadn't lessened. In fact, it had doubled in strength, and even now he felt that tug to his heart. "But that's selfish, isn't it? She deserves everything good in life, and some of that she'll never find with me." At least he'd spoken it and could now process it and eventually accept it.

The cat flipped over onto her back, paws in the air with a come hither look in her eyes.

"Oh, no. I'm not such a nodcock to try and stroke your belly again. You bite me every time I fall for it." Instead, he shook one of her front paws and then patted her head. "Back to work. At least on paper, my characters can have the happy ending that I can't."

Wellington wriggled until she laid over his notebook. She flipped her tail and meowed.

"You think a man like me can defy the odds?"

She leveled her blue eyes on him as if daring him and telling him to believe in himself.

Finn sighed. He scratched the cat behind her ears. "What lies between her and me and a glorious ending is a handful of mountains, and I don't have the use of my legs. How can I assume to climb them?"

This time, her meow was more forceful... and then she bit his finger.

"Fine. I'll try, but you needn't be mean about it." Though, in that attempt, if his heart were shattered, would he be able to survive the inevitable sucking darkness a second time knowing Jane wouldn't be there to catch him?

Gooseflesh raced over his skin. It was both terrifying and exhilarating to contemplate.

A knock on the open door wrenched Finn from his musings. He glanced over. "Rodgers, what's amiss?"

"Nothing I can tell. However, Lady Jane has arrived. She

wishes to take you riding."

"I beg your pardon?" His lower jaw dropped slightly open. "Riding, in my condition?"

The valet shrugged. His lips twitched with the same amusement lining his expression. "That is what she said, sir." He plucked a piece of lint from his immaculate brown jacket. "What shall I tell her?"

"Where is she?" Despite the shock of her request, excitement gripped him. He hadn't been riding since the middle of his career in the military.

"The downstairs parlor. I intercepted her while the butler is running an errand and figured there'd be no need to bring her up to the drawing room if you wanted to categorically refuse her offer."

Finn snorted. "Which is a polite way of saying it's rather a bother to convey me between floors." There was no bitterness attached to his statement, only truth.

"Far from it, sir." Rodgers, ever the staunch supporter, grinned. The big man was loyal to a fault. "Do you require assistance?"

"I do, unless you'd like to see me slide down the stairs like a troublesome child." They both shared a laugh, and oh, it was good to finally have reached a place in his life where he could joke about his injury.

"No need for that. I'll summon a footman for the chair." When Rodgers crossed the room toward the bell, Finn sighed.

"That doesn't mean I've agreed to her insane plan." How the devil did she think he could ride with any sort of authority?

A chuckle escaped his friend. "Where the lady is concerned, I've come to believe anything is possible." He yanked on a velvet braided rope. "She has a certain way about her that makes everyone do her bidding, or even rise up to the mark to achieve something better."

"That she does." What was her aim for this outing?

>>>><<<<

TWENTY MINUTES LATER, Finn rolled into the parlor, and his breath caught. Had there ever been a more beautiful sight? Jane sat on a settee that featured a pink crushed velvet cushion. Clad in a riding habit of dark forest green, it featured smart military-inspired lines, black braiding, and frog closures down the bodice. Masculine cuffs and collar completed the gown, and sent desire rushing through his blood. The rather mannish top hat she wore on her upswept Titian hair had a short veil that shaded her eyes and lay gathered in an intricate bow at the back. And damn, if that peek of lace at her throat beneath the habit jacket would drive him insane if he stared too long.

"Good afternoon, Lady Jane," he said in a somewhat strangled voice when he realized he had regained the ability to speak.

"Hello, Major Storme." She rose swiftly to her feet as he came further into the room. With a nod and a smile at Rodgers, who hovered silently behind him, she said, "I came to ask you to go riding with me."

Hell, at this point, if she'd requested that he accompany her to the moon, he'd find a way, merely to please her. *What the devil is wrong with me?* "Out of curiosity, how do you expect I should do that?"

"Pish-posh, Finn. Why not meet your limitations and turn them into challenges?" She waved away his comment as if it were naught but an annoying gnat.

Apparently, she *was* on a course for folly. "Are you mad? Look at me." He gestured to his legs and Bath chair. "This is not the man who rides any longer."

"I *am* looking, and you're handsome enough to make this scheme legitimate."

From the corner, Rodgers tried to cover a loud guffaw with a cough.

"How do you figure?"

Jane blew out a breath that ruffled a few curls on her forehead. What he wouldn't give to pull the pins and combs from her hair and delve his hands again into that heavy mass. "You can sit in front of me. I'll guide the horse with my legs while you handle the reins if you wish for control." She shrugged as his mind jogged to having those legs wrapped once more about his head…

Get hold of yourself, Phineas! That is about as likely to happen as a shark swimming through the Serpentine.

"I… I'm not certain that's a good idea." Had it always been so bloody hot in this room?

"Well, it matters not to me, for I'm going riding regardless, but if you wish to taste this particular brand of freedom, why not give it a go?"

How the devil did she have such a way with words that made him desperate to try everything she suggested? If his pulse surged any harder through his veins, they'd burst open. "Does that mean you'll ride astride?"

"Of course."

"Are you not concerned with someone seeing you in such scandal?" He admired her daring and wished he could have an ounce of her courage.

"Finn." Jane edged closer to him and took his hand. "If I were afraid of wagging tongues or malicious gossip, I wouldn't have done half the things that I have in my life, and thereby would have cheated myself of the joy found therein." She winked. "But if your tender sensibilities are threatened, I shall ride properly until we're ensconced in a private section of Hyde Park."

Rodgers laughed outright at that. He quickly gained his feet and ran from the room with a mumbled, "Excuse me."

Finn's mind was stuck on the picture she would make with the horse between her legs. Would her skirts fly up, show off her ankles and calves? *Oh, dear God, stop this!* He cleared his throat. "You'll think poorly of me if I fail."

"Hardly, but I do want to share this experience with you." She squeezed his fingers. "I'm told that men in your circumstances can increase trunk strength and control, as well as balance and overall posture and endurance by riding."

"Told by whom?"

"Royce." Jane shrugged. "Do you wish to come? You can swear the boys in the mews to secrecy if you fear gossip."

Oh, how tempting was this idea. "I'd never thought of riding as exercise while I'm like... this." The whole plan was mad, insane, outrageous. Horrible, really. Any number of misfortunes could happen. "I could fall." In all likelihood that would happen. And then what? He doubted she'd have the upper body strength to put him back on the horse, and she certainly couldn't carry him.

Jane gave him a smile that brimmed with wickedness as she released his hand. Matching deviltry winked in those green eyes. "Yet you might fly. Which truth would you like to believe?"

"Damn it, woman, you'll be the death of me," he grumbled, knowing full well that he'd agree with her.

"Or I'll usher in a rebirth." She moved slowly to the door. Was it his imagination or did her hips sway in a more exaggerated fashion today?

"Fine." He shoved a hand through his hair. "If you'll ring for a footman, I'll meet you in the mews."

That gave her pause. "You don't wish for me to accompany you?"

Heat surged up the back of his neck. "I'd rather you not see my reliance on a footman for such things as stairs."

"Oh, Finn." She frowned. "I'm not a stranger, and nothing will change my opinion of you. I merely wish to be *with* you." Her shrug only lifted one shoulder. "There comes a time when a man needs to rise above the difficulties facing him and challenge himself to reach new goals. Are you ready for that next step?"

His heart skipped a beat. How was it possible he'd found this remarkable woman and she didn't give one whit about his injury and handicap? "Very well. You win. I'll go riding with you."

"Excellent." With a smile that could have lit all of London,

Jane strode across the room to yank at the bell pull. "You won't regret this."

A HALF HOUR later, they'd gained the tree-shrouded paths of Hyde Park. After entering a gate on the far side and away from the more popular areas, Finn brought the horse to a halt. She situated herself astride behind him. Her arms went around his chest while he manipulated the reins. It was odd, this sensation of knowing such a large animal was beneath him yet not being able to feel it, but it was also most thrilling. In the event that he did fall, Rodgers rode behind them at a discreet distance.

"All right, Major, let's see what you can do," she whispered against the shell of his ear. "Show me what I already know—that you're vital, capable, and every bit a man any woman of the *ton* would be proud to find at her side."

The warmth of her body pressed against his back left him speechless, but he nodded and flicked the reins of a dappled gray mare he'd long gotten to know over the years. They started off at a walk but once he grew more confident, he urged the horse into a trot. Tingling in his right leg returned. Was it his imagination or was he able to slightly dig his heel into the horse's side?

Jane's squeal echoed in his ear. Her hold about his chest tightened. "I knew this was a good idea," she gushed while they followed one path onto another without pause. Her breath warmed his nape, making him ever conscious of her presence.

All too soon, he lost himself to the excitement of riding. The summer breeze, perfumed with the smell of green growing things, whispered over his face and he reveled in it. He tangled the leather reins in his fingers, urging the horse to find her own rhythm as he gave himself over to the whole experience.

His breath came in pants, for he was unaccustomed to the exercise, but he grinned as the world fell away with every *clip clop* of the hooves, each rise and fall of his body that brushed against Jane's. The steady race of his pulse competed with the chirps of the birds in the trees overhead.

Eventually, the path went parallel to the Serpentine in a more private section of the park. The sunlight sparkled on the water like gems tossed away. Had the grass always been so green, or the tree leaves so crisp and sharp? Had the distant laughter from children wading in the shallow part of the river always held such unfettered happiness? Or was it all merely a product of being in Jane's company, the woman who'd turned his world upside down?

Unexpectedly, he lost a piece of his heart to her, couldn't imagine a better place to keep it than in her hands. Finn turned slightly in the saddle so he could look into her face, meet her gaze. "This afternoon is a gift I'll treasure always."

Though she grinned, tears sparkled in her eyes. "If you find that you enjoy riding, you can work your muscles by moving yourself from your chair to the horse's back when you're ready. One of the stable hands can set your chair on a mounting block to make the transition easier." She blinked away the moisture. "You're already well built in your upper body, so this shouldn't be an issue. It'll be good exercise in addition to the riding itself."

Heat swamped him that had nothing to do with the summer sun. "Thank you."

"For what?" Her eyes in the strong afternoon light gleamed like the finest emeralds.

"For coming into my life. For badgering me out of my battered shell. For daring to befriend me despite everything." If he weren't careful, he'd spout romantic poetry and make a cake of himself. That simply wouldn't do.

"You're more than welcome." She grabbed one of his hands and pressed it to his chest. "Do you fell that?"

"What, my heartbeat?"

"Yes. It means that you're alive and you have a purpose, and you are loved." Jane edged herself closer, put her lips to his ear.

"Never forget that, Finn. I rather like having you in my life as well."

He inhaled sharply. Was that a roundabout declaration from her? How could a man tell? More to the point, did he believe he could return her feelings despite everything? Not having the answers, and not caring that Rodgers lurked some distance behind them, he lifted his hand from his chest to hook around the back of her head, and he pulled her in for a quick but meaningful kiss. Once he released her, he grinned. "Shall we continue?"

Did he refer to their relationship or the riding? Perhaps it didn't matter.

"I can't think of anything I'd rather do."

CHAPTER FOURTEEN

July 22, 1817

"**M**Y LADY, THE Duke of Ballantrae is here to see you." The butler couldn't quite keep a note of excitement from his somber tone. "I've put him in the drawing room."

Good heavens, the man is persistent.

Jane glanced up from the letters she currently wrote in the morning room. "Thank you. I'll attend him presently."

"Shall I have tea brought up?"

"Not just yet." No need to encourage the duke to linger.

Once the butler left, she sighed, replaced the pen in its holder, put the stopper on the inkwell, and then stood. Her gown of robin's egg blue stopped her annoyance from growing. Why couldn't it have been Finn who'd come to call? She hadn't seen him for two days.

Not since the idyllic afternoon when they'd gone riding in Hyde Park. Finn had been the epitome of joy in those moments. As his confidence had grown the longer they'd wandered, he'd stolen another piece of her heart. If the only thing that came of their relationship was showing him other sorts of freedom he could indulge in, then she'd count herself happy, but oh how she wanted to do so much more with him.

Then reality came crashing through her thoughts, for the

Duke of Ballantrae waited for her downstairs. He was the man her father wished her to marry, and duty told her the same, as did her sense of self-preservation. Yet...

No matter what decision she made, someone would feel hurt or disappointed, including her. Why was everything so difficult?

With the air of someone needing to do a difficult task and have it over with, Jane made her way to the drawing room. The various shades of blue immediately soothed her troubled spirit, but the second her gaze fell on the blonde Adonis of a duke, her stomach knotted. Oh, he was handsome to a fault and no doubt had coffers brimming over with wealth, plus he commanded position and power for all his newly-minted status, but nothing about him appealed, and he certainly didn't make her soul dance.

However, neither had Finn, yet she refused to ignore the connection between them. It was more than she had with the duke.

"Ah, Lady Jane. There you are." The duke turned as she entered the room from where he'd been contemplating something beyond the windows. A sweet bouquet of flowers was clutched in one hand. "I was beginning to think you were ignoring me."

"That is impossible, Your Grace." Impossible due to his habit of calling on her or finding her at any given society event.

"That color suits you." He smiled and the gesture only added to his gorgeous looks. "In fact, I can't think of any color you've worn that didn't."

Her cheeks heated, which stoked her annoyance. She didn't want to feel anything for this man let alone harbor a reaction to something he said. "Thank you for noticing." Finn always did as well, but with the major, that admiration was reflected in his eyes or the way he subtly stopped breathing for a few seconds. The duke remained unaffected, his face a mask of polite inquiry. No doubt those sorts of things were ingrained into him from birth. "Uh, is there a particular reason you've called today?"

The sooner she could shuttle him out of the house, the sooner she could concoct a reason to either seek Finn out or invent a reason that he should call upon her.

"Of course. How silly of me not to be forthright." His voice wasn't as deep as Finn's, but neither was it unpleasant. The duke came toward her, stopping within two feet of her, and then handed her the floral tribute. "Lady Jane, I wish permission to pay my addresses to you. We've known each other throughout society for many months, and I would like to know you better personally."

Dear Lord. The pressure of what he left unsaid weighed heavy on her shoulders. No doubt he, as well as her father, expected them to make an announcement any day regarding an engagement. The urge to cast up her accounts grew strong. She held it off by swallowing a few times in succession, and when that worked moderately, she brought the flowers to her nose and inhaled their summertime scent. Cold panic welled in her chest as she stared at him over the blooms. What to do? "How interesting." *That* was all she would say?

One of the duke's golden eyebrows rose as confusion crossed his face. "Your father indicated you were receptive to my intentions."

My father doesn't know the first thing about me anymore. She'd changed by increments since the advent of Finn, and she rather liked the woman she was growing into. "Would it be acceptable if I gave you my answer at your ball?" It was the biggest societal event this summer. Every notable member of the *ton* who remained in Town had no doubt been invited. She rushed on before he could respond. "Just now I'm not feeling myself. Too many worries are pressing on my mind. I don't wish to make such a large decision until I can think it through." None of it was a lie, per se, but it would give her more time to separate the threads of her life and see clearly.

Duty to her father and her position or follow where her heart would go?

"Ah, understandable." The confusion cleared from his expression, replaced with masculine indulgence. "That is perfectly acceptable. I look forward to seeing you again."

"As do I." *Really, Jane, don't lead this man on.* She cast a look about the room, and spying a vase on one of the nearby tables, she rested the bouquet inside it, making a mental note to carry the whole thing upstairs with her later.

"Good." Ballantrae drifted close once more, took her hand, lifted it to his lips, and then kissed the back. "Four days seems too long, but I'm certain the time will pass in a twinkling." When he released her hand, Jane gawked at him.

Even she couldn't deny that was a rather nice gesture, and her romantic heart beat a little faster. "Enjoy the day, Your Grace."

"I shall try, though doing so is difficult without having the opportunity to see you again soon." With a smile, he quit the room.

"Goodness." Jane collapsed into the nearest chair as the strength in her knees gave out. She fanned her face with a hand. Yes, he was everything a duke should be, and he certainly was charming enough, but would he set her afire like Finn did?

"Ah, Jane!" Her father sailed into the room, his gloves and top hat in hand. "I'm on way out to parliament for a vote. Should run late into the wee hours, but I saw Ballantrae leaving. He told me you'd give him a decision at his ball."

"I did say that," she replied in a quiet voice. Confusion ran amok through her brain, but her heart hurt as if she'd betrayed Finn.

"Well, I'm pleased to hear it." He beamed as he drew on his gloves. "To think my daughter might be a duchess!" His chuckle echoed in the room. "I'm glad you've come to your senses and have stopped chasing Major Storme. Knew you'd put duty ahead of all else."

Jane merely looked at him, incapable of speech. What was she to do now?

"I'll see you on the morrow," her father went on, oblivious of her split attention. "You've made me proud."

"Shouldn't you be pleased with any man I've taken a liking to, especially if he's won my heart?" she whispered, but her father had already gone. An ache formed over her temples. Jane rubbed her fingers over the spots. Perhaps a megrim would send her to bed for a week, thereby causing her to miss the ball altogether. But that would also mean she wouldn't have a chance to see Finn.

No sooner than she'd sunk into maudlin thoughts did the butler return. "My lady, Miss Spencer is here to see you. Shall I show her in here?"

Oh, dear heavens, would she never know a moment's peace today?

Jane stifled a groan and sat up straight in the chair. "That's fine. Thank you, Boswell." Perhaps talking to Fanny would help clear her mind and make her feel better about the choice she needed to make. When her friend came into the room, her face wreathed in a smile, and the jonquil color of her gown filling the space with cheerfulness, Jane sprang from her chair. "Fanny!" She rushed over the floor to give the other woman a tight hug. "It's been an age."

"I meant to call sooner, but life has a way of finding other things to fill our time."

"You have no idea," Jane murmured. She pulled Fanny over to a low sofa and tugged her down as she sat. "Why are you so happy?"

"I saw the Duke of Ballantrae leaving as I approached your house." Her eyes widened. "Has he declared himself?"

"Not exactly, but I'm certain it's coming."

"Why does that make you look as if your favorite dog died?" Fanny frowned. "The duke will be this Season's greatest catch."

Why should she settle for a catch when she could have a gentle hero with a heart of gold, complete with tarnished armor?

"Fanny, I need your advice." She took in a deep breath and then let it out slowly. "I'm so confused." With another sigh, she began. "Ballantrae is charming, is perfection like a Greek god, and has an impressive title to be sure."

"Of course!" Her friend nodded. "Go on."

"He wants to pay his addresses, wants even more to pursue an engagement. My father has already endorsed the match."

"But?"

Jane bit her bottom lip. "I have no feelings for him."

Fanny snorted. "No doubt they'll come in time."

"What if they don't?" A lifetime of years stretched before her in her mind, and the best she could summon for the duke was respect, perhaps admiration, and if they were fortunate, a certain affection. But would it change into love?

Her friend shrugged. "You'll have the freedom to look elsewhere for that."

As if she could separate the needs of her heart from the needs of her body or mind. "Or shall I pursue the heat and fun that is between Major Storme and me? He's not shown evidence of wishing for a match, but I have feelings for him that can easily slip past infatuation with very little encouragement."

"What?" Fanny's dark eyebrows rose. "Have you been seeing the major this whole time?"

Heat slapped at Jane's cheeks. "Yes." Quickly, she detailed a few of their outings but left out the evening at the musicale when she and Finn explored intimacy. "I even met his mother a couple of days ago. She's a lovely woman and wants the best for her sons." She shrugged. "I think the countess is worried about the major."

"Understandable. He can't look after himself." Fanny patted her hand, even though Jane sputtered with annoyance at the flash judgment. "Can the major act as a man should... *in that way*?" She titled her head to one side. "What about children should you want them? If he is unable to father them..."

It was on the tip of her tongue to reveal all to Fanny, but it felt too personal, something that only she and Finn had shared, and she wanted to horde that treasure to her heart. "Does it matter? Why can I not *only* want Finn? Why must I weigh things like physical intimacy and the possibility of children against what I feel for him?"

"In a perfect world, feelings and love would be enough." Fanny's expression was the most serious Jane had ever seen it. "However, you and I, as well as the major, exist within the *ton*. Nothing is perfect, and there is a reason for everything. It's how we were raised, how our parents were raised, and their parents before us. Women aren't afforded the choice of free will most times. We marry for position and for duty, to further a man's bloodlines and name, to play at being a pretty hostess in a glittering house, for that's what we've been bred to do."

The headache grew with intensity. "What if I wish for more? To do more? Be *more* than society dictates I should be?" Cold dread and panic twisted up her spine to fill her chest. "To find my own path that wasn't laid out by my father?"

"Then you'll end up disappointing everyone around you, including yourself if you are honest." Fanny's frank summation didn't improve her outlook.

Jane touched a fingertip to her heart pendant. "After two failed engagements, I now wonder if I have strength enough to perhaps risk my heart again."

"That is indeed an issue. The duke appears hale and hearty while the major already battles health concerns."

"Not to mention the demons in his mind. No doubt seeing years of battle will do that to a man." The duke hadn't felt the call to follow the drum. Was that a black mark against his character?

"It's quite simple, really. Do you think the major will fulfil every longing you have? Can he provide a life for you that you've grown accustomed to? If he can't, you'll have your answer regardless of how you feel."

"But—"

Fanny squeezed her fingers. "Security is better than love, and you'll have that with the duke, but poverty and want will kill even the fondest of feelings, especially if the major isn't able to somehow make a living. He doesn't hold a title nor will he unless his brother dies."

Tears sprang to Jane's eyes. "I don't have the answers, or at least I'm not ready to face the answers I should give." She didn't want to toss Finn away merely due to the fact that he wasn't a whole man.

"You'll have everything you need with the duke," Fanny said with the shake of her head. "Nothing we do is easy; I know that, but at times, you must make a decision even if you hate every moment of it."

Love or security? A comfortable life or constant worry? Possible motherhood or finding contentment with her clinic work?

But I won't have Finn. Her heart ached as if squeezed by an invisible vice. *Why must I decide?*

"I'm sorry you must go through this, but consider yourself lucky to have such a dilemma." Fanny shrugged. Sadness clouded her eyes for a second, gone with her next blink. "You have two men. I've never been given a chance for one."

"Oh, Fanny, I'm sorry to have dumped this upon you." The thought occurred to her that Trey would be a perfect match for her friend, but she didn't have the strength or wherewithal to play matchmaker just now. Not when her own life was in such chaos.

"It's all right. I hope that whatever decision you make, you'll find happiness."

Before Jane could form a response, Boswell once more appeared at the door.

"My lady, Major Storme has arrived wishing to see you. Shall I show him in?"

Dear heavens, he'd called on her! That was an extraordinary step for him. She exchanged a glance with Fanny as her heartbeat accelerated and tingles of anticipation danced down her spine. "I..."

Her friend rose with a smile. "I'll come 'round in a few days, unless you need me sooner." She winked. "Good luck."

"Thank you." Jane looked at Boswell as Fanny left the room

with her limping gait. "Please show the major in. And order tea. I'm suddenly famished." Having one day a week for at-home visits was exhausting.

"Very good, my lady." The butler vanished, and Jane sagged into the sofa a moment to catch her breath.

The second Finn wheeled himself into the room, her heart leaped at the sight of him, and oh, how handsome he was! A charcoal jacket of superfine hugged his shoulders and torso to show them off splendidly. His waistcoat of steel blue drew her attention to his lean abdomen, while trousers in a lighter shade of gray encased his legs, set off by impeccably shined boots. But what caught and held her gaze were his sapphire eyes and the spark of mischief there.

"I'm so happy you've come." Giddiness rose in her chest as she stood. But *why* was he here?

"Our schedules didn't allow an earlier meeting, so I decided to change that." Finn moved slowly across the room. "Come and sit with me." His voice dropped to a whisper. "I've rather missed you."

A thrill shot down her spine. "How sweet." It was easily the most romantic string of words he'd said to her. Only then did she see the posy resting in his lap of flowers in varying shades of purple. "Let us sit here." She led the way to a low sofa of crushed navy velvet with curved bolster pillow arms. He gave her the nosegay, and she accepted it with a trembling hand. No sooner had Finn lifted himself out of his chair and settled on the sofa, looking for all the world like a beau come to call, than Boswell returned with a silver tea service.

The butler set it on an ivory-inlaid table near her location. "Will there be anything else, my lady?"

"No, thank you. But please, I don't wish to be disturbed for the next hour. All these interruptions of the afternoon have me at sixes and sevens. I need time to gather my thoughts." Jane brought the purple flowers to her nose before tenderly laying the offering on the same table where the duke's bouquet waited.

"Very well. I'll see to it." With a nod, the butler departed. He pulled the doors closed behind him.

Once she made certain Finn was comfortable, she poured him out a cup of tea and then handed it to him. "I'll return shortly." With feet that didn't feel as if they touched the floor, she lightly ran across the room and turned the key in the lock. Catching his expression of confusion, she giggled and darted to the connecting door at the side, giving it the same treatment. "I'm merely ensuring we will not know distraction."

"I wonder why that is?" he murmured and took a sip of tea.

Dear heavens, he was mouth-watering sitting there, watching her with a hooded gaze. The shades of blue in the room perfectly complimented his color and brought out a depth to his eyes. She shivered while she returned. Heat infused her person when she took up residence on the cushion beside him. "Everything I could ever need is right here," she finally replied with a fair amount of fire blazing in her cheeks. Had she said too much?

A wicked light glimmered in his eye. "I would have to agree." One of his midnight eyebrows rose. "Will you take tea with me?"

"Yes. And perhaps after we could indulge in other... things." Was that too forward? Jane knew what she wanted. Life was too short to feign a demure attitude.

"That can be arranged." He patted his jacket. "I've brought the items you sent in the event you might wish to..." His words trailed off, but a flush crept above his collar.

"Wonderful!" If the butterflies in her belly wouldn't settle down, she'd give into hysterical giggles, but she settled beside him again and attempted to act calm as she drank her tea.

"You, my lady, are incorrigible." He selected a small jam cake from the plate. "I must say I'm never quite certain what you'll do next, but I know I can't wait to discover what it will be."

Her heart trembled as did the hand holding her teacup. Amber liquid sloshed over the rim of the cup to dot and stain her gown. "Drat." With more haste than grace, she set her teacup on the table. Then she snapped open a crisp, ironed serviette and dabbed at the spill. Finn gasped. His own teacup sagged in his lax hand while his eyes took on a faraway look.

"Finn?" Gently, Jane took the cup from his hand and set it down. Droplets of sweat formed on his upper lip. One trickled down from one temple. For all intents and purposes, he was frozen in a moment she couldn't see. His breathing came hard and fast. One of his hands gripped the sofa cushion while the other curled into a fist on his knee.

"It's all right." She finger-combed the hair away from his forehead. When he whimpered, the sound tugged at her chest. "You're safe. The battle is over," she whispered in soothing tones. All the while she stroked her fingers along the side of his face and neck. "I'm here with you and won't leave."

Several moments went by as Finn fought with his demons. Eventually, he came back to himself. He blinked at her, confusion lining his expression until recognition dawned. When she put a serviette into his hand, he mopped at his face. Embarrassment seeped into his expression. "I apologize. Sometimes the night-mares happen due to a particular sound, a smell. I never know what will set them off or when they'll come."

She rubbed a hand along his back. "Do you wish to talk about it?" Oh, how she wished he would let her in so she could help.

"Not right now, for it would spoil our time together."

"If you're sure?"

"I am." He rearranged himself until his back was against the bolstered arm of the sofa with his legs stretched out in front of him behind her. "Come here and let me hold you."

"Oh?" How utterly decadent.

Finn nodded and when she stood, he shifted his legs with his hands until they were splayed with the right one bent at the knee. "Usually after a nightmare happens, I have Wellington to comfort me, but I'll take you in her place today."

"I'd be honored." Gingerly, Jane sat between his splayed thighs, and when he encouraged her to lean back against his chest, she sighed. "This is nice."

"Agreed." Then he collected a book that had been resting on a table behind him. "Fairy stories, eh?" His chuckle rumbled through her chest. "Would you allow me to read to you?"

"That sounds lovely."

"Once upon a time..."

How utterly romantic. She lost another piece of her heart to him. There was something to be said for a man who indulged her passions for fiction with nary a grumble. In an abstract part of her mind, she wondered what the duke would say about a woman reading, then she didn't care as she lost herself to Finn's words.

CHAPTER FIFTEEN

HAVING HER BACK in his arms felt better than it should have. So much so that his concentration on the story he read wavered. Quickly closing the book, Finn tossed it in the direction of the table nearby, not caring that it thudded to the floor. "Of course, they lived happily ever after and every problem they've ever encountered melted away as if by magic," he said in a low voice while brushing his lips along the side of Jane's neck.

"Were you tired of the story?" She turned her head in the attempt to look at him. A small frown had taken possession of her mouth.

"I was not, but I did find something more pressing to take my attention."

"Oh?" A shiver racked her body, and he grinned.

"See if you can guess what." As she settled against him once more, Finn caressed his fingers up and down her left arm. Her skin was as soft as satin, and her orange blossom perfume filled the air around him, reminding him of summer days when there wasn't a care in the world. She murmured something unintelligible, and he shifted, raising her arm so that he could draw the fingers of his other hand up and down the inside of that limb. "This is highly illicit, you know."

"How so?" Her eyes had fluttered closed as he transferred his attentions to her other arm.

"You've already had an admirer who's come before me to-day."

"Ah."

Hot jealousy lanced through his chest, but he strove to keep his emotions in check. "I should bow out and let Ballantrae win you uncontested." The duke was the best choice for her. Was he being a cad for continuing to hang about?

"Please don't. I am a woman grown. Why can I not make a decision for myself?"

Finn frowned at the budding panic rising in her voice. "Perhaps I'm not the *right* choice." But then, they hadn't discussed a future between them, nor had they spoken of anything permanent. He certainly hadn't declared himself. What would he say? That he thought he could fall for her but didn't know yet? That even if he did, how could he expect her to throw away her life on him?

She laid her hand on his left knee. Damn, but he wished he could feel that touch. "I know my own mind, Finn. Please don't ruin that with a lecture on what I *should* do."

"Very well." For the moment, desire overrode his common sense. There was something about Jane that he craved, wanted—needed—for his continued existence, but if there came a time when it was clear Ballantrae wanted her more, he would give her up if it meant seeing her happy.

If he couldn't give her that.

When she nestled her head into his chest and against his cheek, the warmth of her scattered his tortured thoughts. He applied himself to the task of arousing her, for that had been the driving force that had pried him from his own home to make a social call when he'd never done such before.

Daring much, Finn drew his fingers along the bodice of her gown. The filmy tulle that trimmed the garment tickled his palm but made it all too easy to slip his hand inside and brush a nipple with a finger. At her quick inhalation, he grinned. "Are you in great need yet, my lady?" he whispered against the shell of her ear.

"I soon will be." She tightened her hand on his knee.

"Good. There is nothing more beautiful than a woman flushed with desire and lost in release." The realization struck him as if he'd been given a blow. Pleasuring a woman didn't hinge on a man's ability to use his prick. It was how he made her feel and his aptitude in wrapping her in a web of sensation, to employ his attention to her body, mind, and spirit.

He withdrew his hand to tug the bodice down and easily free her breasts from the fabric. The second Finn took those full globes into his hands, she uttered a shuddering sigh as if she'd wanted him to do that very thing for a long time. Gently, he squeezed them, smashed them together while the dusky nipples hardened. He rolled those pebbled buds, first at their base, and when she softly moaned her pleasure, he applied more pressure to the tips.

"Oh, Finn." Her breathless whisper encouraged him to continue his play, and with each new touch, every caress and stroke of his fingers on her quivering flesh, she arched her back, her legs bending at the knees. "You make me feel…" She didn't finish the thought, for he flicked his thumbs over her nipples, teasing them with varying levels of friction.

"Mmhmm." He grinned as she shivered. Oh, there was so much he wanted to do to her, hours he could fill by sending her close to the edge with his fingers and mouth. He nuzzled beneath her jaw, nipping, and nibbling the satiny skin there while he slipped his hands down her body, and as he licked the side of her neck, kissed that fragrant flesh, he drew up her skirts, finding his way through the yards of fabric until he could skim his fingers over the silky skin of her thighs.

He explored the ribboned garters that held up her embroidered white stockings, wished their positions were reversed so he could kiss and nip every inch of her legs, but he would save that treat for another time. Jane's soft moans of approval urged him onward, and he grinned. She was so responsive to his touch. It both flattered and humbled him. When he brushed his fingers through the red curls hiding her sex and she spread open her thighs, she trembled in his hold.

"Please say you wish to put on your cock ring," she said in an urgent whisper. "I want you so much."

"Not just yet." He lightly bit her earlobe then sucked and soothed that fleshy bit. "But I will use something else you gave me." As she tried to twist around to see him, he tsked his tongue. "No peeking." After giving one of her nipples a pinch that had her gasping, he delved his hand into the interior pocket of his jacket. Seconds later he withdrew the wooden phallus that was sheathed in a thin covering of supple leather that didn't compromise the shape of the shaft nor change the integrity of the tool's stones.

He rubbed the leather over a nipple so she could see what he intended, then drew the object down her torso, over the fabric of her skirting, and rested it on her mons. "Are you certain you wish for me to employ this? It's not conventional and—"

"I want whatever you'll give me." She guided his free hand back to her breast. "Please."

The word broke through the last of his reserve. "Imagine it's me, moving inside you," he whispered into her ear. "But mind you don't become too loud. Somehow I don't think your butler would appear pleased to see you splayed out like this."

Finn circled the phallus tip around her hidden button and then slid it down, resting it at her entrance. "God, you're so beautiful." Making certain he held it in a firm grip by the wooden stones, with a flick of his hand, he penetrated her as deep as he could go. "How does that feel? If it's uncomfortable, we'll stop." He had no idea what such a device would feel like on sensitive flesh, but if she enjoyed it—

"Please continue." She touched a hand to his, pressing it against her body, holding the toy inside her. "It's not as soft as a man, but it's... nice."

"Good." He moved his hand, sliding the phallus in and out until he found a rhythm he liked, and she enjoyed. Once he'd become accustomed to it, he let himself relax and watch Jane's face. With each stroke, he'd roll or pinch her nipple. Sometimes he'd kiss her neck, nibble the soft skin. When she lifted her hips to match his thrusting, his breath caught. He remembered what the act had felt like, and in his mind's eye he saw himself on top of her, making love to her body as he did with the leather-covered toy. His chest tightened. Heat spread through his torso. As he worked her over with the phallus, he slid his other hand down to play with her swollen bud, further bringing her to the brink with exquisite torture.

"Oh, Finn, oh, oh…" Jane bucked her hips against his hand. "Oh!" She sucked in a breath, no doubt in anticipation to scream out her pleasure, but at the last second, she turned her head, pressed her face into his neck as her body shuddered and she shattered in his arms.

A rush of affection rolled over him. He held her close while she came down from her release. As discreetly as he could, Finn removed the phallus, let it drop to the floor. Perhaps he *could* adapt to this new way of giving her pleasure. As bizarre as it was, he felt closer to her now than he had on their failed first attempt, and in that thought came the new realization intimacy was merely the act of being together in whatever capacity they chose.

"That was amazing," she whispered as she turned in his arms. Jane snaked a hand around his nape and drew him down for a lingering kiss. When she pulled away, she smiled. "*You* were amazing." A couple of the combs had come loose from her hair, allowing some of her lovely tresses to tumble about her shoulders. Already she had the look of a woman who'd been thoroughly ruined.

Perhaps he wasn't as useless a man as he'd thought, and it had taken her to make him see that. Another piece of his heart flew into her keeping.

"I'm not certain I was." How could she say that when it hadn't been him doing those things to her body? Well, it had been, but not in the usual way.

"Trust me. You were." Then she kissed him again, and he was lost on another wave of bonding. She burrowed her hands beneath his clothing. Slowly, as she devoured his mouth, she caressed his chest, his abdomen, worried his nipples with her fingertips and nails.

Oh, God, had they always been so sensitive? Hot, urgent sensation filled him. The feelings swamped him, and he reveled in them, for he hadn't thought he could enjoy anything having to do with intercourse. This was different, but as satisfying only in a new way.

"I'm anxious to try the ring." Jane kneeled between his legs on the sofa as she made swift work with the buttons of his frontfalls. "One of these days, I want to see you naked, Finn." Mischief twinkled in her eyes. "Not that I mind these quick trysts." When she unpinned the towel shrouding his privates, the heat of embarrassment burned his cheeks.

Would he ever become accustomed to this? "Jane, I…" He reached for her hands, but she batted him away.

"There is no shame, just you." When his shaft fell out of the fabric, she wrapped her fingers around him. "Let me do this for you." Up and down she worked his shaft, and he was helpless beneath her ministrations.

Never had he known how erotic watching a woman fondle him would be. Before, the whole of his concentration had been worrying over when he could bury himself inside a woman's warmth before he lost control, but now, all his previous thinking had been challenged. There was more to closeness than that, more to the trust and promise such physicality brought.

She licked the underside of his member, squeezed his stones, sucked at his tip. At no time did she appear disgusted by his inability to feel. In fact, the delight and desire in her emerald eyes stole his breath. Little by little, as he grew more aroused, he hardened. "Now, Finn. Put it on, unless you'd like me to do it?"

"No." He could barely speak, so great was his wonder. With a shaking hand, he yanked the leather aid from his pocket. "I've practiced a few times so it would be easier if you and I came together."

"I'm proud of you." She released him so he could manipulate the sheath onto his erect member and then pull his stones through the leather loop.

Once he'd tied the ends that would keep him hard, he looked at her. "I think I'm ready to try again." For the first time since his injury, his prick maintained its rigid shape. Due to the ring, the skin was turning a shade of red. He held her face between his hands and brought her over his body. "Without you believing in me, encouraging me in this and so many other things—"

"Hush." Jane straddled his waist. She kissed him with abandon, and he quickly followed her lead. Their tongues dueled for dominance until they both panted with need. "If this is successful, you can share your experience and give other men in your same situation hope."

"That hadn't occurred to me." Now that she'd mentioned it, he marveled at the opportunities to change other men's fate as his had been changed. Then every thought flew out of his head when she guided his tip into place and gently eased herself down his shaft, fully impaling herself.

"Oh, goodness." Intense pleasure lined her face. A shudder of need went through her, and she began to move. Up and down, faster and faster she rode him.

Though he couldn't feel her on his member or lap, he watched her, and his mouth went dry from the ravishing picture she made. She leaned over him, her hands firmly planted on his shoulders as he reclined against the sofa arm and bolster, and since her breasts were there, he cupped them, squeezed them, suckled and nipped the nipples while she ground on him.

Annoyance visited him, for he couldn't thrust into her lush body, but when she opened her eyes and smiled at him in that special way she had, he tossed the emotion away. It no longer served him; there was no more reason for it. With her steadfast belief and unwavering support, she'd upended his world, polished it, and set him back into it while encouraging him to try again.

Quick tears stung the backs of his eyes. No one had given him so much while wanting so little. Finn blinked them away and lost himself in her. As he stared, *something* was exchanged between them, something that pulled at his soul, touching him deeply. He gripped her hips, helping her to move more effectively, guiding her. Needing to send her over again, he delved a hand between them to play with her button once more. Apparently, that added stimulation was enough to break her, for she shuddered, her breath labored, her cheeks flushed. Her body stiffened, her eyes drifted closed, and when she opened her mouth, he yanked her down on top of him, kissing her hard, taking her scream into himself.

The scrape of her pebbled nipples, the rasp of her escaped hair against his bared chest sent heighted awareness through him, adding to the pleasure-filled sensation he'd reaped during their joining. Tingles zipped through his right leg. That foot twitched, but he had no time to gawk in wonder, for she went limp in his hold. A long, satisfied breath escaped; her warm breath skated across his cheek.

Shock sank into him, for having her in his arms after such an act was a transcendent experience. A juddering sigh left his throat. How had he been so fortunate as to meet this woman? "Ah, Jane, what are you doing to me?" he whispered into her hair and gathered her even closer. It grew more difficult to think she might belong to the duke. For the first time he allowed himself to dream, to see her by his side years into the future.

For long moments, the only sound in the room was their breathing and the frantic beat of his heart. Eventually, she stirred. Jane lifted her head and met his gaze. "I'm not nearly done with you, Phineas Storme." After a quick brush of her lips over his, she slipped off his lap. A wobble of her knees when she attempted to stand made him grin with supreme masculine satisfaction. "I had no idea how potent you could be."

Without comment, he untied the cock ring and removed the

sheath. He had no idea if he'd come, for there was copious moisture present, but it was interesting to think about. "I do what I can." She'd found pleasure at his hand, and what was more, he was happy for the first time since his injury—happy and content.

He snagged a serviette from the table then wrapped the ring and the phallus in it and tucked the pieces into his interior jacket pocket for cleaning later. After setting his clothing to rights while she did the same, he gave into a grin. "I don't know about you, but this has been a most pleasant teatime."

"You, Major, are too adorable for your own good." She shocked him into silence when she returned to the sofa and stretched out next to him. "I intend to enjoy the remainder of my uninterrupted hour with you, but if I fall asleep, please wake me. I don't trust Boswell not to have footmen burst the door open."

"I promise." He wrapped his right arm around her and held her close. She rested her head on his chest. Intimacy was what a person made it, but was what they'd attained here today enough for a possible future?

Chapter Sixteen

July 24, 1817

"**I** CAN'T DO this," Jane whispered as she clenched her gloved hands tightly in her lap. The carriage in which she sat rolled ponderously through the crowded Mayfair streets toward St. James Square. It was the evening of the Duke of Ballantrae's annual summer ball, and the time had come for her to tender an answer to his question of two days ago.

I can't consign my life to being his duchess.

The conspicuous absence of their father was noted, but he would arrive at the ball later once his business endeavor had concluded. A light rain was falling, rendering the passing world soft and blurred around the edges. Her brothers, Royce and Trey, stared back at her through the dimly lit interior of the closed coach. Both were dressed immaculately in the requisite dark evening clothes. Royce had chosen a burgundy waistcoat while Trey had selected one of peridot green. Other than that, they resembled the twins they used to pretend to be back in childhood days.

"You'll need to pinpoint the crux of your nerves," Royce said with a specific tilt of his mouth that heralded teasing. "In the last weeks, you've been more at sixes and sevens than I've ever seen you."

She bit her bottom lip. "It's a twofold problem." For the span of a few heartbeats, she traced the watered silk pattern of her emerald gown with a fingertip. The emerald and diamonds of her bracelet sparkled at her wrist, as did the silver embroidered scrolls lining the hem of her gown and the bodice. "I'm afraid I cannot accept the duke's intent to court me."

Trey snorted. "That's a bit of a stupid move, little sister. The bloke is rich. If you can manage to have him sponsor our clinic, do you know how much good we can do?"

A shaft of guilt stabbed deeper into her chest. "I'd thought of that too." It was a strangled sort of whisper.

"Father is near bursting with pride at the impending match," Royce said. "You can't do better than Ballantrae."

"I don't want *better*, I want happy." She turned her face to the window. The heavy black velvet drapes were drawn open. Droplets of rain clung to the glass, racing down with each bump and bounce of the coach. "I don't love the duke."

Two days ago, her world had been completely upended by the major. What had begun as a teatime respite, made cozy with him reading her a fairy story, had ended with her sated in the best possible way. The fact that the devices her brothers had given her for Finn's problem had worked astonished her. She'd been able to ride him and his erection had held strong for the length of time needed, which meant enjoying penetrative intercourse had become possible, but more startling and infinitely more wonderful was the connection they'd shared. Her soul had shivered with it, as if it had recognized his and had welcomed him with enthusiasm.

As if she'd finally come home from an eternity of wandering.

That meant something.

Never in any of the meetings she'd taken with the duke thus far had he produced any such reaction, not even on a smaller scale.

"Does it matter?" Trey asked with indifference in his voice. "Love takes time. Enjoy a long engagement with Ballantrae if you wish."

"What if I already know love with another right now?"

When Royce leaned forward and placed a hand on her knee, she looked at him. "Major Storme holds your heart." It wasn't a question.

"Yes."

"Ah." He sat back. "Has he declared himself?"

"No." And there was the rub. She had no idea how he felt about her, for though his other emotions were easy enough to read, anything that smacked of love or romance he held close to his chest—if he had them at all for her.

"Dashed coil, that."

"Thank you for that wise commentary." Sarcasm clung heavy to the retort. She needed advice, not obvious statements. "What should I do?" The world she'd been born into demanded she put duty over all else. Wasn't that the English way? Yet the romantic in her, the woman who'd fallen in love with fairy stories and tales of old knights of daring, beseeched her to follow where her heart led.

"What can any of us do?" Royce glanced at Trey, who shrugged. "I will be an earl someday despite my calling as a doctor. Once that happens, I'm duty-bound to take a wife and start my nursery. Will my dreams be forfeit to tradition? As much as I would like to say no, you and I both know what the outcome will be." He shrugged. "Trey is the most fortunate of us all. He's the spare, the middle child. He has freedom neither of us will know."

"Ah, yes, the freedoms a one-armed man has." Trey shook his head. "What does it matter? If you both live your lives by the dictates of someone else, then life will be long indeed." He leaned forward until Jane looked at him. "I've come to know the major better since he started working at the clinic with us."

"And?" She could hardly squeeze the word out from her tight throat. Tonight, her path would either open before her or she'd see it blocked and closed.

"A man who isn't thinking along the lines of love doesn't look at a woman like he does you when you're not paying attention."

Tiny trembles moved through her belly. "Meaning?" When had she been reduced to one-word inquiries in response to conversation?

"If the major hasn't realized that he's in love with you by now, he soon will." Trey shrugged. "Perhaps he needs proper motivation to make a definitive move."

Royce snorted. "Some men are stubborn and refuse to fall."

Hope bloomed and blossomed in her chest as she stared at her brothers. Would Finn ask for her hand if he felt that he might lose her? A thread of excitement climbed her spine. And if he did, would she accept? "Papa will be livid if I choose the major."

"Of course, he will," Royce agreed with a vigorous nod. "The duke is the catch of the summer, and if you could land him before the Season officially opens, all the better. There are already entries in the betting book at White's on who you'll choose."

Oh, dear heavens. Heat infused her cheeks. "Will Papa lose face if I don't accept the duke's offer?"

Both Royce and Trey laughed at that.

"Absolutely he will. He and Ballantrae have been thick as thieves at White's these past weeks. From their perspective, it's all but a done deal."

The urge to retch grew strong. Jane swallowed a few times to keep the hot bile down. "Do you... uh, suppose he might disown me if I don't follow his dictate?" Her last two engagements had been of her own making. Though the men were upstanding fellows, neither of them had been of *ton* stock. The first had been a wealthy merchant's son, while the other had been a decorated soldier who'd attained the rank of captain. Since they'd both ended in heartbreak, was she an idiot for not going after a title?

"I doubt it, but he'll make all our lives miserable for a time." Royce's expression sobered. "He might revoke your privilege to work in the clinic though. Already he sees it as an excessive freedom that a woman shouldn't partake of." As quick tears sprang to her eyes, he leaned forward and clasped her hand over the narrow aisle. "I know how difficult life is to navigate for you. I've witnessed your struggles over the past few years, but I will tell you this. If the major makes you happy, don't discount that. Such a thing is difficult to come by; you've seen that with your own eyes working at the clinic. So when you find it, you must cling to it fiercely."

"Even if it means choosing such a future will come with more challenges than not?"

This time it was Trey who brought comfort. He touched her foot with his. "Dearest sister, nothing grand in life ever comes easy. Remember that and make your own decision. Royce and I will support you no matter what."

"Thank you." Jane caught an escaped tear with her glove and once more turned her attention to the window as the coach approached St. James Place. Was she strong enough to make the right decision? She lifted a hand to touch her grandmother's heart pendant except she hadn't worn it tonight. A diamond and emerald necklace graced her neck instead, for the pendant hadn't matched the gown, and she'd wanted something fine and expensive for the evening.

Perhaps once she saw Finn tonight, she would know beyond a doubt what she should do... even if her heart had already decided.

GOLDEN CANDLELIGHT ILLUMINATED the Ballantrae townhouse. Due to the crush of people, every window had been thrown open to encourage the refreshing, cool summer air despite the persistent light rain. Everywhere Jane turned, couples milled through the corridors and filled the rooms, all clad in glittering finery and rich fabrics. Laughter and the buzz of excited conversation filled the air, and that energy transferred to her until anticipation thrummed through her veins. The strong scents of perfumes, pomades, and powders tickled her nose as she glided through the throng in search for one particular person while her brothers separated to find their own amusements.

When someone called her name, she craned her neck. As her gaze fell on Fanny, she gave a spirited wave, but since too many people separated her from her friend to easily join her, she kept walking toward the ballroom. The crowd waiting at the door surged, but once she finally entered, the brilliance of the décor took her breath away.

Oil paintings featuring pastoral landscapes hung in heavy gilt frames. Grand mirrors interspersed the paintings, which gave the already large room a bigger, airier feel. A huge crystal chandelier sparkled with mad brilliance in the middle of the high ceiling. Crown molding gave the room the feeling of opulence as did the delicate papering on the walls featuring moss green stripes. On the ivory stripes, scrolling ivy, tiny painted tulips in pink and blue, and the occasional peach cherub peeking out from the floral accents. Not to mention how lovely the highly polished parquet floor reflected the candlelight.

"Good heavens," she whispered to herself as she slipped to one side of the room. A string quartet currently played a lively country reel. Couples moved and skipped through the steps, providing even more decadence to the atmosphere. She poked at her upswept hair with a finger, for the combs itched and her scalp hurt from the weight of her tresses.

"It really is quite something, isn't it?"

The tenor wasn't the voice she'd been hoping to hear. A quick glance at the speaker had her stifling a groan. "Good evening, Your Grace." His blonde hair glimmered even more golden in the soft light, and dressed in perfection as he was, he'd turn any woman's head.

And possibly steal their hearts.

"Good evening, Lady Jane." He took possession of her hand and brought her gloved fingers to his lips. "You are perfection in that color."

"Thank you." It would be all too easy to follow societal assumptions and allow the duke to offer for her. With a tiny shake of her head to clear her thoughts, she gently slipped her hand from his. "You're quite popular from the looks of the crush here tonight."

"Indeed." A smile curved his lips. "Can I hope you'll promise me a dance or two this evening? I'd hoped to reserve them before your card is filled."

She lifted her hand, prepared to offer him the requisite dance card, but it wasn't dangling from her wrist. "Drat. It seems I've forgotten to bring it, but I'll allow you any dance you choose." Would that snag Finn's attention enough so that he might declare himself?

"I would enjoy that very much." His eyes glittered with intensity. "We have something important to discuss tonight." When someone hailed him, he glanced beyond her and lifted a hand in greeting. "I must go. The pressures of hosting an event takes me away from you."

Jane nodded. The relief that coursed down her spine was telling. "Until then."

"I'll count down the minutes."

Once he'd moved away, her shoulders sagged. Was it folly to keep him at arm's length? Her mind was more confused than ever. Not wishing to remain stationary and thereby encourage another visit from the duke, she continued to edge about the ballroom. A knot of young ladies clad in pastel colors tittered and gossiped behind fans. Their gazes were drawn to the duke across the room where he conversed with an older peer. *Good luck, ladies. Perhaps one of you might win him.* She offered a group of young bucks a smile, but most of them were paying attention to the ladies. Widows and matchmaking mamas alike all vied to capture the duke's attention, for who among them wouldn't wish to land a duke?

Then the country reel ended and the crowd on the dance

floor temporarily disbursed in lieu of another set. Through the shifting bodies a flash in the candlelight caught her eye.

Finn.

In that moment, when her gaze met his across the room and he grinned, she knew exactly what she wanted beyond all doubt. Her heart skipped a beat while an answering shiver echoed deep inside and made her very soul dance with joy. Heated awareness skittered over her skin as he wheeled his chair toward her over the parquet floor, regardless of the next dance that set up or the couples he displaced in the process.

A ripple of murmurs rode the air as many others followed his progress, for he was resplendent tonight in the soft illumination. Tiny raindrops sparkled on the shoulders of his black evening jacket, for he must have been caught in the rain while waiting for his chair before entering the house. As lean and handsome as he'd ever been, he looked even better, for he'd made a concerted effort at taming his wild hair and keeping his cravat neatly knotted. The silver embroidery winked on an emerald satin waistcoat that matched the exact color of her gown. How had he known? But the wicked light in his sapphire eyes had the power to turn her bones to mush and accelerate her heartbeat.

Finally, he'd traversed the floor and came to a stop before her. "Good evening, Lady Jane. You are easily the most beautiful woman in the room tonight."

Oh, dear Lord, has he always been so charming? Butterflies danced through her belly as heat filled her cheeks, "Thank you for the compliment." She forgot how to breathe when he took up her hand and shuttled it to his lips in a similar manner the duke had done, but prickling awareness zipped over her skin now. "You're quite dashing yourself." Her hand trembled in his, and she couldn't stop staring at him. "Is your mother in attendance? I'd like to say hello."

"She is. My brother Drew came as well, with his new wife, Sarah."

"Oh?" How interesting. "What is she like? How is he acting?

Are they truly in love?" There was so much she wished to know about his family, but using their limited time together talking of that seemed a waste of precious minutes.

Finn shrugged. "From what I can tell, she's what Drew needs, and yes, he looks a besotted fool when he's around her." Wonder wove through his voice. "I can only hope it will last."

"I'm sure it will. Love never steers one wrong." She could barely squeeze out the whispered response from her suddenly tight throat.

After what seemed a scandalous amount of time, Finn released her fingers. "I saw you talking with Ballantrae as I came in." Perhaps a touch of bitterness had entered his voice, but the spark of jealousy in his eyes betrayed his interest.

She tamped on the urge to show her pleasure. "He greeted me briefly. I promised him a dance. Then he left." It was best to stick to the facts. Would that prompt a motion from the major?

"I see." Finn glanced about the area before returning his regard to her. Gone was the jealousy. In its place, blatant need battled with longing. "I'm told the first waltz of the night will begin soon." He lifted an eyebrow. "Would you do me the honor?"

"Of dancing with you?"

"Well, of spending the time with me while we listen to the strains of the waltz." A hint of vulnerability shadowed his dear face. "We can either enjoy it from the sides of the room here, or we can remove to the rather impressive terrace beyond the doors."

If her heart beat any faster, it would jump out of her chest. "But the rain…"

"If I haven't missed my guess, it appears the precipitation has stopped." The slow grin that curved his lips sent a spiral of need through her insides. "Quite fortuitous, don't you think?"

"Yes." Was that an answer to his question or the offer of a dance?

He offered a gloved hand. "Shall we? I'd like to make haste

lest other couples have the same idea."

"I can't think of a single reason why we shouldn't." Jane slipped her fingers into his palm, and when he closed his around hers, a sigh shuddered from her. This man was her future, she'd swear to it. "I'm glad you came tonight," she said in a choked whisper, for being with him was overwhelming now that she'd finally come to a decision.

"So am I, if only to see you again." He slowly wheeled himself around the sides of the room toward the open terrace doors. "I've thought of nothing else since I saw you last."

"Neither have I." Docilely, she walked beside him. Peace enveloped her to further confirm that choosing Finn was exactly what she'd always needed to do. But would he agree and make an offer?

At the doors, he paused and gestured her ahead. "After you, my lady."

Heat crept into her cheeks as she passed him and went outside. Shadows crept through most of the area. Buttery soft illumination from the room barely reached beyond the doors. The rain had slackened to a barely there mist, and she was grateful for the trace of moisture that cooled her warm skin. She hadn't yet gained the middle of the smooth flagstones before he came to a stop.

"The musicians are beginning the waltz." His baritone sent a thrill though her belly, and when she turned to face him, he patted his lap. "Shall we begin?"

The remainder of her confusion fell away, disappeared into the air as she nodded. "I cannot wait."

Was there any wonder she loved him to distraction?

CHAPTER SEVENTEEN

FINN COULD HARDLY form a coherent thought, let alone words, for Jane was the most beautiful woman he'd ever laid eyes upon. Every time she moved, the jewels at her throat and wrist sparkled, as did the silver embroidery that lined her gown. Emeralds glittered in her hair, much like they'd done the first time he'd met her, but oh how those russet strands called to him! His fingers itched to encourage those tresses down so that they'd fall like a molten waterfall.

But that was for another time.

He waited, trepidation filling his chest, while she looked at him, eyes luminous with emotion he couldn't read well in the dim light. Then, with an angelic smile, she slipped onto his lap. Her silk skirting flowed over his legs and down one side of his Bath chair, her orange blossom scent surrounded him, and he wrapped his arms around her. She felt right, as if he'd been searching for her all his life. As the first strains of the waltz drifted out to their location, a trace of insecurity crept in.

"I apologize if this dance isn't conventional."

"Do hush, Major Storme," she whispered. The pleasant tones of her voice sent a wave of anticipation through him. When she laid one gloved hand on his chest and rested the other on his shoulder, a tiny sigh shuddered from her. "I couldn't ask for a better interlude or a more dashing man to spend it with."

"I'm glad to hear that." Finn set his hands on the wheels of his chair. His confidence soared when he was in her company. He wheeled them about the terrace in tight circles, and when the soft notes of her laughter rang in his ears, he finally knew the meaning of true happiness. That it took the advent of this petite, voluptuous, kind-hearted, forward-thinking earl's daughter to open his eyes was amazing, and he'd be forever grateful to her for that alone.

To say nothing of how she'd turned his life upside down to affect change.

He soon lost himself to the magic the string quartet made, and while couples twirled around the ballroom in a myriad of colors, he performed loops and circles with his Bath chair, the luckiest man of all, for he had Jane on his lap, and she held his heart in her hands.

Over and over, he traversed the flagstone terrace. In his mind's eye, he saw them dancing across the floor as if his legs had never been affected on that fateful day on the battlefield, but soon the image faded. For the first time since his injury, his reality wasn't as horrible as he'd once assumed. Now that he and Jane had navigated the pitfalls and ruts of intercourse and had declared victory over the obstacles, light glimmered in the darkness.

When he met her gaze and saw everything he'd ever wanted in another person clouding her emerald depths, his heart shuddered. Would that he could whisk her away to a secluded room and show her how much she meant to him, but unlike other society events, this one was too well attended for that. He brought the chair to a stop in the shadows. Awareness of her raced over his skin and tingled through his chest. Muscles in his right leg jumped, and he was able to flex his toes for a brief time. Later, if they were afforded a more private moment alone, he would show her the evidence of the nerve renewal. It heralded a better life ahead. When she continued to look at him as if she wished to devour him alive, he forced a hard swallow.

The words he'd wanted to say hovered on the tip of his

tongue, but cold fear crept in to steal them from him. What if he told her the contents of his heart and she rejected him after all? It was well and good for a lady to pretend, but when it came down to brass tacks and she thought about her future and everything he couldn't give her, would she turn down his offer?

So, he kept his own counsel and instead wrapped his arms around her. As the music inside the ballroom reached a crescendo, Finn claimed her lips in a series of deep, drugging kisses designed to show her how he felt. He hoped to God she was as receptive in that as she'd been in everything else.

All too soon, their embrace grew heated, for her touch turned his blood molten. He stroked a hand up and down her back while he cupped a breast with the other, teasing its peak with a thumb. When a low moan escaped her, she increased the ferocity of the kiss. She slipped her hands over his chest, restlessly roving, and he knew her well enough to assume she'd put him in enough dishabille that she could shove her hands beneath his clothing.

When she glanced her fingers along his waistcoat pocket, she paused and drew back. "What's this?"

Oh, God. She must have felt the outline of the emerald ring he'd dropped into the pocket by habit. Finn froze for a fraction of a second, but in that time, she'd stuck a gloved finger into the slit and then withdrew the ring. Warning bells sounded in his head, for what he couldn't say, but a soldier always knew when danger threatened.

Her breath caught as she held the bauble aloft. The dim light caught the gem, illuminating its shine. "Is this what I think it is?"

"If an engagement ring is what you're thinking, then yes." At least that was the truth. "However, it's not what you think." When he attempted to take the ring from her, she held it out of his reach.

"Does this mean you're declaring yourself?" Excitement wove through her voice as she stared first at the ring and then into his eyes. "It's such a great time for this, and it matches my dress. What a darling man you are."

Mortification and self-loathing mixed within his chest to from a hot mass that threatened to choke him. "It's not for you." He hadn't meant for the words to sound as blunt as they did, but there was nothing for it.

"What?" All color leeched from her face. The dim light couldn't hide that sudden pallor. "What do you mean?" The light that had danced in her eyes faded.

How could he explain without marring the exquisite moment they'd shared? Further, he did want to admit to yet another failing on his part, not when he'd been on the cusp of asking for her hand and needed to put forth his best showing. "Suffice it to say, this ring was never intended for you. I don't wish to explain why just now."

Tears welled in Jane's eyes. "Do you have a mistress?"

"No." He shook his head to reinforce the denial. How could she even think such a thing when she was the only woman he'd ever wanted?

"Then why do you have a ring meant for another woman when you haven't shown any sort of deep feelings for the woman in your lap?" Ah, that was why. He'd been rubbish in giving her any sort of clue or indication of how he felt. "Me, who seconds ago kissed you?" Hurt clung to her quiet tones, and in the anemic light, a tear slipped over the curve of her cheek, leaving a wet trail behind.

Foreboding slid through his chest in a cold tide. Fear prickled his skin and had the hair on his nape standing at attention. His pulse pounded loud in his ears. Every second he didn't respond sent another nail into the coffin of his dying hopes for the future. "I can't say." Any affection she held for him would turn to disgust and possibly hate if he told the tale now.

"Oh, Finn." With a barely stifled sob, Jane slid off his lap. She tossed the ring at him. It lodged itself in the folds of his cravat. "If you can't manage to trust me or open yourself fully to me by this point, we have no chance for any sort of future." Another tear fell to her cheek, and he died a thousand deaths with that one drop.

"Have you been playing with my affections, my heart, this whole time?"

"No, of course not. I..." What? Was a coward, plain and simple? Had so much ill-fortune in his past that he couldn't bear to think he might have mucked this up too?

She backed away a few steps. "Then why do you have an engagement ring if not to give it to me?" The tremor in her tones tugged at his heart.

With his hand shaking from dread and panic, he plucked the ring from his person and stuffed it back into his pocket. "I... I..." Those icy fingers of fear wrapped around his throat, cutting off his words and the explanation that could have brought her back to him.

"Answer me this: have you recently seen the woman to whom the ring belongs?"

"Yes." It wasn't a lie, but it wasn't the truth as she believed. However, that one little word taken out of context was damning, and the chilly silence that brewed between them was evidence of that.

"I see." She scrubbed at the moisture on her cheeks. "Devil take you, Finn. I thought you were different; I'd hope you'd be... more."

It was all too easy to fall back on old ways of thinking. "Of course I'm not. I can't be more of anything, now can I?" The flooding bitterness in his voice was evident to his own ears.

She blew out a breath. "It was never about the state of your body, the use of your legs, or anything like that. Haven't you realized that by now?" When he didn't answer, for panic filled his chest, she shook her head. "Please don't seek me out for the remainder of the evening. I'm too furious with you to talk politely."

"Jane, wait. Truly, it's not like that." Due to his own stupidity and cowardice, he was losing the best thing to ever happen to him, but fear kept him rooted to the spot and his tongue glued to the roof of his mouth.

"Yet you won't rectify the situation, and without honesty, I have nothing more to say to you." Without another word, she turned and stormed into the ballroom amidst a flurry of skirting.

Pieces of his heart crumbled off the whole to tumble about his feet. A shiver racked his shoulders. With her defection, it was as if the sun had hidden behind thick clouds. With nothing else to do, Finn wheeled himself into the room. Despite glancing at the crowd, he didn't immediately spy Jane. Had she fled to a retiring room, perhaps hidden herself away into a quiet area to sob out her grief? Emotion clogged his throat, lodged in the center of his chest like a ball of tar. He'd been the greatest nodcock to not explain the significance of that ring, and the consequence of that decision would haunt him for the rest of his life.

It felt much like it had after his regiment suffered defeats from the enemy on the fields of battle. He moved as if in a dream, maneuvering his chair along the sides of the ballroom without a clear destination in mind. What would he do without her?

"Oh, Phineas, I'm so glad I found you."

With a barely stifled groan, he turned his head as his mother joined him. "What can I do for you, Mother?"

"Why are you not with Lady Jane?" At least she didn't mince words, but the fact that she didn't sent the knife twisting deeper into his broken heart.

"She and I have had a disagreement." There was no point in creating a lie. Speaking it aloud didn't provide relief from the hurt battering him.

"I'm sorry to hear that." His mother frowned. "Perhaps you should circulate and talk to others. It will help. There are plenty of lovely young ladies in attendance tonight. Ballantrae has invited many of the *ton's* elite."

"Well, bully for him." He did *not* wish to hear anything concerning the duke. "However, I'm not of a mind to seek out anyone else tonight." With a wave of his hand, he dismissed his mother. "Go have fun. You deserve to enjoy yourself."

She frowned and touched a hand to his shoulder. "Is there

any way you can make up with the lady?"

"I'm not sure." Another wave of desolation swept over him, and he steeled himself against it.

"Try, Phineas." Compassion pooled in her eyes. "When you find someone who fits you like a comfortable glove, fight for her."

The urge to talk with his mother, to tell her everything and ask for her advice, grew strong, but he tamped on it. Nothing could change what had happened. "I'll take that under advisement."

She melted into the crowd and soon she'd been snapped up by an older viscount, who led her out onto the dance floor. They took up position near Drew and his wife. As Finn moved his gaze along the other couples, jealousy slammed into his chest. Ballantrae was partnering Jane for this set. She smiled up into his face, and he already looked the besotted fool.

"Oh, God." He rubbed at his chest above his continually breaking heart.

"They make a handsome pair, don't they?"

Finn glanced at the man who'd come abreast of him, and his shoulders slumped. "Doctor Marsden. Good evening." He swung his attention back to the couple, and another few pieces of his heart tumbled to the floor. "They are quite nice." The words barely escaped his tight throat. All he wanted to do was rage at the heavens and ask why this debacle could happen.

"I'm honestly surprised she's not with you at the moment," the surgeon continued as if he couldn't sense that Finn's world was collapsing with every passing second.

"Why is that?"

"When my sister is in your company, she's lit from within." He gestured toward the dance floor with his chin. "That is not the case now."

Finn flicked his gaze to Jane. It was true. He'd never noticed it before, but she didn't seem as sunny or as spirited as she was when with him. Though she smiled and laughed with the duke, the gaiety didn't reflect in her eyes. "Regardless, she has made her choice."

"Will you sit there and accept it even though you know it's the wrong one?" the surgeon asked in a quiet voice.

"Why do you assume that? He'll give her the life she should have."

"Because he doesn't love her like you do."

As those words sank into his brain, Finn gasped as an overwhelming realization smacked him upside the head. The remainder of his heart squeezed so hard he struggled to breathe as he watched her go through the steps of the dance with Ballantrae. *I love her.* He hadn't thought about it in those terms before, but it was undeniably true. "It doesn't matter. Nothing can come of it. She thinks that life is nothing but fairy stories where everyone will come out happy and with a romance at the end." Depression roared to life inside him, bringing the ever-present shroud of darkness with it.

"Why shouldn't she? My sister has hope, and that is nothing to sneeze at. Everyone should have the same, especially if one is brave enough to see its value."

He hadn't declared himself due to fear of failing her when it mattered most, out of fear of not ever being the man he was growing into, out of fear of his past mistakes and his inability to save his friend, out of fear that because the relationship with his brother was strained that he might muck it up with Jane. "Perhaps I lack the courage she needs."

"Then you're a greater fool than I'd thought." The doctor clamped a hand on Finn's shoulder and turned his chair until their gazes connected. "Where is the bravery and daring you had on those battlefields, Major? Where is the unwavering duty in doing what was right? Pursuing the woman you love is no different, but it *will* take effort."

"I don't want her to become merely a companion or to trap her into a half-marriage. I can't give her everything she deserves." His chest hurt from uttering the words aloud to her brother of all people.

"Then think instead of everything you *can* give her. That's worth something."

"You know nothing about it." He shook his head as the voices therein grew louder, told him he was worthless. "What if I *do* convince her to be with me and I leave her alone if I can't fight back my depression."

"Only you can make that decision." The doctor patted Finn's shoulder. Speculation clouded his eyes. "At the end of your life, though, do you truly want to have such regrets?"

"Will it change anything?"

"You tell me." The other man shrugged. "Are you man enough to fight one last time? Fight for everything you've ever wanted?" With a nod of encouragement, the doctor slipped away.

Finn watched Jane slide by on the dance floor in Ballantrae's arms, and his chest constricted. Ice coated the remainder of his heart. If she didn't want him, he didn't need her. "Removing myself from the picture is perhaps the best decision for all of us," he whispered to himself and then gasped at the cold desolation that plowed into him.

The longer he monitored the dancing, the deeper he sank into darkness. Of course she would choose the duke. Who wouldn't? He had working legs and would give her beautiful children. As the dance finally came to an end, Jane allowed Ballantrae to escort her off the floor and then out of the room, presumably to seek out refreshments. Another few pieces of Finn's heart crashed to the floor.

He transferred his gaze throughout the room. Drew had his head bent close to his wife's. Whatever he said made the plain-looking woman laugh. She glanced up into his face, and even from his position across the room, Finn recognized the affection between them. Jealousy stabbed through him with the accuracy of a saber's blade. He reeled from the feeling. Then his attention fell to his mother. She tittered at something the older viscount said as he led her onto the floor for another dance.

God, I'm a drain on them all. They're perfectly happy without me looming in the background like a wet rug.

Well, not anymore. He straightened in the Bath chair as best he could. The black thoughts could have at him for all he cared— all any of them cared. With quick, determined pushes at his wheels, he moved through the ballroom and then out into the corridor beyond. Thank goodness he didn't spy Jane on his way. It would have further broken him. When he reached the entry hall, he summoned a footman, loath to disturb Rodgers, who was no doubt enjoying himself down in the servants' hall.

"Please see that the Hadleigh coach is brought around. I wish to leave."

The young man nodded. "At once, Major Storme."

There was only one path left for him at this point. Emotions continued to batter him from within—hurt, anger, despair, envy. They formed a perfect storm that caught him up in the tide. The bleakness of depression raged around him, dropped darkness over his eyes until he couldn't see a way out. Negative voices in his head told him he wasn't good enough, that he didn't deserve any sort of happiness, that no one cared for him because he was too broken for their notice.

His defenses were down enough that he believed every word. The constant fight had drained him, and losing Jane had left him bare, vulnerable, grasping for something that would help pull him out of the sucking quagmire.

But there was no one there to save him this time.

By the time the coach was brought around, and the footman had helped him into it, Finn had made up his mind. "Please see that the Bath chair is strapped to the back." He'd only need it for one last trip.

"Of course, sir."

While the footman did as bid, Finn yanked the small note-book from the interior pocket of his jacket. When he took up the nub of a pencil, he sighed and turned to a blank page. He wouldn't fail on the second attempt to end his life. Before he could change his mind, he dashed off a brief note to his mother that simply said, "I'm sorry." Another note, this one to Jane, stated, "I wish I could have been the man you needed."

As soon as the footman returned to the open coach door, Finn ripped out the notes and handed them to the younger man. "Please see that my mother receives these in an hour."

"I will." The footman tucked the papers away. He swung the door closed. "Where to?" he asked through the window glass.

"Hyde Park. I ask that you don't reveal my destination if someone asks."

"I won't, sir."

"Good." Finn sat back as the footman relayed the information to the driver.

Drowning should be relatively easy, for he had no plans to struggle, and his legs wouldn't work anyway. He bit down on his middle knuckle to keep from crying out against the plan and the pain hammering his chest.

I'm so sorry, Jane.

After all, what had he to live for now?

CHAPTER EIGHTEEN

J ANE ACCEPTED A flute of champagne from the duke as she stifled a sigh. Thoughts went through her mind like ponies on a loop but they only served to confuse her more. The events of the evening had been exhausting, yet her chest felt empty as if someone had stolen her heart and absconded with it like a thief in the night.

Above everything, she remained furious at Finn for deceiving her. She couldn't believe he'd been playing games with her for the last few weeks. What sort of man would carry around an engagement ring for one woman while courting another? If that's even what he'd been doing with her. That simply wasn't the type of man he was.

Or so she'd thought. She'd left him sitting on that terrace with shame and despair in his eyes as if the story behind the ring hadn't mattered. But he'd refused to explain; what was she to think? On the other hand, hadn't all her dealings with the major come about from patience and persistence? She hadn't given him either tonight, for he'd broken her heart, and that hurt had prompted her to flee, put space between them lest she suffer more. It had been years since her heart had been shattered, and she didn't much like the feeling.

Finding time alone to sort through her scattered thoughts proved a challenge, for the duke had claimed her hand for a dance and she hadn't the strength or wherewithal to refuse. He'd managed to lift her spirits, but only just, for every step she'd taken with him had reminded her of the waltz she'd shared with Finn. Tears had been close to falling. If the duke had noticed, he'd been too polite to mention them.

When the champagne's bubbles tickled her nose, she shifted her attention back to the world around her and realized Ballantrae stared at her with a smile curving his chiseled lips. "I beg your pardon. I've been woolgathering."

This isn't how the story is supposed to go. Why can Finn not see that he's every bit as good as the duke? She sighed. Why didn't she tell him that instead of leaving him in the heat of the moment?

"Then I must do better in securing the whole of your attention." He finished the last of his champagne. After setting his empty flute on the table he turned his dazzling ice blue gaze on her. "Have you given further thought to my wish to pay my addresses to you?"

Merciful heavens, her reprieve had expired. Before she answered, she gulped down the remainder of her beverage, and when the bubbles stung her throat, Jane gasped. The duke gently tugged the empty flute from her hand and set it next to his. She would be a proper ninny not to accept his suit. Marriage to the duke meant security and position, and her father already liked him, where he'd warned her away from Finn.

But…

She raised a gloved hand to touch the heart pendant and belatedly remembered she hadn't worn the piece this evening. *Follow your heart, girl, no matter what is expected of you. Duty can hang. Your heart will always know where to call home.* Her grandmother's words rang in her ears, now more poignant than ever. As she held the duke's gaze, her eyes filled with tears.

I love Phineas Storme.

Home was wherever Finn was, even if he was currently acting the nodcock. She couldn't imagine a future without the major in it. What she needed right now was to find him, make up with him, and demand he explain himself so they could repair the rift in their relationship before it grew larger. Her brother was right. Nothing worth having came easy, not even in the stories she adored, but she was fully prepared for every challenge and obstacle.

"Dearest Henry." She laid a hand on his arm and hoped to goodness that was his Christian name. The facts in her head were quite jumbled, especially when every beat of her heart called out for Finn. "You are a wonderful man and an even more lovely catch…"

"Yet?" Insecurity flashed in his eyes that weren't the right shade of blue.

"But you aren't all of that for me," she finished rather lamely. What a terrible thing to break someone's heart, and what a horrible burden it was.

"I see." A muscle in his cheek jumped when he clenched his teeth. "Is there someone else?" He flicked his gaze to the people milling about and watching them with interest in their expressions before looking at her again.

It was all too complicated to try and explain. "There is the *hope* of someone else." She squeezed her fingers on his arm that had gone as taut and rigid as his posture. "You deserve a woman who will give you the whole of her attention and heart. I apologize for not telling you the truth sooner."

"I appreciate your candor now." The duke bowed from the waist. He took up her hand and brought the gloved fingers to his lips. "Then I wish you all the best in life. I hope you find what you're searching for."

"Thank you." The tears gathering in her eyes spilled onto her cheeks. She brushed them away as the heat of embarrassment sank in. Why was choosing a man so deuced emotional and trying? "Would that you discover the perfect lady for you."

"I thought I had, but my heart still beats so I'm not yet dead." A tiny smile curved his lips, but the gaiety from the dance they'd shared had faded. "Life must go on." With a nod, he took his leave.

Oh drat, drat, drat.

Second thoughts plagued Jane's mind. She twisted her hands together as she worried. The duke had vanished into the crowded ballroom. Would he dance with someone else? Her heart went out to him, for as the host of the event, he couldn't very well slip away to lick his wounds in private. Had she made the right choice? There was every chance that by turning the duke away, she'd end this night without either man.

Oh, falling in love is a terrible thing, even if it has brilliant potential.

Barely had she decided to dash into a ladies' retiring room to regain her composure before seeking out Finn, when his mother rushed over to her with panic in her expression.

"Lady Hadleigh, what's wrong?" Knots formed in her belly, for she *knew* Finn was involved.

The older woman took a few deep breaths before speaking. "Do you know where Phineas is?" She glanced about the immediate area. "I'd hoped he'd come and found you after your disagreement."

Warmth invaded Jane's cheeks. "He told you what happened?"

"Not in so many words; just that you'd had some sort of falling out. I advised him to fight for you."

"He did not. I haven't seen him since I left the terrace after our quarrel." A ball of unshed tears formed in her throat. She swallowed them down else she'd become a watering pot. "Why do you ask?"

"This." Lady Hadleigh shoved two slips of paper into Jane's hand. They'd no doubt been torn from the journal Finn always carried. "After I read them, I searched everywhere. My son is no longer in attendance." Fear wove through her voice and reflected in her eyes.

Jane glanced over the notes. Her stomach bottomed out at the one addressed to her. *"I wish I could have been the man you needed.*" As her hand shook, she glanced at Lady Hadleigh. Cold foreboding dripped down her spine. "What does this mean?"

"I can pretend not to discern the direction of his thoughts, but deep down you and I both know what he intends." Desperation lined her expression, and it fed her own worry. "Did you see where he went after you parted?"

"I'm sorry, but no." Jane looked at the notes again. A shiver racked her shoulders. The sounds of the string quartet, the laughter and conversation, it all faded while her mind dwelled on the possibility that Finn had left with the intent to put an end to his life. Her chin trembled as she raised her gaze to meet his mother's. "Perhaps he's gone home, to collect his thoughts." Her heart hammered painfully behind her ribcage, for in her soul she knew he hadn't. When caught up in depression, there was no logic to guide him, and if he'd thought he was alone, that everyone he knew had abandoned him for their own entertainment, that she was going to accept the duke's hand...

Oh, God, please don't let him die.

"It's possible, I suppose," the countess said, and her frantic tones yanked Jane back into the present. "The footman who helped him into our coach refused to say. I don't wish to seek out Ballantrae and involve him, but I will if the threat of having the footman sacked loosens his lips."

Jane frowned. "That's not advisable." She'd rather not find herself in the duke's vicinity again so soon. "Perhaps Finn was fatigued and did indeed seek his bed." Quickly, she grabbed a flute of champagne and took a deep sip, hoping to stave off the inevitable urge to retch when every muscle in her body told her to run, to find him—to save him because her life would never be the same without him. "Where's his valet? Surely he wouldn't have left without Rodgers."

"He's still here. I've had him summoned."

"I see." Jane glanced at the notes again as knots pulled tight in her belly. *Oh, Finn, you must try to have faith in us.* "I wish he would have asked for help, but I understand why he wouldn't.

The mind is a tricky place."

The countess' chin wobbled. "I must go home post haste."

Jane rested the flute on the table. "I'm coming with you." She stuffed the notes into her reticule.

For a tiny second, the countess smiled. "I rather thought you might."

Rodgers ran up to their location, his expression a mix of wariness and dread. "How can I be of service, my ladies?" The fact that he encompassed both of them in his glance spoke volumes.

"My son is missing."

The valet gawked. "He left without telling me?"

"Apparently." Jane nodded. "We're leaving immediately for the Hadleigh townhouse."

"I'll make the arrangements at once." He sprang away, loping through the crowds in the corridor like a man possessed.

The countess sighed. "We must inform Andrew. He'll want to accompany us."

THOUGH THE TRIP to the Hadleigh townhouse took a quarter of an hour, to Jane, it seemed as if a lifetime had passed. Urgency held her captive but also guided her footsteps as she hitched her skirting and ran up the stairs after the dowager and Finn's brother, Andrew. The new countess waited for them at the foot of the stairs.

However, Finn's room was empty. It had an air of not being inhabited for hours. A second Bath chair—slightly different in design that the one he'd used earlier that evening—waited near his bed. Several books rested on his nightstand, and from their titles on the spines, they were all fairy stories. A worn leather notebook lay beside the books. The coverlet hadn't been disturbed. In the center of the bed, a gray-blue cat watched them with light blue eyes, as if she didn't trust any of them. When her glance landed on Andrew, she uttered an offended meow, jumped off the bed, and slipped beneath it.

"Ah, that must be Wellington," Jane murmured, but there was no time to make the feline's acquaintance.

Rodgers checked a few places in the apartment and the adjoining dressing room. "Nothing is out of place or missing," he announced when he returned.

The dowager pressed her hands to her cheeks. Anguish shadowed her eyes. "Where would he have gone?"

Jane patted her shoulder in an ineffectual show of support. "Does he have a special place in London where he might hide himself away and reflect?"

"Not that I know of." Lady Hadleigh shook her head. Defeat lined her expression making her seem older than her years. "That is to say, I have no idea. Ever since he returned from various rehabilitation hospitals, I haven't truly known him as the man he is now."

Andrew cleared his throat. For a moment, Jane had forgotten he was there, but his big presence filled the room. When both she and the dowager looked at him, he said, "Finn would go to Hyde Park."

"Why?" Jane gawked at the earl, the man Finn both respected and loathed.

He landed his stormy gaze on her and she took an involuntary step backward. "Father used to take us fishing as boys whenever we were at the Derbyshire property, but we talked of life instead of doing much fishing."

"How does that translate to Finn going to Hyde Park?" Perhaps she was dense, but she couldn't connect the pieces.

The earl glowered. "Water is the key. Staring out over the water makes a man think."

"Ah." The knots tightened in her belly as worry circled through her insides. Once all the ruminating was finished, would Finn kill himself by drowning? Hot sour bile climbed the back of her throat. Quickly, she swallowed. "We're wasting time here.

Let's go."

THERE'D BEEN NO talking in the coach on the ride to Hyde Park, which went faster than usual, for the earl had implored the driver to throw caution to the wind and drive to the park with haste. He'd also ordered the man to aim for a little used gate, for Finn would wish for privacy.

By the time they'd arrived, a light rain had started once more. Jane drew her thin wrap about her shoulders as she alighted from the coach. Clouds obscured the moon and starlight, rendering the park as dark as pitch. In the distance, the gentle lapping of the Serpentine against its banks reached her ears, as did the drum of the rain upon tree leaves.

Trembles of unease played her spine as she followed the earl and Lady Hadleigh, as well Rodgers over the wet ground. Her dainty satin slippers were soon wet, but she didn't care. She had no need of any of the luxuries of life, for without Finn it was all meaningless.

And then she saw him, sitting in his Bath chair at the bank. Unfortunately, he'd chosen the deepest end of the Serpentine for his final act. She sucked in a breath. "Finn," she whispered.

"Damnation." Andrew forged forward through the under-growth. "What the hell are you thinking, Finn? You've worried our mother, and once more you're selfishly putting your life at risk."

"Oh, that man has absolutely no sense of timing or compassion." She darted past the others, and when she caught up to the earl, she yanked on his arm. "That is *not* the way to handle this." Not caring she made a terrible mistake in man-handling an earl, she dragged him away from Finn until they'd rejoined the dowager and Rodgers.

"What the devil is the meaning of this?" the earl exclaimed in tones that probably echoed through the park. "I am the head of this family and I'll say what I please."

Jane glared at him. Too bad his wife had elected to remain behind, not wishing to tramp about in the weather. The man needed a tether. "You haven't been there for Finn in a manner that he needed, haven't supported him in more years than you can probably count." If she were already in the soup, dressing him down wouldn't matter. "Quite frankly, you don't have that privilege now, Your Lordship."

She held up a hand when he sputtered to find a comment, but she then addressed the dowager. "I don't know you well, but Finn also doesn't need a mother's intrusion or her best intentions either."

The earl snorted. "I suppose you think he needs you? The woman who has no doubt prompted this bit of madness?"

Heat burned in Jane's cheeks. Perhaps that was true enough. She pushed the thought away. "Absolutely he does, and I need him. I think I always have." Tears choked her. "Go home, Your Lordship. Take your mother and return to the townhouse. Wait for us there."

"I will not." The earl crossed his arms at his chest.

"Andrew, please," the dowager pleaded. "What she says has merit. She's become close to Finn over the weeks."

Jane pressed her lips together as she trembled with cold and fear. "Rodgers can remain here to help with logistics, but I promise you this. I *will* bring Finn home alive." For she wouldn't accept anything less. Her own life would be empty without him. Wasn't that what heroines in her favorite books did, rescue their men? Then it all became too much. Tears welled in her eyes. A sob escaped no matter how hard she tried to mask her emotion. "At least I hope to, but we quarreled, and he keeps too many secrets... I don't see how any of that will resolve itself."

"Oh, you poor thing." The dowager stepped forward. She slipped her arms around Jane and hugged her. "Shh. You've been so strong when confronted with all of this, and you need to be, perhaps always will where my son is concerned."

"Yes." For one second, Jane let her emotions run unchecked. She cried against the countess' shoulder, for she sorely needed a mother's counsel at the moment. "I don't know how to be any way else. Finn's in a bad place right now, but I believe he won't always be. I hope I can reach him because..." Another sob escaped. "I love him, my lady. If he's not with me..."

"I understand." The dowager set her at arm's length and held her gaze despite the men who looked on. "Love isn't the walk in the wildflowers and rainbows everyone hopes it will be. It's complicated and painful and it makes us feel wretched much of the time."

"Exactly." Jane wiped at her eyes.

The countess' smile was tight and didn't reach her eyes. "Go to Finn. Save him. Tell him what's in your heart while I talk some sense into my other son." She looked at the earl, who huffed out a breath. When she rested her gaze once more on Jane, she squeezed her hands. "Welcome to the family. It's so nice to have females underfoot instead of males."

Jane shook her head as confusion swirled through her thoughts. "Finn hasn't declared himself."

"He will."

"But the way things are right now—"

"Don't give up hope, and don't give up on my son." She released Jane's hands. "Time is of the essence, so we'll go. I'll be sure to send the coach back here for you."

As they boarded the vehicle, Jane turned to Rodgers. "Stay here. Let me talk to him first. Then come once three quarters of an hour have passed. No matter what you might hear, don't come for us sooner than that lest it push Finn over the edge."

"God be with you, my lady," the valet murmured. "I can't imagine life without my friend." Emotion graveled his voice.

"Agreed, but I *will* bring him home."

"If anyone can, it's you."

Jane swallowed down the fear lodged in her throat. She

tramped through the underbrush in the attempt to find a path, but there was none this far from the more popular areas. The dark pressed in on her while the sounds of nocturnal birds sent her heartbeat soaring. The scurrying of rodent feet ramped the fear brewing in her belly. Oh, she hated the dark! So many creeping, crawling things were abroad that gooseflesh raced over her skin.

When she reached the spot where she'd last seen Finn, her heart sank to find only barren grass. The annoying man had left! "Finn?" She followed the bank of the Serpentine. He couldn't have gone far. The ground was wet and muddy in spots; the tracks of his wheels clear evidence of his passing. "Finn, where are you?"

Oh, why did it need be so dark out here?

When an owl hooted nearby, she jumped and emitted a tiny squeal of alarm. She hastened her steps, and as she rounded the curve of the lake, she spotted him behind a grouping of shrubbery and small trees. "Thank God." For the moment, he sat in his chair.

"Go away. I don't wish to see you."

Well, too damn bad. "And I don't wish to leave things as they are between us. We're going to talk." Though fear wrapped its icy fingers around her heart, she slowly approached him. "I refuse to lose you this way."

Nothing else except bringing him home and securing his promise was acceptable.

CHAPTER NINETEEN

T HE LAST PERSON he wished to see right now was Jane. Several more pieces of his heart shattered as she crept closer. Since the nighttime world around him had been relatively silent, and a former military man didn't forget how to train his ears for the slightest change in atmosphere, he'd caught bits and pieces of her conversation with his brother. She'd told Andrew off with an ease that spoke to previous contretemps with her own brothers and she'd braved the dark in order to reach him. Was there nothing she wouldn't do? His chest tightened. It hurt to breathe, especially when he wanted her so much, he could barely function.

But she didn't belong to him, and he had no right to think such things. Not anymore. "Go away, Jane." He refused to look at her. "I'm sure you have a duke waiting for you, who most likely isn't best pleased to have you running through the rain on my behalf." The remainder of his heart squeezed painfully as he died a little more inside. "You'll make a wonderful duchess."

He wouldn't be there to see it. *Thank God.*

"Finn—"

He shook his head. "However, before you follow him into marital bliss, let me say that the duke isn't the man for you." Finn held up a hand before she could protest. "I don't feel he'll support your endeavors at the clinic, and it would break what's left of my heart if you didn't have the chance to follow them." There, at least he'd said his piece.

Not that it mattered.

"While I appreciate your confidence in my abilities and my path, we'll never know what sort of duchess I'd be," she said in a soft voice as she came abreast of his chair.

"Why?" He frowned and finally looked up at her. The silk of her gown clung to her figure thanks to the rain. At the last second, he stifled a groan of pure appreciation. Would that he had a future with her... or one time more with her.

"I turned Ballantrae down." There was no dissembling in her tone nor in her expression. Concern wrinkled her smooth brow and pulled at the corners of her kissable lips.

"You're having me on." Finn shook his head even as a thread of optimism moved through his chest. It had to be a mistake. "No woman in her right mind would throw over a duke."

She touched a hand to his shoulder. Finn started from the contact. "Then call me insane if you wish, for I did exactly that."

"Whyever for?" He couldn't understand her reasoning.

Even in the inky darkness, her eyes were soft and luminous, filled with emotion he couldn't quite see let alone hope for. "Because I love you, you great lummox."

"What?" Shock slammed into him. "I don't believe you. No woman could ever love me as I am."

"So you think." Jane moved a hand to his hair, combing it with her fingers into a style she apparently preferred. He tamped down any reaction to her touch, for it was torture. "You are as vital to me as breathing, Finn, yet you'd throw that away because of the voices in your head." She leaned close and fit her lips to his ear. "They lie. I never do. Even from the first, I've been forthright in everything I've said or done."

He struggled against the conflicting emotions that threatened to tear him apart. It was always a fight, and one he wasn't winning. "Those voices are quite loud at times. There is only one way to make them stop."

"I can be louder." She knelt by his chair despite the wet earth and the mud. When she sought his gaze, he shivered. "I'll shout them down if you wish it."

A tiny grin pulled at one corner of his mouth. "If only it were that easy."

She laid a hand on his left knee. Of course, he couldn't feel the touch, and he never would. "I know it's not, and it probably will never be, but you have to keep fighting because this world would be a sad place without you in it."

"I'm so tired, Jane." He shook his head. "Of the voices, of the guilt I carry, of the animosity between me and my brothers, of the shame, of the knowing I'm not good enough."

"Fight. For you. For me. Can't you see how much good is waiting for you?" Her voice broke from emotion, and that tiny tremor stabbed through him like a knife. "Oh Finn, you are worth so much more than your darkness."

He'd done that to her, made her cry, and that couldn't happen again. Loving someone meant too much heartbreak and grief. *I can't bear to see her experience that.* "No." Finn shook his head. She was meant for happiness and sunshine, not what she'd reap with him. "I can't be the man you want. Nothing good will come from that."

A sob escaped her. "You're the man I need. I'd choose you time and time again because you're wonderful and a part of me I can never let go, a part of me that's critical for my own growth."

"But my past, what I've done… the ring…"

"None of it matters as long as I have you."

Oh, God. Warmth rolled through his chest. He should tell her how he felt, that he loved her too, but the cacophony in his head grew louder. *Do you really think she truly wants you? She's lying, telling you what you want to hear so you won't put an end to it all.* Finn pressed his hands over his ears and rocked back and forth. *Only in death will you know peace.*

"How can what you say be true?" he managed to gasp out. "You left me like so much rubbish tonight."

"What was my recourse? You're keeping secrets from me! In

that moment, I was hurt, my heart broken when I thought of you with another woman, marrying her." Tears sparkled on her cheeks. "You refused to talk to me. I can't help you if I don't know how you're hurting." Frustration rang in her voice. She pressed closer until her face was near his. "Don't shut me out, Finn."

You couldn't make your best friend's girl happy. Why do you assume you can do the same for Jane? You, as half a man.

She shook her head. "Suicide doesn't take away the pain. Death merely passes it along to someone else, which makes it twice as painful."

In a remote part of his brain where logic dwelled, he knew she told the truth. "It's all too much." He couldn't bear to tell her how he'd failed yet again, so he maneuvered his body to the edge of his chair. The voices in his head goaded him onward. He looked at the dark expanse of the Serpentine. In mere moments, it would be over, and he'd know peace and blessed silence. "I can't. If you don't already hate me, feel disgust for me, you will if our relationship were to continue." He swallowed hard as his throat closed with unshed tears. "Goodbye, Jane."

"Oh no you don't, you stubborn arse." She leaped to her feet, hurried to face him the second Finn leaned forward and left the chair. Jane took the brunt of his weight in her arms, but it was too much for her to hold. She struggled to find purchase on the muddy bank. Fear reflected in her eyes as her feet slipped. His momentum held, and they both fell into the Serpentine. Her brief scream tugged at his heart before the water closing over her head stole the sound.

Damnation. Above everything, he couldn't let her drown because of him. The shock of the water jolted him out of his tortured thoughts enough to think clearly. He grabbed her about the waist as she struggled. The frantic pounding of his heart was a welcome feeling. Once her head broke the surface, he used his other arm to guide them. "Help me to the bank. I can do the rest." Thankfully, the water was just over five feet deep, for they hadn't had time to wade out further.

"You're really trying my patience, Major." The darling wom-an must have hit the bottom, but she was too short to stand and breathe at the same time. But his Jane had never given up before. She pushed and ultimately pulled him toward safety. "Once your arse is safe, you *will* tell me what I want to know."

"Agreed." He'd been an idiot. The dunk in the water had brought a realization along with clarity. *I don't want to die.*

Once she'd scrambled onto the bank, lying there on her side with her chest heaving, Finn pulled himself on the slippery grass with his arms. His right leg tingled; the muscles ached. He was able to move the leg slightly to help haul himself out, but there was no time to marvel at the occurrence. The unexpected exercise as well as the gambit of emotions had left him exhausted. He flopped upon the grass, and when he discovered a second wave of strength, he used his forearms and elbows to move over to her location, where he collapsed with his head on her hip, lying on his side so he could look into her face.

"I'm so very sorry, Jane," he said between wheezing for air.

"I won't accept that until you tell me about the ring." She coughed, wiped at the moisture on her face, leaving a streak of mud behind on her cheek. "And so help me if you've been toying with my emotions all along—"

He took one of her hands, the poor glove wet and muddy, and brought it to his lips. "I swear I haven't."

"Good. We *must* have trust between us going forward."

"You'll have it." He blew out a breath. "The story of the ring is wrapped up in the Battle of Waterloo." Hopefully, he could make short work of the tale and spare her the gorier details.

She squeezed his hand. "If you find yourself lost, remember I'm here."

"I know that now." For long moments he laid there as he pondered how to begin. "I met Edward four years before that battle while in France. I'd made captain by that time and had a nice allotment of men under my command. We struck up a close friendship, for the horrors of war were never more concentrated than in that country." A shudder moved through his body. "He reminded me of Brand, so that probably made it easier."

"Was it horrid there?"

"Sometimes. The winters were the worst. Supply lines were interrupted on both fronts. Food and clothing shortages plagued us, as did the lack of proper munitions." He drew his thumb over her knuckles. "At times there was an unspoken truce to halt the fighting until both sides had what they needed. But not always. The French were bastards at war, and savage at that."

Finn closed his eyes while images of brutalized bodies of soldiers littered fields they'd had no choice but to march through, the forms already picked clean of clothes, boots, or anything of value—even sometimes teeth—for the ground was too frozen to give them proper burials. "Getting to know Edward better helped pass the time and balanced out the atrocities. We shared letters received from home. He had a girl in England he intended to marry."

"Oh, no. How sad," Jane murmured.

"War rarely births happy stories." He held onto her hand as if she were the only thing keeping him tethered to this world. Perhaps she was. "The war dragged on. We'd been fortunate to survive for as long as we did, but we were experienced and knew what to do." Panic built in his chest, for he was coming to the crux of the story. "My promotion to major came two weeks prior to Waterloo." He shook his head. "God, Wellington was magnificent. Fearless. He had a way about him that imbued us with confidence and strength. We knew fighting for England and those we'd left behind was the most important job we had."

"Because of you, Napoleon never stepped foot on English soil."

"Every battle was hard fought. None so grand or as bloody as Waterloo." His breath rasped loud as he struggled from the memories. "Two nights before the battle, I promised Edward I'd look after him and keep him safe so he could go home and life a happy life with his woman. He gave me the ring and told me that if he didn't make it out, to find his girl and give her the ring."

"There was no way you could have kept that promise though. War is unpredictable." Her dulcet tones in the dark washed over him and saw him calm.

"I agree. However, the promise was made. Then we found ourselves in the battle for our very lives." His body shook from reaction or perhaps cold. "We were at it hours, days even. I thought both Edward and I would make it out unscathed, where I'd already lost so many men under my command." The pain of loss lodged in his chest, but perhaps finally speaking about it would help soothe the memories. "We'd been amassing for another charge, Wellington barking commands from horseback, when a cannon ball exploded into a wheeled cart nearby. In the few seconds when my attention was taken by that, the French came over a ridge. I was hit, the ball going into my back to tear up my spine. Immediately, I fell."

The acrid scent of cannon fire clogged his nose. Echoes and screams of the dying and wounded rang in his ears. Frantic whinnies of terrified horses danced through his consciousness.

"God, there was so much blood on the ground. It was slippery and vile. So many men slaughtered. I couldn't think from the agonizing pain that gripped me. When I realized I'd lost the use of my legs, I looked for Edward. He stood not five feet away, staring down a charge by himself. I called out to warn him to run, but it was no use. They were upon him with the advantage. Some of my fellows rushed to his aid, but he'd already been struck. I tried to go to him, check on him, but two of my own men pulled me back behind our lines. Because of that, I survived while Edward didn't. Shortly after, I passed out from the pain."

Tears flowed down his cheeks. No longer did he feel the pressure of her hand in his. "I couldn't keep my promise, couldn't say goodbye. I failed."

"Oh, Finn, you didn't. I think Edward knew you were a man of honor and of your word."

"Ha. Some honor. I was dragged off the field like a sack of potatoes, sent back to England through France in a horse-cart filled with other wounded men like me. Some of whom didn't survive the journey."

"Sometimes, it's not about the ones we lose, it's about the ones we save too. I know you saved more men than you lost," she said in a soft voice. "Remember that."

"I'll try." He swallowed again and tried to shift, for the muscles in his right leg ached fiercely, the nerves felt like fire. The scent of rotting, diseased flesh and blood filled his nose. "It took nearly two years for my recuperation." As the tears continued to flow, Finn dug the ring from his waistcoat pocket. "A handful of days ago I finally called upon the lady he'd loved. I'd been too much of a coward to do it before then. When I presented her the ring, she refused it, was bitter about Edward's death. She said that he'd told her in a letter I would take care of her in his stead. When she saw my chair, she refused me too—not that I knew of Edward's promise in that regard. She blamed me for Edward's loss." He took a shuddering breath. "That added to my guilt and pushed me further into darkness. I didn't know what to do after that."

The soft sounds of Jane's weeping pulled at his chest. "Why didn't you tell me?"

He shrugged. "It was another failure, and they were rapidly mounting since I'd met you. Why would I want another one to come to light? Eventually, you would look at me differently; you'd wish to rid yourself of me."

"Oh, Finn." She sniffed and wiped at her nose, leaving a streak of mud behind. "You haven't failed me."

"Really?" Finn snorted. "Not even during intimacy? Surely, you've noted the difference, the decided lack of what it should be." Bitterness filled his statement. He closed his eyes against the creeping exhaustion, but the voices in his head had quieted somewhat.

"Both times we were together were amazing in their own

right, because of you."

"Thank you for that kindness, even if it is only pity." He couldn't keep the cynicism from his voice, for he refused to give into hope.

"Dear Lord, you are the most stubborn, aggravating man I've ever known!"

Her exclamation made him grin. She was glorious when annoyed with him. The edge of the emerald bit into his palm as he clutched it in his hand. "Also, I have stalled on my novel." He snorted and popped open his eyes to contemplate the darkness overhead. Light rain fell upon his face, cooling his overheated skin—a great equalizer. It fell on everyone. At least that was something. "London doesn't need another failed writer."

"Why do you believe you've been unsuccessful in that? Creating a story takes time."

"The damned heroine won't do what I want. She's too independent, too confident, too… she's *you*, and I have no idea how to finish the tale."

"Still looking at life through a negative mist." A chuckle escaped her, the sound welcoming and inviting. "Don't you think you owe it to yourself and me to finish that book then?"

"I don't know." At least that was the truth.

After a few moments of silence, she spoke again. "Why are you afraid, Finn? Why didn't you tell me all this before? It's hardly damning against you. Horrible things happen during war. That isn't a crime, and it's completely understandable." She paused, once more finding his hand in the darkness. "Why haven't you told me the truth, the one sitting on your heart even now?"

How did she know? Was he that easy to read? But then, she'd already confessed her feelings for him. Perhaps that allowed her to see past his insecurities and everything keeping him from her. "I didn't wish to present you with the pile of my disasters and disappointments. I have nothing of consequence to my name to give you—"

"—Medals, ribbons, accommodations—"

"Bah!" He shook his head on the soft pillow of her hip. "They don't matter if I'm confined to this chair."

She huffed. "They are a part of you, earned on those faraway battlefields because you care, because you *are* brave, because you did what others refused to do." Another sob escaped her. "Why can't you realize you're full of potential even now? That you're good enough for me already? If you don't, there is no hope for a future for you or between us."

"I didn't believe it before." His breath was uneven as his pulse raced as the truth pummeled into him. "When I hit the water just now, I knew for a certainty that I didn't wish to die. And I think…"

"Yes?" Her eyes glittered in the darkness.

"I think the bravest thing I can do in my life is continuing to live, when I wanted to die, for now I have purpose." And he would have never seen that unless he'd met Jane.

"That is something I can agree with you upon." She combed her fingers through his wet hair. "Life is before you, Finn. I'd like for you to remain in it to experience every marvel that's waiting."

"I'm beginning to want that too." God, she was unbelievable, and he needed her like a starving man needed a scrap of bread. "While I struggle, how I proceed while fighting those demons I brought back from the war, I can help other men like me. That's something to live for."

"It's quite gallant to be sure," she was quick to agree. Her gaze twinkled in the dim light. "Is there perhaps another reason you've decided that living holds merit?"

The conversation he'd tried to avoid on the duke's terrace hours ago had come due. Jane deserved honesty. She deserved to know the contents of his heart even if it would render him vulnerable to pain and possible rejection. "I would like the chance to pay *my* addresses to you. If that's agreeable?"

"Finally!" She squeezed his fingers. "I would enjoy that very much."

"As would I." Had it been too easy? He'd expected emotional

outbursts and accusations, but there was only her, accepting him for the man that he was, loving him… as she always had.

Her gaze met his. "I want to go home. I'm cold and wet."

"That's understandable." He didn't stir; neither did she.

"And I'd like for you to go home as well, make things right with your family. They love you, and in the last few weeks, you've given them a fright. Don't discount how they care for you even if it's not the way you assume they should." She sniffed again. "We are all trying in the only way we know how."

Heat smacked his cheeks. "I realize that too, and I promise I'll talk with them. I do miss my brothers." He held up the emerald ring. "What about this?"

Jane patted his head. "Let that part of your past go but keep the good memories. They're the only things worth remembering."

Was there any wonder why he'd loved her? Finn chucked the ring into the Serpentine without second thought. It made a soft *plop* as it sank, and as it did, portions of his heart that had housed that guilt were suddenly empty, free for filling with happier, brighter things.

A few minutes later, Rodgers came out of the underbrush with a slight cough. "Good evening, Major. The lady instructed me to wait three quarters of an hour before arriving on the scene. Do you require assistance?" He nodded at Jane. "My lady."

Never had he been more elated to see his friend. "Yes, and I'm grateful for it, as well as you, Rodgers. I heartily apologize for making you worry."

"Think nothing of it, sir," the valet said as he approached and offered Finn a hand. "All of us go through the valley at some point. It's the people who are waiting for us on the other side that make the difference."

"Indeed, they do. Let's go home."

He had a new life to begin planning, and a wonderful woman to declare his love to.

CHAPTER TWENTY

July 26, 1817

J ANE STARED AT her visage in the dressing table mirror and
sighed. Slight purple smudges marred the skin beneath her
eyes, a testament to her sleepless nights since she'd rescued Finn
from the Serpentine. Though there was color in her cheeks, her
lips were pale. She bit them to encourage a pink hue, but the lines
of exhaustion and worry on her face had no such easy fix.

She glanced again at the brief note the butler had handed her
three hours ago. It was from Finn's mother. *If you were to call on
my son today, I'm quite certain it would be worth your time.*

That was all it said. Heat infused her cheeks, giving them
more of a healthy color. Did she dare to hope what the outcome
of such a meeting might be? Though Finn had opened his heart
and told her the secret haunting him, he hadn't declared himself
nor had he uttered those three little words she was desperate to
hear from him.

There was nothing for it. The answer she sought would never
be found in the dressing table mirror. She hadn't seen the major
for two days, nor had she any word from him. How had he fared
since she'd left him that evening? Had his mental state improved?

Her maid bustled in with a freshly pressed gown over her
arm. "This royal blue will make certain you're noticed, my lady."

"Let's hope you're right." Jane stood, stifling the want to groan from the soreness of her muscles. That unexpected plunge into the Serpentine had taken more of a toll on her body than she'd assumed. With a tiny tug at her upswept coif, she encouraged a tendril to curl at each temple, as well as a tiny becoming curl over her forehead. "However, I rather think sleeping for a few days sounds like just the thing."

The younger woman snorted. "Not now. Not when you might come home engaged." She helped Jane to don the gown and then made quick work of the line of tiny pearl buttons along the back. "Speaking of which, your father is looking for you."

"I imagine he is." Jane's smile was a grim affair. "However, he can bloody well wait. It's about time I saw to my own fate instead of anyone else's." Her father hadn't been best pleased to discover she'd refused Ballantrae's suit. He'd lectured her for close to two hours the afternoon following the ball, while she'd sat humbly in his study and let him rail.

It wouldn't be the last time she'd disappoint him, for if she did become engaged to the major this afternoon, she be certain to appraise him of that fact as well as her intent to continue working at the clinic alongside her brothers and Finn.

"Father needs to understand that times are changing, as are the people who are living through them." She fastened her grandmother's heart pendant around her neck and studied the effect in the mirror. It would do.

"You're a braver woman than me, my lady." The maid handed Jane a pair of ivory kid gloves and a shawl of the softest ivory silk.

"Mmm, I don't know about that." She slipped her stocking-covered feet into a pair of matching royal blue slippers. "Father will bluster at anything, I think. He needs a hobby, perhaps." Or a new wife. Someone to bully him and challenge him.

"Well, you're a vision today. I wish you luck."

"Thank you." She scratched at her head where one of the silver combs dug into her scalp. "I hope to have news to announce by dinner."

"Shall I call for a carriage, my lady?"

"No, I'll walk. It's not far, and it's not raining. I intend to enjoy every moment of it." With that, Jane left her bedchamber and minutes later began the walk through Mayfair. With every step, her heart beat faster and flutters filled her stomach. What if she'd misinterpreted the dowager's note?

By the time she arrived at the Hadleigh townhouse and rapped on the green-painted door, her nerves felt strung too tight.

When the door swung open and the butler stared at her from down the length of his long nose, she trembled. "I'm here to see Major Storme."

"Follow me." This time he admitted her without argument. Instead of being shown to a parlor or even the drawing room as she'd expected when they'd mounted the stairs, she trailed after him to the next level. When she asked their destination, the butler remained silent. Then, as they approached the door she recognized from the other night as Finn's bedchamber, the butler paused. "Although Major Storme doesn't feel up to receiving guests and is resting from his ordeal, he wanted to see you. Ring if you have need of anything."

How extremely odd. Worry flooded her being. Had he further damaged himself? Lifting a shaking hand, Jane knocked softly on the wooden panel. When bid to enter, she did so.

"Hullo, Jane. Please close the door."

She frowned but did as bid. When she turned, she studied him with a critical eye. Finn sat upright on his bed. A flowing linen shirt covered his upper half while his lower half was hidden beneath the bed's coverlet. His midnight hair stuck up at all angles, whether by accident or design she couldn't hazard a guess. "What's wrong?" She didn't move from the door, for something about the situation made the baby-fine hairs on her nape prickle.

"Nothing."

Jane didn't quite trust the wicked twinkle in his sapphire eyes. "Then why was I shown in here instead of a more proper location?" She'd never been one to adhere to societal rules and neither was she a prude, but this smacked of something personal and quite intimate.

His shrug was a thing of beauty. In fact, the dratted man acted as if nothing out of sorts had happened. "I don't feel like getting out of bed." A decidedly roguish grin curved his lips. "Why didn't you call on me yesterday?"

"I thought perhaps you'd need more time after... everything." She propped her hands on her hips. "Besides, *you* could have called on *me*."

He rolled his eyes heavenward. "I'm lazy."

"Arse." After everything she'd done for him, he couldn't manage to dress and leave the house?

"I won't deny that." He crooked his index finger in a come-hither fashion. "Come over here so I don't feel as if I'm shouting."

With a healthy dose of wariness, Jane moved to his bed as he maneuvered his legs over the side while throwing the coverlet off him. *Oh, dear Lord.* The sprinkling of dark hair on his pale legs captured her attention. "Where is your family?" Not for worlds would she admit to the note his mother had sent.

"They've gone visiting. No doubt they'll return by dinner. Mother said something about wishing to take tea with a friend and to show off Andrew's new wife."

"Ah." *Something* was in the wind, and it wasn't the coincidence of his family being conveniently out of pocket during her call. "What on Earth is wrong with you?" She narrowed her eyes and peered closer at him. "Have you taken too much laudanum? You're acting strangely, even for you."

"Haven't touched the stuff for some weeks now." His smile nearly knocked her on her bum. As it was, butterflies fluttered madly in her lower belly. "I'm happy."

"Happy?" That word and Finn didn't readily go together.

"Yes. Also, I want to show you this." He struggled off the side of the bed.

"Oh, please don't—"

"Look." He held up a hand to keep her from rushing at him while he stood awkwardly on his right leg. Though his balance wavered and his leg shook, he grabbed onto the nightstand and took a tiny hopping step while his other leg dragged.

"What... what does this mean?" she asked in a barely there whisper.

The grin he flashed could have lit the London sky in the darkest night. "The leg works slightly though it's a bit unreliable at present. Nothing else does, but I'm grateful."

She could do nothing except gawk at him. "How?"

"Not sure." Finn settled on the edge of the bed once more. When he shrugged, the placket of his shirt fell open to reveal a tuff of dark chest hair. "Royce came yesterday to examine the leg as well as the rest of me. He said the nerves might have repaired partially since inflammation from the original wound finally receded, but since nothing else has feeling, it's likely that damage is permanent." Excitement wove through his voice. "I never thought anything of the sort was possible."

"And Royce didn't tell me?" Her eyebrows soared.

"I asked him not to in the event it was my imagination."

"I can't believe it." She pressed a gloved hand to her mouth as she stared at him in awe. "Good for you."

"For *us*, sweeting." He winked. "However, I'm not a whole man, even if I might walk with the help of a crutch someday. Plus, I'll always need the chair."

Trembles played up and down her spine. "You are as whole as you need to be. I've told you that before."

"That's what I'd hoped you say." Taking possession of her hands, Finn slowly peeled first one glove off and then the other. They dropped to the floor, then he tugged her close, snaked his arms around her and began working the tiny buttons at the back of her dress from their holes.

Jane swallowed to encourage moisture into her suddenly dry throat. "What are you doing?" She could hardly manage the whisper, for it took all her concentration to stand upright. His presence was everywhere, heightening her need.

"Taking shameless advantage of the situation. Also, I intend to show you how I feel about you, so you'll have absolutely no more misgivings about me."

"What if I already don't have any doubts?" She shivered when her gown gaped open.

Desire darkened his eyes. "Then our enjoyment of what's about to happen will be that much greater."

One by one, her garments fell away: gown, lace-edged petti-coat, stays, and then finally her shift. They all dropped to the floor at her feet with barely a whisper. Jane stood before him in her slippers, stockings, garters, and nothing but her dignity. For long seconds he raked his gaze up and down her person until goose-flesh popped on her skin and her nipples slowly tightened.

"Well? This is the first time you're seeing me *sans* clothes." Did her curves make her less desirable? Did he not like that she wasn't as thin as some of the diamonds in the *ton*?

"You're like a Renaissance painting by a master," he breathed, and he devoured her with his eyes. "Soft and rounded in all the right places, and too gorgeous to waste on a man like me."

"Hush." She pressed a forefinger to his lips, and when he took that digit into the warm cavern of his mouth and sucked, she gasped. Her knees wobbled. A throb of need pulsed between her legs.

"I've waited so long for this, and you haven't disappointed." Emotion graveled his voice. He grabbed her hips and pulled her close into the vee of his splayed legs. "I can't wait to explore every damn inch of you." Finn then proceeded to pleasure her breasts with his fingers, tongue, and teeth.

Heated sensation rolled through her body while she stood before him, afraid if she moved the dream would shift and she'd wake up. When he danced his fingers over the sides of her breasts, swept his palms along her hips, her bum, the outside of her thighs, a sigh escaped her. With a tiny moan, she rested her hands on his shoulders. If he didn't take her to bed soon, she'd melt into a puddle on the floor.

"You're only missing one thing."

"What's that." Her eyelids were heavy from desire. Oh, when would he touch her again?

"This." Finn methodically plucked the combs and pins from her hair. He tossed them away, and they pinged all over the floor. As the red waves tumbled down around her body, he groaned and tangled his fingers into the tresses. "You're beautiful, a siren, a goddess, a wood sprite of my very own, escaped from a storybook exclusively for me." He tugged on her hair, tilting her head backward, and when he claimed her lips, his kiss hard and demanding, she was lost.

For several minutes she kissed him back, following his lead and chasing his tongue as he did the same to her. With each heated pass, every nip and nibble, pressure coiled and stacked in her lower belly searching for an outlet. When she wrenched away merely to breathe, her hunger for him had only increased.

"Finn, stop for a moment. Let me catch up."

"Oh, no." His strong hands were at her waist. "We're barely getting started."

Jane squealed when he tossed her onto the bed. She landed on her back in the midst of soft down pillows. The luxurious sheets were decadent against her bare skin. He pulled himself beside her, kissed her lips again, and urged her onto her stomach. Excitement coursed through her veins. Where had this man come from who had a sudden verve for physical intimacy? With a gentle hand, he parted her legs, then his fingers were at her sex and in her channel, tenderly pumping, driving her wild, stretching and exploring, while he coaxed that tiny bundle of nerves out of hiding. "What are you doing?" The inquiry was breathless, for her traitorous body immediately responded to his overtures. Warning tremors began deep inside her core. Oh, she wanted this man above everything in life, but could she survive this new intensity?

Finn chuckled. The sound reverberated in her chest. "Preparing to worship your form."

"Shouldn't we talk first?" Every word she'd wished to utter flew right out of her head, for how could she think, breathe, do anything else when he created such magic? She writhed from his touch, bucked against his hand. "Love me," she whispered, needing him more than anything in the world, hoping that her words would prompt his.

He moved the mass of her hair from her back and kissed her nape. "I rather think I've been endeavoring to do that all along, but I only just realized how."

"Oh, Finn." How romantic he was! All too soon, her body tensed from his constant ministrations. The quick pressure that had built from his first touch broke and she shattered with a gentle release that had her pressing her face into a pillow to muffle her scream of repletion. "It was so fast. I had no idea…"

"That was only the beginning, love," Finn replied as he encouraged her onto her back. If she were concerned that he hadn't said the words, the look in his eyes completely obliterated the worry. Such love lingered there that it stole her breath and renewed the contractions inside. *This* was the man she knew he could he. *This* was the man she'd always wanted. *This* was her Finn.

Oh, dear Lord, I think I'm in a spot of bother. And she couldn't be happier.

CHAPTER TWENTY-ONE

T HE ENDEARMENT HAD felt all too natural, and Finn couldn't wait to use it another thousand times as their future unfolded. Beyond that, giving her pleasure had become one of his favorite responsibilities. Watching those emotions dance through her expression heightened his own feelings. As love and affection and need crashed together in her gorgeous emerald eyes, he couldn't imagine a place where he belonged more than with her.

"Ah, Jane, how much I adore you." Unable to stop his grin, he pulled himself on top of her, his mid-chest resting between her splayed legs. "You were made for being loved—by me." Finn teased and tortured her tempting curves with his mouth, teeth, and tongue until she writhed beneath him or alternately guided his head to where she wanted him the most. He explored every inch of her body that smelled like summer, from the gentle swell of her belly to the fullness of her breasts to the nice roundness of her hips. Once he was done, he did it all over again because she was his.

He would officially ask for that right later.

Intense joy welled through his chest from the new freedom he'd found with her. Now that he understood making a woman happy and content went beyond physically lying with her, penetrating her, showing off his prowess, he'd broken away from of some of the fetters that had previously bound him. Intimacy was in how a man spent time with his lady, how he attended to her needs, how he treated her outside of the bedroom, and he reveled in the knowledge. It was a challenge to him, a game perhaps, to see how many times he could make her find release, how many times he could send her flying into bliss, for witnessing this woman—his woman—in the throes of passion was its own reward.

Why have I never grasped this concept before?

For long moments, Finn gave thorough attention to her breasts and nipples, loving her body with abandon. Those dusky pink tips hardened from his touch, and when he rolled them between his thumbs and forefingers, took those full, quivering globes in his hands and explored every inch of them with his mouth, she trembled from the play; his name was a litany on her lips.

This was the woman he'd dreamed of those nights in hospitals when he thought his life was over. The longer he was with her, the more he thanked God she'd come into his life to turn his upside down and set him on an even greater path.

"Ah, Jane, you have no idea how much I've changed because of you."

She uttered a murmured response he couldn't make out, for her eyes were mere slits while her hands randomly plucked at the bedding, but he didn't stop his exquisite torture. Once more he sent her to the edge and left her wanting, but oh he would give her so much more this afternoon.

"Dear God, Finn, you're... wonderful." In a daze, Jane blinked open her eyes as he lifted off. "I need..."

"I know."

As she'd always instinctually known when they came together, she worked with him to provide him better access. Gathering pillows, she reclined against them, her back arched, her bum and hips elevated, her legs spread and in the perfect position for him to devour her.

"In the past I'd tell you that I don't deserve you, but I've since learned it's not a true statement." He met her gaze and grinned. Never had he felt so happy or uninhibited. "The two of us together will become a force—a storm if you will—and I've finally seen my worth because you've dared to love me." The fact that his voice broke on the last words was a testament to his own state of mind.

Then, he turned his attention to her, the woman who'd changed everything. Like a man who was finally offered his favorite dish after being held prisoner for years, he feasted. Finn gripped her thighs, splaying her further open and delved his head between them, licking, suckling, tasting the very essence of the woman he loved and adored beyond reason. When he penetrated her warmth with his tongue, she uttered his name, but a moan stole it away. Over and over, he thrust into her, while flicking that tiny swollen button with a finger. Her responses to his attentions sent satisfaction through his chest, and still he worked to bring her to new heights of ecstasy.

"Oh Finn, oh Finn, oh *Finn*..." Jane bucked her hips, putting herself more firmly into his care.

With a smug chuckle against her flesh, he renewed his attentions. He suckled that little nubbin while thrusting two fingers into her core. Quickly, he found a rhythm he liked, and she obviously enjoyed it, for soon her whole body shook. Her thighs quivered at his cheeks, and her feminine walls fluttered, gently at first, then with more force the longer he teased with his tongue.

"Finn!" She came undone in spectacular fashion, biting into the heel of her hand to keep her screams at bay.

Was there ever a more beautiful sight than seeing a woman shatter from his hand? Because he was an arse, or perhaps because he adored the hell out of her, he didn't relent his exquisite handling, not until he'd brought her to the edge and sent her over once more.

When he finally lifted off, Jane sagged into the pillows, her body flushed and limp, her breathing ragged, tears rolling down her cheeks and into her ears, but she was the vision he'd seen shortly after meeting her—naked in his bed with her glorious red hair spread out on his pillows.

"Oh, you wicked, wicked man," she managed to gasp after some minutes had passed. "Prepare for retribution."

His heart squeezed. She matched him in every way, treated him as an equal. "We'll see who gives quarter first." How had he been so fortunate to win her? Some of his confidence faltered as she clambered to her knees and pushed him onto his back. What if after all of this, she didn't wish to marry him, for he'd planned to ask her after bedding her, which was the reason for his family vacating the townhouse.

"No losing yourself to dark thoughts that will steal your bravery." Jane wasn't a hesitant miss in matters of physical pleasure, and he adored that about her. A woman who knew her own mind was attractive and drugging.

Anticipation buzzed through him as she yanked off his loose linen shirt and tossed it away. "I've wanted to explore your body for so long." She licked and nibbled and nipped her way over his chest until it was his turn to shudder with need. How was it possible when he couldn't feel anything with his prick? She peppered his face with kisses, explored beneath his jaw until she found a spot that apparently had the power to drive him insane, and when she touched the tip of her tongue to one of his flat nipples, he inhaled sharply.

"Oh, God, I never knew…" His chest tightened as she flicked the hardened nub with her tongue, and with her fingers, she worried the other, plucking, twisting, pushing him toward the brink as he'd done to her. Finn gasped at the sensations she invoked, marveled at the waves of pleasure breaking over him that had nothing to do with his member or his stones. "My thinking was flawed," he rasped out. "I assumed a man could only find stimulation through his equipage."

"Surprise, dearest." She winked and continued to separate him from his sanity.

In intimacy, as with everything else, one must be creative and play up one's advantages. Jane had that in spades.

Dear Lord, what is happening to me?

He was going to perish from the relentless throbs of longing and need in his chest. Tingles crept along his upper back and nape to heighten the pleasure she brought him. When she left off from his nipples to kiss his neck, gently nip his earlobe, his upper body nearly arched off the bed. He was powerless to stop her even if he'd wanted to.

Holding his gaze, Jane walked her fingers down his body. He enjoyed the light sensations until she hit his navel and all feeling ceased. She paused at the towel he wore. "Do you mind?"

"No." Finn shook his head. "I apologize if it is distasteful."

"We all have bodily functions. I'm not embarrassed." Nimble fingers undid the pins at the sides. She let down the front of the towel and then took his member in her hand while he watched. Though he couldn't feel her working him over, he saw it, and that in itself sent heated desire through his chest, to say nothing of the thoughts racing in his mind.

Did every man think it the height of scandal to witness a woman fondle their bits? His breath caught when she gathered her hair over one shoulder and then slowly, oh so slowly took his hardening shaft into her mouth. He lost the ability to breathe, to swallow, to think, to exist as she bobbed up and down his length. *Oh, God*, it was too much even though he couldn't feel it, as he remembered what the act had been like. He hooked a hand around her nape and guided her more fully onto his erection.

"Jane…" She met his gaze as she worked him over. Amusement sparkled in those emerald depths as if she were having the most marvelous time. Every shattered piece of his heart came back together, glued into place by the love she selflessly gave. Tears crowded his throat. If she didn't leave off, his chest would burst open, he was certain of it.

How was it possible to feel so differently during intercourse yet experience the same intensity?

She came off him and slanted him a look that brimmed with

naughtiness. The raw need shadowing her face gave rise to his own. "Quickly, put on your ring. If I don't have you right now, I'm going to explode." The urgency in her voice quickened his pulse.

Knowing that this woman wanted him so badly both exhilarated and humbled him, and he fell deeper into love with her. "I'll be a moment." Finn fumbled for the decorative box on his bedside table. When he grabbed the sheath and ring, he fit the supple leather to his shaft and tied the loop around his stones as fast as he could. The result was a proud, stiff erection that saluted the ceiling, ready and waiting. "Ride me, my lady."

"Gladly." Jane's eyes held a slightly crazed look, a clear testament to her desire. "You understand I don't want you merely to stem my desire, don't you? I need you for much more than sexual congress." She mounted him, her knees on either side of his hips, and when she took him in hand, he gasped.

How well he remembered what it used to feel like. "I want you to glean everything you need from me, like I do from you."

"We're well matched." Then she moved, bouncing up and down his length, ever faster, always deeper. Her glorious full breasts jiggled, tempting him.

Finn took them in his hands, squeezing, kneading, worrying the stiff tips with the pads of his thumbs. When she leaned over him, her hair and her breasts dragged over his chest. A moan escaped him. God, the sensation was exquisite and quite torturous at the same time. The new position must have hit the right place, for Jane shuddered and gyrated her hips against his, rocking faster and more urgently. He gripped her waist, helping when he could, watching her as she unabashedly took enjoyment from the act of joining with him.

Tears sprang to his eyes. She was magnificent, and he loved her. So much. Not once had she let his reality prevent her from befriending him, loving him, enjoying his company, pushing him to be the man only she saw. He'd put those barriers around himself, but never more would they—or his doubts and fears—

come between them.

"Finn, yes! Oh, oh yes!" Her body stiffened. She cried out as she found release, hard if her joyous, light-filled expression was any indication. Shivers racked her form, then she collapsed against him, her ragged breathing tickling his ear.

Odd sensations whooshed over him. Heat filled him like a wave, an all-consuming fire. His ears roared. Tingles danced over his arms, ushering in gooseflesh, and the most intense pleasure pushed through his chest, his head, heating his neck and face. Finn gawked at the ceiling as his upper body shuddered and a sense of repletion sank into him. Was it possible he was spending yet in a different way than he'd known before? When one didn't concentrate on one's shaft and stones, was this how it felt?

"This is... fascinating and amazing," he managed to whisper through the pulses.

And so peaceful. He took a shaky breath, wrapping his arms around her. Perhaps he *could* have a fulfilled sexual life after all. Never would he have discovered that until the advent of Jane. Because she persisted and refused to give up on him.

I love her.

Eventually, she moved off him with a soft sigh. "I don't think I'll be able to move for a while." Exhaustion wove through her voice.

"Then I must have done something right." Finn removed the cock ring and sheath from his flagging member. After tossing the aid into the box, he pulled her tight against him. "Thank you."

"What for?" Her body, snuggled into his, made him grin. She rested a hand on his chest and her head on his shoulder. "You deserved the coupling as much as I did."

"Not for that." Gently, he brushed locks of her silky hair from her face so he could press a kiss to her temple. "For never giving up on me."

"I couldn't. Since the first, I've felt a connection between us."

So had he, but he'd been too much a coward to recognize it for what it was. "You peered into the heart of this Storme and completely stole it, but there is something I would say to you."

"I'm listening." Her warm breath skated over his chest and renewed his awareness of her.

"When I'd thought you'd choose Ballantrae over me, I was afraid, for if I lost you, I might revert to the man I was before I met you, the man trapped by depression and racked with bitterness, a man without hope." His throat constricted, for it was difficult to share his most private thoughts. They didn't reflect well on him. "I need your sun and your warmth."

Her fingers stilled on his chest. "How can I be that when you nearly left my life that night, Finn? When you assumed no one cared about you, that I didn't care?" The waver in her voice tugged at his heart. "Tough times will come. Setbacks too, but you can't think to solve each one of those by attempting to kill yourself. That isn't the answer."

"I know that now. Because of you." He cleared his throat. "You've completely changed how I think, how I look at life... and my family."

"Life has changed for us both," she said softly. "As I've given you light, you have shared your darkness with me. We're in balance. You've opened my eyes, ripped the blinders from them and forced me to look at the world differently." She lifted on one arm to hold his gaze. "I'm not the same woman I was when we met."

"No, you're better." And he hoped to God he could make her happy.

"No."

"Then, perfect."

She snorted. "Hardly. I have flaws and prejudices I need to work on, perspectives that need to be changed."

"To me, you're perfect... and perfect *for* me."

Affection softened her gaze. "There's no such thing as perfection, and even if there was, I wouldn't want you to put me on a pedestal. I'm much too real for all that."

"Ah, Jane." He cupped her cheek, encouraged her close so he

could brush his lips over hers. "With us together, excellence is possible. It might not be perfect in the definitive sense, but it's happiness and that is a good start."

"What are you trying to say, Major?" A frown tugged her kiss-swollen lips downward.

"Just this." He shifted his position, pulled himself up to lounge against a mound of pillows to better look at her. "I love you beyond reason, and I'd like to spend the next twenty or thirty years of my life making you happy. If you'll have me."

"Hmm, I don't know. For a writer who knows words have very specific meaning, that was rather poorly done of you." A wicked twinkle glimmered in her eyes as she maneuvered into a sitting position. "How *exactly* do you want me in your life?"

Of course, she would dwell on the semantics. "Marry me. It won't be easy, but I *can* promise you we'll have contentment and happiness and sunny days too."

She studied him for the space of too many heartbeats before finally nodding. "I can't think of a reason why I shouldn't." Her smile was as bright as the summer sun outside. "Yes, I'll marry you, Phineas Storme." When she threw herself into his arms and kissed him with the same vigor that he claimed her lips, his chest tightened with profound joy.

"I don't know where we'll go from here, for marrying me will mean a step down in position for you," he began, but when she pressed a forefinger to his lips, he left off.

"I won't have you ruining this moment with doubts. We'll work everything out. My father, however, will be furious, but I can convince him." Her smile never dimmed as she combed a shock of hair away from his forehead. "But you must know right now my path is leading me to the clinic. I won't sway from that."

"Never would I dream of dissuading you. Follow your dreams, Jane, as I will do the same." Finn kissed her, for no other reason than he could. "I'll be there with you, and I also hope to finish my book. You never know. It might prove a wild success."

She giggled. "My husband-to-be, a famous author."

"It sounds rather nice." Gently, he eased her into his arms and drew her back with him against the pillows. "Should you wish for children..." That one thing marred his happiness of the moment. "I'm not certain I can father them."

"I haven't given the matter of children much thought, but imagine all the fun we'll have in discovering whether or not you can." The throaty purr of her words had renewed desire tightening his chest.

"Oh, and there is a ring. Mother let me have my pick of the Hadleigh jewelry." He glanced at his nightstand, but other than the decorative box containing the toys she'd given him, the wood was suspiciously empty. "Wellington loves shiny things. She must have run off with it, but I chose a ruby cut into the shape of a heart set in gold filagree, for you won mine from the very first."

"How romantic." Her eyes filled with tears. "My grandmother would be pleased, for she always told me to follow mine. I did and it led me to you."

Finn hugged her close. They remained like that for long moments until the chime of a long case clock announced the four o'clock hour. "My family will return home soon. We should at least try to look less scandalous. No doubt Mother will wish to help plan the wedding."

"I can't wait." Then Jane giggled again, for Wellington had jumped up onto the bed and cautiously approached her.

"Jane, may I present Wellington, my best friend. I hope the two most important ladies in my life can find a friendship." When his fiancée put out a hand and the cat sniffed her fingers, he sighed.

He was so damned fortunate. To think he could find love and even happiness. It didn't solve all his problems, and neither would it completely banish the depression, but it would go a long way into fighting it. With a grin at Jane, who scratched Wellington beneath her chin, he settled into the pillows.

I can't wait to find out what happens next.

The End

Other Regency-era stories by Sandra Sookoo coming soon from Dragonblade Publishing

Storme Brothers series
The Soul of a Storme (coming June 2021)
The Heart of a Storme (coming August 2021)
The Look of a Storme (coming October 2021)
A Storme's Christmas Legacy (coming November 2021)
The Sting of a Storme (coming January 2022)
The Touch of a Storme (coming March 2022)
The Fury of a Storme (coming May 2022)

Willful Winterbournes series
Romancing Miss Quill (coming June 2022)
Pursing Mr. Mattingly (coming August 2022)
Courting Lady Yeardly (coming October 2022)
Teasing Miss Atherby (coming late 2022)

About the Author

Sandra Sookoo is a *USA Today* bestselling author who firmly believes every person deserves acceptance and a happy ending. Most days you can find her creating scandal and mischief in the Regency-era, serendipity and happenstance in Victorian America or snarky, sweet humor in the contemporary world. Most recently she's moved into infusing her books with mystery and intrigue. Reading is a lot like eating fine chocolates—you can't just have one. Good thing books don't have calories!

When she's not wearing out computer keyboards, Sandra spends time with her real-life Prince Charming in central Indiana where she's been known to goof off and make moments count because the key to life is laughter. A Disney fan since the age of ten, when her soul gets bogged down and her imagination flags, a trip to Walt Disney World is in order. Nothing fuels her dreams more than the land of eternal happy endings, hope and love stories.

Stay in Touch

Sign up for Sandra's bi-monthly newsletter and you'll be given exclusive excerpts, cover reveals before the general public as well as opportunities to enter contests you won't find anywhere else.

Just send an email to sandrasookoo@yahoo.com with SUBSCRIBE in the subject line.

Or follow/friend her on social media:
Facebook: facebook.com/sandra.sookoo
Facebook Author Page: facebook.com/sandrasookooauthor
Pinterest: pinterest.com/sandrasookoo
Instagram: instagram.com/sandrasookoo
BookBub Page: bookbub.com/authors/sandra-sookoo

www.ingramcontent.com/pod-product-compliance
Lightning Source LLC
Chambersburg PA
CBHW071752190726
48292CB00003B/952